INK

With You Forever
By
David Charlesworth

Needle Falls
By
D E McCluskey

INK

ISBN 978-1-914381-49-2

Dammaged Productions
www.dammaged.com

INK

WITH YOU FOREVER

David Charlesworth

For Kath Taaffe …
The luckiest girl in the whole world

Prologue

MORNING WAS STILL a distant dream to the city, and though she slumbered, still, she lived and breathed. Her streets were filled with those who never truly slept, the revellers, the workers, and, sadly, those who were simply trying to survive to see one more morning.

One of the latter sat huddled and shuddering in one of the many alleyways that snaked through the roads by the docks. She lay there, soaked to the bone, as water chugged from a broken pipe somewhere far above, funnelling the torrential rain into the doorway she'd sought refuge in. A single sodium light, a remnant from a far older time, stood as a lone watchman in that dark corner of the city, its weak orange glow barely reaching the girl.

It was no wonder, then, that Charlie did not see her at first. She appeared, at a casual glance, to be a mere bundle of rags. And Charlie, exhausted from a long night shunting freight, was moving on autopilot. His mind was focused solely on the prospect of collapsing into his bed.

Then the rags began to sob.

Despite this, Charlie did not stop. Not entirely, though his pace did slow. The city was rife with homeless, and he was not entirely apathetic to their plight. He had found himself living payday to payday himself, and rumours of layoffs at the docks abounded. If those wicked whispers became manifest, he could easily see himself slipping through the cracks of society and, not long after, joining the ranks of the destitute and forgotten.

Something about the girl caught his eye. Though the clothes she wore were soaking and filthy, they were *new*. Her designer trainers had only been on the market for a couple of weeks at most, and the grime on her jacket was fresh. It was likely she had a home to get back to but had found herself unable. Perhaps she was drunk and lost? Whilst homelessness was something Charlie could sympathise with, he had no firsthand experience in that department. Drinking too much and waking up outside on a cold, wet floor, on the other hand? That was something he was more familiar with than he would like to admit.

'You all right, love?' he said, finally stopping.

Slowly, the girl raised her head. It took some effort, as the hooded jacket she wore appeared to weigh a tonne with how much water it had absorbed. The girl's face was revealed, but even in the dim light of the alley, her appearance was striking. Electric-blue hair tumbled down across a face that was encroached by tattoos snaking up from her neck. Lips, laden with metal hoops, quivered as she tried but failed to form words. Her eyes were swollen and red from crying, but still, Charlie knew this girl. How could he not? It had been impossible to even glance at a social media app and not see her face. Amber had been missing for days now. Her mother had died quite suddenly, and she had fled her home, leaving her father and brother in a state of distress.

'Amber?' he asked.

With a weak nod, she confirmed her name.

'Are you all right?'

'I'm tired,' she whispered.

'Yeah,' was all Charlie managed to say.

He would gladly admit that he was the last person who should be trying to console a lost teenage girl. He barely knew what to say to his mother when they would have their monthly calls, so what hope did he have of finding the right words here? He paused, trying to conjure something warm and positive to say, but instead, the alley spoke for him. The wind brought with it Amber's sobs, which echoed out from behind him, and above, the wailing creaking of rusted pipes grew louder.

'Oh God,' Amber cried out, though her voice was lost in the cacophony.

'It's all right,' Charlie said, trying to sound as though he knew what he was doing. 'I'll call someone and they'll … People have been looking for you.'

'I know.'

Shaking from the effort, the girl braced herself against the rain-slick wall and rose to her feet. Charlie moved forward to try and help her, but the look of horror on her face caused him to pause. He stepped back and glanced up the alleyway from where he had just come, hoping for someone to help share this burden, perhaps even relieve him of it, but all he found were the dancing sprites of broken raindrops leaping from the cobbled ground.

In that brief moment of distraction, Amber had staggered from her hiding place. She stared past Charlie and screamed before turning on her heels and racing away, skittering and splashing down the flooding road.

Once more, he turned to see what had spooked the girl, and his heart lurched. There was someone there. It was a pale shade of a naked figure in the darkness at the end of the alley, arm outstretched and reaching for him. Within a blink, the vision vanished, and he found himself alone.

Exhaustion, he rationalised. Between the long shift he had just completed, the wet, the cold, and the lost girl, his mind was slipping into a state of sleep-deprived stupor. Tucking his head into his chest, Charlie resumed his trudge home. After a well-deserved sleep, he would find someone on social media who knew the girl and inform them where he'd seen her. Hopefully, she would be somewhere relatively close by and easily located.

~~~~

Amber's dead body would be found the following morning.

Her passing would forever play on Charlie's mind. He would often wonder if he could have done more to help the girl, chiding his lack of foresight. His guilt was unfounded, however. As there was nothing more he could have done for her that night. There was nothing anybody could have done to save her from what would come to pass. Her death was as guaranteed as the rising morning sun.
~~~~

INK

1.

THERE WAS A brief sense of panic when Gemma awoke, lost as she was within that period where dreams and reality bleed into one another. She took in her surroundings and found them entirely alien and abhorrent.

Everything was wrong. The door was beside her instead of across from the bed. The walls were adorned with printed canvases depicting city skylines instead of ragged posters of pop-punk bands held up with tape. And most egregious of all, the curtains were as thin as crepe paper and did little to halt the cruel presence of the encroaching daylight. It illuminated not only the room but her mind as well, reminding her where she was.

Despite how odd it appeared, it *was* her bedroom and had been for close to three weeks now. Her mind was still rebelling against the idea, however. She had spent countless nights in that very same room, but now that it was *hers*, there was no shaking the feeling that everything was just ever so slightly out of place. Or perhaps, more likely, it was Gemma who did not fit in.

In a daze, she cast her blankets aside, leaving them in a heap. Staggering to the curtains, she cast them aside too, allowing the day to greet her fully. However, a stray shadow meant she came face to face with her own reflection instead. It matched how she felt; her short, dyed hair was an explosion of red and orange bursting from her head, and she'd fallen asleep without taking her makeup off again, so her eyes appeared sunken and darker than normal. She ignored the ghoul who met her gaze and looked past it, across the city that lay before her.

There was no sign of any of the iconic landmarks the city was proud to house. No sign of the iconic cathedrals, towers, or parks. Yet the view was a truly gorgeous sight to behold, and one Gemma knew would never lose its allure. For the previous five years, she had been living in a dire little council estate. Upon waking there, the only vista she had was that of a drab concrete yard littered with weeds and pigeon droppings.

From the kitchen, there came the smell of breakfast and Dan's voice calling her to come and eat. He would have to wait if he was expecting a reply; her mind was still wracked with what she dubbed her *morning malady*. Things would refuse to begin working properly again until she filled her belly with coffee and her lungs with smoke. Only then would some sense of normalcy return.

Leaving the bedroom, she made her way through the hall that connected their sleeping quarters to the rest of the apartment. It was a long, cramped umbilical that hummed and shuddered. The plumbing, electrics, and a lift shaft for the entire building ran behind those claustrophobic walls, stretching a further ten floors above them. But it was a small price to pay because the rest of the apartment was a grand open plan affair. Their front door led to the kitchen area that ran into the living room, whose floor to ceiling windows allowed for near day-long natural light. If there was anything bad to say about the flat, it would be that Dan's minimalist décor was ruined somewhat by piles of unopened moving boxes crammed into the corners.

'There you are,' Dan announced as he plated up her toast and eggs at the kitchen island. 'How did you sleep?'

He was already dressed. His hair was coiffed, and he sported a suit that was pressed to perfection. Gemma had no idea how he managed it, but second to the view, the best part of waking up was seeing him. Unfortunately, she was still in the thrall of her morning malady, so there would be no amicable response to his pleasantries.

'Slept like shit,' she said, accepting the plate of food.

'Still?'

With a grunt, she began to devour the offerings, and thankfully, Dan had already prepared a giant mug of coffee.

'Is it the mattress?' he asked. 'I was thinking we should maybe get a new one.'

'It's not the mattress,' she said. Her mind somewhat clearing. 'It's … I don't know. How about you? How are you finding sleeping beside someone full time?'

'Oh, I absolutely love it,' he said. 'Best part is all the snoring.'

'Dickhead,' she replied with a smirk.

They had only been living together for three weeks but had been an item for closer to three years. They may have grated here and there, but they had become comfortable with their morning routines, and her malady was never too much to bear for him.

'I was kept awake this morning, though,' he said. 'It wasn't your snoring this time. Well, not entirely.'

'Oh?' She had been woken up by *it* too, but she held her tongue so as not to pollute his take on the matter.

'The bloody pipes again. I think it's coming from next door. I could hear her crying again, too. I don't know what to do about it. Have you not heard it? Has it not been bothering you?'

Of course it had. It had bothered her the night before. Then all of the week before, and a month before that. The creaking moans from some unknown source, the muffled sobs of a young girl. She had endured much worse in her time. Before moving in with Dan, she had lived in one of the rougher parts of the city. Dogs barking, rave music shaking her walls until all hours of the morning, so much screaming and crying … but this was something different.

So long as it's just the noises, she thought to herself.

'I'm not an arsehole, Gemma. You know that, right?'

'I know,' she laughed. Dan swearing was like catching a glimpse of a unicorn. She was unsure if it was his slightly posh accent that made him unsuitable for the act of cursing, but it always made her laugh.

'If it keeps up, I'll have to say something. To who? I don't know, but I'll be having words, believe me.'

With that, he stood and slipped behind her. He wrapped his arms around her and buried his face into her neck, where he planted a kiss. In response, she let out a contented sigh.

'I should get going,' he said.

'I'll see you tonight,' she replied, still wolfing down her food and coffee.

'Actually …'

He moved to the kitchen cabinets and opened the bottom drawer that was overflowing with miscellaneous utility items. After a brief and cacophonous rummage, he re-emerged. In his fist, he held a box cutter.

‘I’ve got an idea that might help us both sleep better,’ he said, placing the knife on the table.

‘A bad night’s sleep isn’t worth killing ourselves over,’ she said, cocking an eyebrow.

‘No, you drama queen. Unpack your stuff,’ he said, nodding to the boxes. ‘This is *your* home now, after all. Settle in, get comfortable.’

‘Hmm,’ was all she managed to get out.

‘Just do me a favour,’ he said, picking up his briefcase from beside the door. ‘When you *do* unpack, please go easy with the pillows. There’s barely enough room on the couch as it is.’

2.

PULLING A LUNGFUL of smoke into her lungs, Gemma felt her morning malady melt away. She may have had some grievances regarding moving in with Dan, but those, too, slipped from her mind as she experienced the city waking up. She passed through the shadows of centuries-old buildings, their rich histories carved into their stone flanks. Her city had been the crux of the British Empire at one point, her ports trading in priceless wares like tobacco, cotton, rum … and, unfortunately, for a time, the blood of men too. Those dark days passed, thankfully, and as galleons gave way to tankers, the city lost its relevance for a time. Until it once again found itself centre of attention on the world stage, her greatest exports becoming music, culture, and beauty.

Gemma's city was alive. The building shaped valleys she strode through echoed with the pulsing heartbeat of commerce. Shutters clanked as shops opened, vendors called out to one another as they unloaded goods from their trucks, and early birds like herself picked their way amongst the chaos.

Normally, she would have missed all of this. The train station she used whilst living alone would have dropped her off near enough right next to where she worked. It was a soulless jaunt, taking public transport, but this! Being a part of this grand awakening was a truly magical experience. One that was almost enough to drive away her foul morning mood without the need of caffeine and nicotine … *almost.*

Work, for Gemma, came in the guise of serving in a small cafe. It was a job she'd promised herself was nothing but a temporary stopgap after she finished just six months of media studies in university. She had big plans, she convinced herself, and every now and then, she would try to put those plans into motion.

First, she'd tried online blogging but found her creativity drying up once her fingers lay upon her keyboard. Then came a stint of jewellery making. Only her peculiar style of blending punk iconography with nineties TV shows refused to attract many customers. She was ahead of her time with that one, she believed … Sign making, sculpting, painting, printing … She had turned her hand to most things in an attempt to strike out on her own. And now, six years later, she was still working at Caffe a la Eva.

It was a small, independent cafe tucked away down a side street just on the cusp of the city's centre, at a crossroads where the commercial zone gave way to the docklands. The area was an ecosystem all of its own. Theirs was a collection of outcasts and forgotten trades. A vinyl store hummed from dawn until dusk with the throbbing beats of old, obscure bands. A hippy palace that sold bongs, crystals, and dream catchers filled the area with the thick, heavy musk of incense.

Finally, there was a small tattoo parlour. No signs advertised its existence; no neon lights or opening times adorned the small lead-piped window or plain black door. Without knowing it was there, a casual observer could presume it to be an access entry or a small flat. In Gemma's opinion, it was the city's best kept secret. Second only to Eva's cafe, of course.

Inside Eva's, Gemma shed her coat and bag. She loved how her boss had decorated the cafe. It was a small affair, more akin to someone's living room than the larger chain coffee shops that were scattered about town. The original wood shelf fittings that lined the upper border had been painted a warm mahogany, and upon them were lined hanging plants and vines. The chairs and tables, likewise, were repurposed and renovated wood, no two alike. Gemma's favourite spot was the cosy little booth near the back. Just enough sun made it through the windows to bathe everything in a warming, golden glow. That booth, her booth, always caught the light perfectly.

'That you?' came a shrill call from the back.

'It's me,' Gemma replied.

'Why you in so early?'

'I don't know. Maybe my body clock still thinks I live out of town and have to get the train in?'

A cacophony of sound rang out as Eva filled the water urn for the coffee machine. The pipes shrieked and shuddered as they expelled their liquid, and the wooden floor creaked and wailed every time Eva shifted her weight from one foot to another. The building was Georgian, which meant it was gorgeous, tall, yet, above all else, absolutely archaic. It was listed too, which meant no major work could be done to it. So during winter, their single-framed glass windows did little to stave off the cold, and it always sounded as though the whole block was on the cusp of collapse.

'You say something?' Eva asked as she carried the large urn into the front with little effort.

She could be a scary woman, Eva, but only if you refused to take the time to get to know her, which was far from the easiest task. She was imposing, both physically and mentally. She carried her weight with little effort, she did not suffer fools, and she very rarely changed her mind once she'd settled on an opinion. The pair had grown close over the years, but there were still things about her that were a mystery. Her age, for one. If Gemma had to guess, she would place her boss as closer to fifty than forty, especially with how she tried to cling to her youth. She never left the house without a full daubing of makeup and was always done up as glamorously as possible, though it did little to mask her stern features.

'Why you in so early?' Eva asked again.

'I just told … never mind,' Gemma said as she set about placing menus and facing up the stock.

'Honeymoon over, huh? Had to escape before he woke up?'

'What? No.'

'Girl, something's up,' Eva said, scrunching her face as if she caught scent of something foul.

Breath caught in Gemma's lungs. She was weighing up if she was ready to complain about Dan's—no—*their* apartment. But Eva continued, making Gemma's decision for her.

'You two still having sex?'

'Jesus, Eva,' Gemma gasped, though she should have guessed this was where her boss was going to take the conversation.

'It's an innocent question. I'm just asking. You know, what with you two moving in together … that's the first step.'

'First step to what?'

'Splitting up.'

'Eva, we're not—'

'You have sex last night?' Eva cut in.

'I don't even …'

'That's a no.'

'Yeah, I mean … no. No, we didn't have sex last night, but that's—'

'That's the second step. First step, you move in together. Second step, you stop having sex.'

Gemma remained silent, knowing full well Eva was far from done.

'He good in bed?'

'Jesus,' Gemma laughed. She loved Eva. The gall of the woman never got old.

'That was a trick question. I know he is; you told me when we got on those Sambuca shots at Christmas. *He's posh, but he's good in bed. You wouldn't expect that from a posh boy.* Is what you said. Or something like that.'

'Eva …'

'Nu-uh, let me say my piece. Just saying that if your man is good in bed and you have sex all the time, which you did, because you told me that too, but then you move in and it stops … that's a red flag. You could be doing it all day and night, but you're not. *Why not?* That's like, steps three, four, and five right there.'

'Is that why you have four ex-husbands?' Gemma bit back. 'Fucked them all until they waved a white flag?'

'*Three* ex-husbands,' Eva said, playing along. 'And even though I said I'd never marry again, I wouldn't mind a little boy toy. Dan smothering you too much, I'll take him off your hands. He can smother me whenever he wants.'

'You are *not* stealing my boyfriend, Eva. Don't be greedy. And he's not smothering me.'

'He's the one who was pestering you about moving in, right?'

'I guess.'

'And you didn't want this. You've been telling me that for months now that he's been dropping hints or outright begging you to move in, and we both know you like your own space. Now you cave, move in, stop having sex, *and* then he kicks you out of the house early?'

'Don't embellish,' Gemma laughed.

'Just looking out for you, girl.'

Though their back and forth was playful, Gemma knew Eva had her best interests at heart, plus the fact she was right. Moving in with Dan had been a sore spot for the couple for a while now. It wasn't as though he didn't make her happy, far from it. It was just a big move for someone as independent and compulsive as she was. His dream was to own a fairytale home, somewhere that could accommodate both of their families come Christmas, where they could settle in on a cold winter night and watch cosy holiday movies. He had plans for them to start a family too, which was another point of contention altogether, as Gemma barely thought further than her next pay packet.

Theirs was a peculiar match, to say the least. Gemma, the heavily tattooed, pint-sized punk with ever-changing hair and a rebellious streak a mile wide, dating a straightlaced solicitor from down South? On paper, it should have never worked, but it did.

Even their meeting had been complete chance.

The circles in which they moved overlapped by only the tiniest sliver. They had met at a bar one night, each of them supporting a friend of a friend who was performing as part of a vaguely Beatles-esque four-piece band. It was far too light and poppy for Gemma, and far too heavy for Dan, which was why the pair spent much of the night in the smoking area rather than in the crowd by the stage. All it had taken was a brief glance for the pair to recognise their mutual attraction.

Unfortunately, there had been no call for the pair to speak that particular night, and by the time the sun came up, they'd gone their separate ways. At an earlier point in history, that would have been the end of their story, but as luck would have it, they had both been bullied into following the band on social media, and so they met once more, online.

What came next was a slow but sure process. They swapped likes on posts made about the band, chatted in their comments section, then eventually exchanged direct messages. Inevitably, they arranged to meet, and that was where they truly clicked.

Both would admit that, at first, their attraction was more physical and *curiosity* than anything else, their wildly different lifestyles being utterly fascinating. But they made each other laugh. Soon, Dan was watching trashy horror movies and Gemma was tolerating cricket.

Still, there were boundaries. Dan, in particular, could get overly clingy, staying at Gemma's house for days at a time as she held back screams, feeling suffocated and oppressed in her own home. Much the same way she was sure he must have been driven to madness by her lackadaisical approach to keeping on top of the cleaning.

All of this begged the question: why *had* she finally caved and moved in? Sure, her old home was a mould-infested shambles in a terrible neighbourhood, but that had never bothered her before.

Something had changed recently in her house. It was small things at first, a sense of unease and a feeling of being watched. Then came the odd noises, the unexplained creaks and the faint sound of a girl crying. All these things she could have explained away as the neighbours or bad plumbing, if it hadn't been for the shadows. The brief glimpses of *something* out of the corner of her eye as she passed empty rooms at night.

Something had awoken at that property, and she wanted nothing to do with it.

3.

HIDDEN AWAY AS they were, passing trade was something of a pipe dream for the cafe. But their motto of being the city's *best kept secret* was no idle boast. Patrons who did accidentally find themselves gracing Eva's doors would inevitably find themselves returning again and again. Travelling past far more convenient coffee shops and breakfast places, even during times of more treacherous weather. Mere minutes after Gemma had unlocked the front door, a queue began to form. Tradesmen, builders, drivers, and more filled their shop, craving their morning fix of coffee and hot breakfasts. It was a well-practised routine, and the mornings slipped by in what felt like seconds as the surge of patrons began to subside.

It was only then, with the breakfast rush done, that the residents of that small and lost street began to make themselves known. Emerging from their burrows like meerkats, the hippies and record fanatics came to say their hellos and to make idle chatter. They were all outcasts, all of them strange in their own unique ways. None quite as strange as the old tattooist from next door, Vinny.

'Oi oi,' he cried over the ringing bell that hung above the door, preferring to announce his own arrival.

'Hey, honey,' Eva called from the back.

'Heya, Vin,' Gemma said.

Despite his ageing years, he carried himself like a man still in his twenties. He never walked when a swagger was available. When he spoke, his hands gestured with a twitchy energy that could have been misconstrued as drug-fuelled jitters. He was a wiry figure, his features gaunt and hollow. A cruel if apt comparison would be to say he was more a skeleton wearing the loose-fitting skin of a man. His skin was more ink than flesh, his trade pricked across near enough every inch of his body. They were poor advertisements for his services, being almost as old as Vinny himself. They made him appear, at first glance, to be suffering from some sort of ashen disease.

'Gem,' he yelled, ever the one for theatrics. 'Gem. Gemma. My precious Gemstone. How are you today?'

'You know me, Vin. Same old, same old.'

'Nothing wrong with that. Same old. Bit of stability is good. Speaking of …'

'The usual?'

'Oh, go on, then. You've twisted my arm,' his voice perky and singsong at times. Remnants of a fading cockney accent.

As she prepared his drink, Vinny began to pat his palms upon the counter, his ring-laden fingers pounding out a war drum beat. Eva flicked at the tattooist's invasive fingers with her dish cloth.

'Hey,' she barked. 'You scratch my shit, I'll scratch your eyes.'

'Cor, you kinky minx,' he said with a grin, flashing the gold teeth he had in lieu of dentures.

Rolling her eyes, Eva nudged Gemma. 'Control your man.'

'So, Gemstone,' he said, changing the subject. 'How's my latest masterpiece holding up?'

'Oh God, what's she had done now?' Eva said, stopping herself from entering the back room.

Handing Vinny his drink, Gemma shooed away the money he offered her. In return, he all but threw himself over the counter to place the cash beside the till. This ritual had played out near enough daily since the day the pair had met.

'Well, Eva, my darling. Not to toot my own horn or anything, but this may be my finest work to date. Show the woman, Gem.'

'You're an egomaniac. You know that, right?' Gemma said, smiling as she unbuttoned her jeans.

'Oh Lord, what are you about to show me, girl?' Eva said, making a play of covering her eyes.

Compared to Vinny, Gemma was a blank canvas. Ink had been splashed across her body with no rhyme or reason. Most people had some sort of plan when they decided to cover themselves with tattoos. Be it a commemorative sleeve for dead relatives, a leg crammed full of celebrity faces, or a themed back piece, most people approached this permanent alteration with some tact.

Not Gemma.

Why not get a band's logo on her ribcage, even if they were a one-hit wonder from the eighties? Why not get her favourite anime characters depicted as dogs on her shoulder? Why not get piles of doughnuts on her arm, even though she despised them? She only had one life to live, was her reasoning. So when people asked her if the art she'd dedicated permanently to her body had any meaning, she would reply with a proud: *Why should it?* It was something most people could not wrap their heads around. Why would someone scar themselves for life in such a way?

Why? they would ask. All Gemma would say back was: *Why not?* In all her life, there had only been two people who'd accepted that answer genuinely rather than brushing her off. One was Dan; the other was Vinny.

So why not get an outdated meme of *SpongeBob SquarePants* on her thigh?

'What in the hell is that?' Eva said.

'It's …' Gemma began, trying to find the words.

'Looks like cheese with eyes. Girl, why the hell did you get a tattoo of cheese with eyes?'

'It's not cheese, Eva,' Vinny laughed. 'Get with the times.'

Eva just let out a light grunt as a response.

'It's a meme,' Gemma offered.

'Uh-huh?'

'Like … How do I explain this. Have you seen on Facebook when someone—'

'Right,' Eva said, cutting her off.

'She doesn't get it,' Gemma said, turning to Vinny.

'She doesn't get it,' he agreed.

'I don't think I *want* to get it.'

'No, I tell you what,' Vinny said, gesturing with both hands as he spoke. 'I'll tell you what it is, Eva, darling.'

'Go on, amaze me,' she said.

'It's *art*, and it is fucking beautiful.'

'Thank you,' Gemma said, pulling her jeans back up. 'I'm glad someone understands.'

'Art … right. I'll get The Louvre on the phone real quick,' Eva said, shaking her head.

'You taking care of that, Gemstone?' Vinny said.

'I think so,' she replied, voice thick with playful sarcasm as she gestured to the rest of her tattoos. 'Never had ink before, Vin. But I think I'm doing all right.'

'Whoa, whoa, whoa,' he cried out, clutching at his heart. 'You wound me, Gem. Eva, did you hear that? Look at what she's calling *ink*? *This* is ink, but *this* is art.'

Hovering his fingers over Gemma's skin, he traced around some of the faded and sloppily images that ran up and down her arm before stopping and pointing to his work. Even Eva nodded, as the difference was night and day. Vinny's work was precise, his line-work tight, the colours rich and vivid.

'Yeah, I see it,' Eva said. 'I mean, I don't get it, but I see it.'

'There we go. Proof that a master worked on your flesh.'

'Oh God, don't feed his ego.'

'Hang on, though, Vinny,' Eva said, giving Gemma a sly wink. 'What is it? All that shit you've drawn on this poor girl's arm. That yellow cheese thing on her leg … it's a good comic book or whatever, but it's dumb as hell. That on her arm, though? Looks like a chicken scratch or something.'

'Those are runes,' Vinny said, appearing genuinely hurt.

'What the hell are runes?'

'Runes. Sigils, y'know?' Gemma said.

'No, I don't know.'

Swirling patterns laced up and down Gemma's arm, woven into the spaces between her old, amateur ink. *Filler* was the official term for it. Arrows and chevrons in vivid blues and green spiralled and turned in on themselves, and they were adorned with crosses, stars, and crescent moons. They stood out, bold and bright amidst the murky smudges Gemma had once cherished so dearly.

'Let me see,' Vinny said, reaching over and taking her arm in his hands. 'Let's make sure you've taken good care of them.'

'Hey,' Gemma squawked, taken aback by his handsy groping. 'Don't be such a drama queen.'

There was one tattoo in particular Vinny seemed to pore over more than the rest. It was a more complex rune, coloured in with the deepest of reds, so much so that it appeared black in dimmer lights. It ran along the inside of Gemma's forearm. It was long, thin, and incredibly complex. There was a beautiful fractal symmetry to its harsh angles, and despite how long it had taken to inscribe, Vinny had refused to accept any payment for it.

'Lovely stuff,' he said to himself.

From the front door came the tinkling of the bell, heralding the arrival of the start of the lunchtime rush.

'Go on, then,' Eva said. 'You've got your coffee, you've looked at your art, now piss off.'

'Catch you soon, Vin,' Gemma said with a laugh.

'Ladies, take care,' Vinny offered with a grin, taking a bow and gesturing with his cup. 'Gemstone, pop in and see me soon. The studio gets lonely when you're not there.'

4.

PHONE IN HAND, Gemma idly swiped through the silent videos on her social media app, eyes glazed. At her back lay Dan, his body rising and falling. He held her tight, and his rhythmic breathing was a siren call, lulling her into slumber.

What felt like a million miles away, the city continued to hum. Late night commuters drove through her streets as midweek revellers called out to one another over the sound of pub jukeboxes belting out old classics. A little closer to home, she heard the quiet *ping* of the lift reaching their floor and the distant padded footfalls of one of their neighbours pacing the halls.

Twelve floors up and the building was a mere five years old. Gemma tried to convince herself she was safe. It was nothing like her old house. How could an apartment in a new building so far up be haunted? There had been no wars fought here. No hidden graves below the floorboards. Dan was the first tenant too. So there had been no murders at the property.

Nothing would happen that night, she told herself. The noises they'd heard the previous few days could be explained away. It was resonance from the taut cables running through the lift shafts. It was the electrics playing tricks on her mind. It was anything other than the supernatural.

She was safe.

For just a moment, she believed it. A brief moment of comfort was all it took for her conscious mind to release the fearful tension she'd been carrying and allow her to slip away and into slumber.

Gemma woke with a start as Dan gripped her arm tight before pressing a finger to her lips and gently urging her to *shush*. He was kneeling beside her side of the bed, appearing to have warped there in a flash, yet a quick glance at the clock beside her bed showed it was now half three. The world outside their window attested to this, as it lay silent and still. The same could not be said about their apartment. From the hallway, there came sounds of intrusion. They were familiar sounds to Gemma, only they were far more distinct than they had been before. There came the aching sound of metal grinding against metal, accompanied by the soft sobbing of a girl.

'Keep quiet,' Dan urged. His face had lost its colour, though Gemma was unsure if it was due to fright or the moonlight that penetrated the curtains.

'What the fuck?' she managed to whisper.

'Someone's *here.*'

'Who is it?' Gemma's body flooded with adrenaline, snapping her awake.

'I think it's the girl,' he said. 'The one from next door I told you about. Jesus, Gemma … I was going to the toilet, then on my way back, I turned around and she was just *there … naked.* Call the police, yeah? Or maybe an ambulance? I don't know if she's hurt or … Just stay here.'

Kissing her forehead, Dan slipped from the bed and crept to the built-in wardrobe. Fishing about in the darkness, he knocked assorted sports gear over, the clattering ringing out, betraying his actions. Gemma looked from the door to her boyfriend and back again, fearing whoever was in their home with them would appear before Dan found whatever it was he was looking for. The sounds had quietened, and Gemma hoped that might be enough to convince Dan to return to bed and perhaps they could both pass out from exhaustion, and that would be the end of it.

'It'll be all right,' he said, finally retrieving his weapon of choice, a cricket bat—a remnant from his university days. He crept back towards the living room.

Once again, Gemma tried to convince herself that what was happening was mundane. Sure, someone breaking in and violating their sanctuary was grotesque and made her feel sick, but at least it was quantifiable. *The paint has barely dried. How could the apartment be haunted?* But no matter how much she denied it, somewhere deep inside, she knew whatever was in their home would not be ousted by the authorities. Gemma cast her covers aside and stood, ignoring Dan's request to call for help.

Stepping into the hallway that connected their room to the rest of the apartment, Gemma looked for Dan. There was close to twenty feet of darkness between her and the living room. Nothing stirred within that gloom, but she could hear movement. There was the soft padding of Dan's feet coming from the kitchen, but for every two soft *plaps* of skin on tile, there came a third, out of step and echoing from somewhere she could not place.

'She's gone,' she heard Dan say to himself.

Advancing slowly, Gemma found herself lost in that limbo between their rooms. She clutched herself tight as goose flesh rippled across her body. A sudden chill swept through their home. *Had Dan opened one of the windows?* Gemma glanced back, paranoia's claws readied at the nape of her neck. There was nothing there apart from the open door to their bedroom, a cool, blue portal that offered protection under the moonlight. She opened her mouth and tried to call for Dan, to beg that they both dive beneath the still-warm covers and seek refuge there until morning, but her words were interrupted.

A racking, coughing sob came from *somewhere* in the apartment. The location was impossible to pinpoint. She could have sworn it came from inside the walls. *We're twelve floors up*, she pleaded with herself. *There's nothing on the other side of these walls, nothing but cables and air.* Still, the crying continued, and it was not alone. A long note called out, high pitched and piercing. It shot through Gemma, making her feel queasy. It was metal scraping against metal, a squealing, aching noise that felt as if it were coming from all directions.

'Dan?' she finally managed to call out, but there was no reply.

Somewhere, through the cacophony of sound, she heard the front door closing. *He's gone*, she realised. *He's left me here alone.*

'Dan!' she cried again. Still, there was no reply.

She would wait for him in bed. He might have gone to get help and would be back soon. Plus, he did tell her to call the police, so she turned around, ready to retreat, and saw what had been creating the noise.

At the end of the hall, peering around the corner of the door frame from Dan's bedroom, a girl was looking at Gemma. Her skin was so pale it was almost luminescent in the moonlight. She was rail thin, skeletal. As she shifted, the muscles that roiled beneath her flesh moved like snakes in a wet cloth bag, threatening to tear it open. Patches of hair clung to a raw, scabbed scalp. Unfortunately, the locks there were too thin and wavering to hide the horror's haunted and pained face.

The source of the crying was revealed. It emanated from the horror's gaping mouth, which was lipless and round, hanging open and loose like a black hole had been shot through the girl's head. Worst of all were her eyes. Sunken and dark, ringed red and raw from an ever-flowing stream of tears. Gemma saw there was no malice in them. Perhaps that would have been preferable. Instead, they were wide and pleading. Two balls of hot, white agony dotted with pinprick irises.

It took Gemma a second to take in the terrible apparition before her. It took a second longer before she managed to find her voice.

Gemma began to scream.

5.

MORNING BROUGHT WITH it a pure and cleansing light. With the curtains opened, the sun provided the kind of illumination and comfort LED bulbs could only dream of.

Their bodies ached as they woke from their restless dreams. Dan's couch was a boxy, leather ordeal. It suited the minimal aesthetic of his apartment but was torturous when used as a makeshift bed.

Gemma was balled up against Dan's chest, his legs splayed out from under the covers, frozen and numb. Silently, they rose and migrated to the kitchen island. Gemma kept the blanket they'd used around her shoulders, trying in vain to keep the shivers at bay.

Coffee spilled from the decanter and filled her mug. Her shaking hands caused droplets of the scalding liquid to splash her fingers, though she barely noticed. There was more than fear consuming her now; there was a sickly guilt in the pit of her stomach, as the truth would have to come out. The truth of why she was here. Why she had kowtowed to Dan's request to move in with him.

'Hey,' was all Dan said, and it brought Gemma to tears.

Trying to retain her composure, she lowered her head and held her mug tight. The heat burnt her hands, bringing her back into the moment. Dan reached over and held her wrist tight, his fist encompassing it easily.

'I love you,' she said. 'You know that, right?'

'I love you too.'

'I love you, and … and I'm sorry.'

'It's all right,' he said, taking her hands in his. 'Last night was horrible. Whatever happened, whoever that was, she's gone now. I'll make a report, and we'll get the locks changed. It's all right to be scared. It freaked me out too, and I—'

'No. No, Dan, not that. I mean I'm sorry, I should never have come here.'

'All right, what do you mean?'

'I mean moving in. I didn't want this. I wasn't ready for it. It was wrong, and now I've … I've …'

'Hey, that's all right,' he said, standing up and moving his stool closer to her. He took her into his arms, pulling her into his chest.

'It's all right?' she asked.

'I just thought it made sense, y'know. We love each other and spend most of our time together anyway, so why not? You always said we should give it a little more time. Perhaps you were right?'

'I thought you'd be mad.'

'I mean, I'm not happy about it. But not the … I mean, I guess I wish you would have talked to me about how you felt. Is this what last night was about? Was it a cry for help or something?'

'What do you mean?' she asked, pulling herself away from him.

'Saying you saw a girl in our room?'

'No. Dan, that's what I'm getting at. I wanted to get out of my old house, but I thought we were moving too fast. I thought it would be better here, but it clearly isn't. It's worse now and—'

'Calm down,' he said. 'You're rambling.'

'I was so scared, Dan. You asking me to move in was the perfect excuse for me to get away, but …'

'Gemma, please. What are you saying?'

'She followed me, Dan.'

'Who?'

'The girl. From last night.'

'You *know* her?'

'From my old house. She was there too. It was … haunted.'

A smile crept over Dan's face. It was a nervous reaction more than any kind of sly mockery. All the same, it caused Gemma to shake her head.

'What's with the *look?*' she asked.

'Gemma. *Ghosts*, really?'

'Dan!' she snapped. 'You *literally* saw her just a few hours ago. She was *here* in *your* apartment.'

'I saw *a* girl, Gemma. It was next door or something.'

'Naked, Dan? Naked and crying, and then, I don't know, teleporting to the bedroom?'

'You were tired, or—'

'I'm not having this argument with you,' she said, cutting him off. 'We could be here all day going around in circles. Just listen to me. You don't have to believe what I'm saying, but please *listen* because I'm scared, Dan.'

Holding his breath, he gave her a little nod before speaking. 'I have to get dressed,' he said, standing up and moving towards the bedroom.

Standing to follow him, Gemma paused at the cusp of the hallway. Even on the brightest of days, the light never quite filled that passage, and the memory of the night before made her shudder. She was there. In *their bedroom.* Gemma thought about how she may never sleep again for fear of waking up to that ghoul standing over her.

'Dan, you know that house was a shithole,' she called out before swallowing her anxiety and following him to the bedroom. 'The neighbours, the damp, the … well, everything. I wrote it off at first, the things that were happening. It was stress, maybe, or the kids from two doors down playing pranks. I could hear noises … those *exact* same noises we've been hearing here, then it got worse.'

It was clear Dan was in a mood. He went quiet when he was upset with her. He simply pulled on a pair of work trousers and shook his head.

Still, Gemma continued.

'Then I started *seeing* her, Dan. I don't know how I knew it was *her,* but I just did. Little things out of the corner of my eye. *Movement* when I'd pass by a room but nothing there when I looked twice. Sometimes, I'd be watching TV, and I'd see someone ducking away through the door to the kitchen. I felt like I was being watched all the time, and then it would get cold too, and …'

'I'll be working late tonight,' Dan said. She knew he was intentionally avoiding her gaze.

She continued to rant.

'I thought I was going mad. I thought I'd be safe here, with you, in this building. Nobody's been murdered here, Dan. It's new, but I know it wasn't the house now.'

'I love you,' he said, kissing the top of her head yet still not engaging. 'I'll text you later.'

Picking up his keys, he made his way to the front door and opened it. Just before he left for the day, she called him one final time. He turned, and for the first time since she started her tirade about ghosts, they locked eyes.

'It wasn't my house that was haunted,' she said, a nervous laugh escaping her lips as she heard the absurd words coming from her.

'It's me, Dan. *I'm* haunted.'

6.

ABUZZ WITH A nervous and sickly energy, Gemma saw the city in a more sinister light that morning.

Night was reluctant to loosen its grasp on the world, and the streets were empty save for the destitute and the lost, shuffling in their dark corners, hoping to avoid the scornful gaze of those who may dub themselves their *betters*.

Stale booze and the acidic tang of vomit was the city's bouquet that morning. The street sweepers had yet to do their rounds, and as such, the remnants of the previous evening's revelry had been left to ripen and rot, overflowing in the gutters.

Dan had left early, in one of his moods. It was rare for him to reach his boiling point, and even then, he was not one to scream and shout. In rage's stead, there would come a long and intense bout of sullen faux ignorance. He would clam up and refuse to address the matter at hand. Then, over the course of the day, he would talk himself out of his tantrum and return to her a new man. Usually, she would have cherished having the apartment to herself of a morning, but not with the night's horrors so fresh in her mind. So, she had promptly gotten dressed and fled too.

She walked beside a ghost of her own making. Long, black windows of an abandoned lot stretched on for the rest of the road. As she marched, she resisted the urge to glance over into the darkness beyond the glass. Beyond her own pale, warped, and ghoulish visage. The dark now held a terrible promise; somewhere within its realm, the dead girl could be lurking.

Her presence had once been a rare, if perturbing, oddity, but now it had become a regular occurrence. If the ghost was brazen enough to confront her face to horrifying face, then what was stopping the phantasm from manifesting itself wherever and whenever it chose?

Despite her fears, her journey was uneventful. That was, however, until she got to the *Caffe a la Eva's* street. Their quiet little corner of the world had a visitor that morning in the shape of a police car. She paused on the corner, inherently afraid they were there to pick her up. For what? She had no idea. Her greatest crime, as far as she knew, was stealing the odd glass from some of the fancier pubs Dan had taken her to. Obviously, they had no interest in her, but then who?

Creeping towards the cruiser, she guessed they were in the hippy shop. The pungent stench of weed was almost choking at times, so they were an obvious pick, but then she caught sight of Paul and Gaz, the owners. Their huge bearded faces were pressed up against their grimy window, eyes strained and bloodshot, both high as kites. They stopped their gawking and waved as they saw her, then pointed to next door, indicating the police were there to see Vinny.

Slowing her pace, pretending to check her bag for keys, she crept past the tattoo parlour's door. Inside, she caught a glimpse of a detective and a uniformed officer. Although she tried to eavesdrop, she could only make out Vinny's muffled voice, floating through from his back room.

Being as early as she was, there was no sign of Eva. So Gemma only half-heartedly performed her regular morning tasks as she popped back and forth from their stock room to the windows, periodically checking to see if the coast was clear. After what felt like an eternity, she heard the low rumble of a car's engine. As the police drove away, she slipped out and rapped on Vinny's door as hard as she could with her knuckles, hoping to emulate a bobby's knock.

In response, she could hear muffled swearing from Vinny. His cursing was followed by a theatrical show of him trying—and failing—to unbolt the many locks and bolts that secured his shop. She heard the rattling of chains and his voice lowering as he pretended to drop his keys. Letting out a light chuckle, she eventually called out to him.

'It's only me, Vin. I'm not here to pinch you for the hundred kilos of skunk you have in there.'

Almost immediately, the door was unlatched and opened.

'Gemstone, this is a surprise,' he said with a smile, stepping aside and gesturing for her to enter.

'Got a minute?' she asked.

'For you, Gem? I have eternity.'

If not for the leather-bound surgical chair that dominated the room and the rack of tattooing equipment beside it, one could be forgiven for thinking Vinny's studio was some sort of spiritualist retreat. The wooden walls were lined with shelves that housed an extensive collection of religious iconography and trinkets. Scrolls and psychedelic rugs hung where shelves lacked dominion. Even the small window beside the front door was decorated with fragments of coloured glass that caused the morning sun to refract into a kaleidoscopic ray of colours.

Outside, there was no swing-sign or neon marquee to advertise Vinny's trade. The man did not ply business cards either. Nor did he flood social media with videos of his work to attract customers. Vinny had confided in Gemma when their friendship had started that he loved tattooing with all of his heart but had come to loath the act of *being* a tattooist. *Vincent,* as he was known back then, had been *scratching* since he was eighteen. He told her he'd traded his pencils and sketchpads for nasty homemade needles and human flesh. He plied his trade from his kitchen for years until, one night in a Soho pub, he got into a round with an actual ink-slinger known as Bobby the Bastard. As soon as Bobby saw Vincent's work, the real tattooist clobbered Vinny with an ashtray and split his lip wide open. The following day, Bobby took the still-reeling Vinny under his wing as his new apprentice. *It was a different time*, Vinny would laugh.

With the right guidance, Vincent soon became a celebrated and sought after artist in his own right. After a messy split from Bobby the Bastard, Vinny struck out on his own and moved North, opening a studio near the centre of town. In time, his empire grew, and he took on his own apprentices and artists. At its peak, the needles in his shop were buzzing near enough twenty-four hours a day.

Sadly, times changed, and seeing as there were fewer stigmas about having your skin full of ink, more and more he was receiving the same requests from clients—football club badges pricked upon forearms, children's names inscribed upon breasts, *Live, Laugh, Love* punctured into so many thighs.

There was no passion there anymore. Both from the public and himself. Getting a tattoo was no longer about defying the order of things and making yourself unique, he said. It had become as mundane and pedestrian and as *punk* as buying a loud shirt. And so he sold the studio and decided on a solitary, almost *pious* life. His client base was now only those who were serious about dedicating their flesh to the *art* rather than the *act.* He now worked on a strict referral basis, and those who wanted to go under the master's needles would be thoroughly vetted and understood that whatever Vinny said would go and he had the right to refuse their requests for any reason.

Obviously, Gemma would have never been allowed within a hundred miles of Vinny's chair normally. It was something he had been very blunt about when the pair had first met. As a client, he'd said, she was everything he loathed, but as a friend … she was welcome in his home and chair anytime.

'You're up and about early,' he said. 'Want a coffee? Tea?'

'*You* making *me* a drink? You want a tattoo in return?'

'Gemma, I would fucking love that. Only two problems, though, love. One, I don't think I have anywhere left but my bum to work on, and I wouldn't wish that sight on even my worst enemies. Two, when was the last time you practised?'

'Well …'

Not long after the pair had become close, she had bought her own tattoo machine. It was a cheap affair from Amazon, but the idea was for her to practice and get to some sort of workable level. Vinny had said he would take the girl in and train her further. Not to work for him, of course, but any studio in the city would have snapped her up, knowing the prestige she had come from. However, like most things, that dream had fallen by the wayside, lost in a deluge of distractions and more pressing needs to be fulfilled.

'How about I just make you a cuppa and we'll leave it at that?'

'Deal.'

Settling on the couch, Gemma nestled into the mound of pillows that were piled within its soft recess. She wanted to drift off there and then as exhaustion threatened to claim her. The only thing that kept her rallied was the promise of gossip regarding why the police had been quizzing her friend.

Across from where she sat, Vinny had vanished into the back room. It was a small affair with plain brick walls that were lined with wire racks holding countless bottles of ink of every colour imaginable. Vinny was a reserved man and loathed people encroaching upon his private room, even those as close as Gemma. It was rare to see him leave the studio, which led the residents of the street to speculate that Vinny lived in his studio, bedding down on the rarely glimpsed old, worn-out mattress he kept back there.

'So, Vinny …' she said, letting the question's prelude hang in the air.

'Gemma?' he replied, his voice sly, knowing what was coming.

'What have you been up to?'

'With regards to … oh, you mean *vis-a-vis* the plod?'

'Yes, Vin, *vis-a-vis* the police.'

'Well,' he began, slipping out of the room and closing the door to hide the rattle of the boiling kettle. 'You see the news the other day?'

'No? I mean, maybe …'

'The girl they found dead down the road in town. She was by the bus depot, outside that all night chicken place, yeah?'

'Oh God, yeah. I saw her on all the socials. She ran away from home or something. Yeah … Jesus.'

'Well, I knew her,' he said, the click of the kettle punctuating his confession.

'I'm sorry. Were you and her close?'

'A bit,' he said, vanishing into the back, emerging a few long moments later, mugs in tow. He passed one to Gemma before sitting himself on his tattoo chair. 'Working on a back piece for her. I'd already done a sleeve and a leg, and she wanted something commemorative on her back for her dead granny.'

'What happened?'

'Just old age, I think. She looked about a hundred in the photo reference.'

'The girl, Vinny. Not her nan.'

'Oh, no idea, Gemstone. Never go into much detail, the plod,' he said with a chuckle. 'Oldest trick in the book. *They* say nothing so when *you* say something, they can pinch you for it.'

'This not your first time dealing with the police, then?'

'Far from it. But they're just doing their rounds, y'know? Chasing up the last people in contact with her and the like. It's not as bad as it used to be in the eighties and nineties. But us lot? Tattoo enthusiasts, body modders, piercers, and all that, we're still seen as a bit shady, aren't we?'

'Vinny, you *are* shady,' Gemma teased as she drank her coffee.

'Yeah, I *am*. And proud of it. Still … profiling, innit? I should complain, really. But then again, who'd listen? Anyway, enough about me, Gem. Why are you up so early?'

'God …' was all Gemma could get out. A single, exhausted word said with so much force it all but deflated her.

It was an apt word too, as all around her were effigies depicting various deities and idols, false or otherwise. A fat Buddha sat laughing beside an emaciated Christ hanging, bloodied, from a crucifix. Next was a miniature Shinto shrine beset by long, worn-out joss sticks. In accompaniment was the golden, many-faced visage of Brahma. Vinny was very *new age*. Which had become an ironic label, as Gemma had found it could only be applied to old people. She had known Vinny to speak of *energies* and *fate* in the past, but she had never heard him speak definitively on the subject of religion, God, or the afterlife.

'You believe in any of this?' she asked, gesturing to the shelves. 'Like, in particular or as a whole?'

'Bloody hell, that a heavy question for this early in the morning.'

'More of an afternoon topic of conversation?'

'I'd say more of a *two in the morning and we're both off our tits on micro-dots* question, honestly.'

'Jesus, that would be the last thing I'd need right now.'

'You fretting about your mortality, Gem? Bad timing, them coppers asking about that poor girl if you are.'

'I don't know, Vin. I really don't know.'

'Well, I believe, if that helps at all,' he said, gesturing with his mug to the walls. 'I don't know about a big bloke with a long, white beard who sits on his arse on a golden throne all day. But I think … no, scratch that. I *know* there's more to the universe than what we can see. I *know* there's more waiting for us after we shake this mortal coil.'

'Yeah?'

'Well, like I said, it's more a thing I'd talk about when having a little dabble with acid. Or better yet, some DMT. You try telling me with a straight face that all there is to existence is football and *I'm a Celebrity* after you've seen the physical world melt away and you've spoken to the machine elves. Nah. There's more to everything than we'll ever know, Gemstone.'

Silently, Gemma sipped her coffee. The urge to spill her soul was strong. She was sure Vinny would take her seriously, yet the shadow of doubt loomed large and dark. Only a few hours had passed since the events of the night before, yet already she thought they would sound farcical should she try to relay them. After all, what ailed her was not some deep, philosophical introspection on life and death. She was talking about things that went *bump in the night*. Surely, with all of Vinny's years and wisdom, he would find such stories insulting.

'I guess …' she began, measuring her words, 'I'm a little worried, Vinny. Death is meant to be the end, isn't it? Maybe not the end of existing, like you say, but an end to *this*. An end to shit television and football … and pain.'

'Yeah,' he said, lowering his head. His eyes had become unfocussed, and Gemma was worried she may have struck a nerve.

Joining him, she gazed into the diminished pool of coffee she held in her hands. Seeing Vinny's reaction made her think of the ghostly girl and her look of sorrow. As terrifying as experiencing a phantasmic intruder had been, what had stuck with her was the look of suffering and anguish on the girl's face. If she was any indication of the afterlife, then there was no comfort to be found in death.

'Gemma,' Vinny said, his voice slow and measured for once. 'I'll not ask what's up. I don't know if it's you or your boyfriend who has something wrong or whatever. I don't want to pry. All I can say is no matter what comes next, whatever is waiting for us when we die, you've got to love. Here, in the now. Make every minute count. Love every minute. Love yourself. Love others.'

'Thank you, Vinny,' she said with a smile.

'Did it help?' He smiled back. 'My old hippy bollocks?'

Surprising herself, Gemma laughed.

'It did, actually. Thank you.'

7.

THERE HAD BEEN no lies when Gemma had told Vinny his words had comforted her. For a scant few hours, the previous night's ordeal had slipped from her mind; they had become a warm and comforting ideal of life after death. However, as those dreams began to cool off and the day drew on, she felt a cold gnawing in the pit of her soul as she contemplated returning to the flat … and Dan.

Thankfully, their day had been hectic, thanks to a new construction project starting around the corner from their street. Both Gemma and Eva had been rushed off their feet; so not only had Gemma not given much thought to Dan's lack of communication, Eva had little time to pry into her business. Now, the pair found themselves alone in a silent café, and Gemma contemplated her next move.

In her hand, she held her phone. Dan had sent one text, just after lunch time. *Home late*, it read. Which meant he was still in a mood and unwilling to talk things out. He would find the biggest case he could and bury his head in it until the witching hour before getting a cab home.

Behind her, she could hear Eva preparing for the following morning. In between the rattle of pans and bursts of water from the creaking pipes, her boss would drag in large lungsful of air. Gemma knew what she was doing. She would prepare herself before an inquisition, measuring how much breath she would need for each invasive question she was about to levy and preparing the perfect counterargument for any evasive manoeuvres her quarry could pull to avoid divulging the information she required. To wait too long in her presence would be folly, Gemma knew. Eva was a bloodhound when it came to gossip and would wear her down with ease, extracting the truth, no matter how ridiculous, from her.

Escape was her only option. With all the grace of a wounded doe, Gemma snatched up her things from the counter and clattered through the front door, shouting her goodbyes and apologies as she went. She heard Eva calling out for her to 'get back here,' but Gemma knew it would be far easier to get forgiveness in the morning than permission in the here and now.

After putting a street or two between herself and the cafe, Gemma slowed, putting her mind to work, pondering on what to do next. The thought of waiting alone in the flat turned her stomach, but she had no desire in seeing any of her friends either. She just wanted some time and space to measure her thoughts and feelings. Then inspiration hit her. Because, as she walked, the overwhelming spirit of the city swept over her and she felt herself drowning within her vibes. Music and cheering drowned out any doubts she may have had about the evening, and it was clear now. So obvious how she would weather her personal storm. She would have a few drinks. Just a couple, she promised herself. She would wait for Dan to finish work and meet him outside the apartment, then they would retire to bed. Even if he was still not in the mood to talk, that would be fine, as long as they were together, at least …

~~~

The bell for last order caused Gemma to jolt awake in her seat. For the last hour, she had been nursing a Guiness, fighting off the exhaustion that had been attempting to shut her down. At some point, she had clearly lost that battle.

Shuffling out of her little corner, Gemma placed her glass upon the bar and waved goodbye to the landlord before making it to the door. Stepping out in the chilly night air, she unlocked her phone and waited for the deluge of missed calls and texts from Dan. Her favourite place to drink was infamous for its lack of phone signal. No wave of beep and buzzing came, however. Her device let out a single chirp. A lone message from Dan, who had gotten home an hour ago. *Going to bed. Love you. Take care,* it said, without any kisses.
~~~

Things are serious, then, Gemma thought. Her mind may have been fuzzy from the booze, but she instinctually knew that no kisses on a text meant he was still upset. Be it her antics from the night before or the revelation that she had never truly wanted to move in with him, she was unable to say. She knew waking him up to talk about it would be a bad idea.

These were the thoughts that overwhelmed her as she staggered through the front door to Dan's apartment. Between that and Dutch courage, she had no qualms about navigating her way towards the kitchen island in the darkness. She dumped her bag and coat upon the floor before staggering to the bathroom to relieve herself. The full extent of her drunkenness hit when she attempted to stand up. Even if she *wanted* to make it to bed, her rebellious body would ensure that would never happen. Luckily, however, the couch was opposite the bathroom door, just across from the open plan kitchen, facing into the apartment. Summoning all her strength and will, she lurched from one room to the next, allowing momentum to carry her forward, staggering across the hardwood floor before collapsing on the sofa and promptly passing out.

Hours passed as she lay there, oblivious to the world.

Oblivious to her breath steaming at her lips as the temperature dropped.

Oblivious to the sound of metal raking across metal.

Oblivious to the pale shape that shifted within the darkness of the apartment.

Consciousness tried to reclaim Gemma, but only after that shape began to cry. The cold and the screech of pipes could be dismissed, but something deep within her, something primal, reacted to those sobs. The grief they brought was universal and understandable, even to dreamers. Her eyes fluttered open, fighting against the gunk and eyelash glue welding them shut. The room swam into some sort of focus despite the gloom. Her mind was more of a blur than her surroundings, however. Memories of her drinking session were lost completely, and her current situation was barely registering.

Perhaps, then, that was why she didn't panic when she found herself unable to move. She had never suffered from sleep paralysis but had heard of the phenomenon. Shadows danced across the opposite wall as the curtains danced gently from a rogue breeze. The moonlight cutting through the powder-blue cloth doused the room in a peculiar shifting cool light, and she thought herself submerged beneath a gently roiling sea.

Somehow, this made perfect sense in her addled mind. The chill that seeped into her joints was from the icy waters, clearly. The aching howl of metal was the result of a passing submarine—what else could it be? Who could it be wailing? Someone inside the sub or a lost creature passing by. Some sad and lonely fish having found itself trapped within an aquarium twelve floors above ground?

For the briefest of moments, she presumed it to be her own crying. Only, that was impossible. She could hear her own breath coming as a half-wheezing snore. Her neck was cricked, and she was lying in an awkward position, her chin buried into her clavicle.

In an instant, she realised nothing about that conjured scenario was true. There was no water, no submarine, and certainly no lost mermaids crying out to her. She knew these noises and feelings all too intimately. Gone was that sub-nautical dream, replaced by a very real waking nightmare. She tried to squirm, but her body remained rigid, disobedient. She tried to call out to Dan, yet all that came forth was another wheezing snore. All she could manage was to scan the room and attempt to temper the dread that was slowly consuming her.

Across from where she'd collapsed lay the long, dark hallway leading to their bedroom, and even though she knew Dan was somewhere deep within that darkness, the moonlight failed to penetrate the shadows, and the passage appeared as a void. For now, she could not look away, terrified of what may come skittering out of the nothingness. She was certain, with every blink, *something* was drawing closer, but she was simply unable to see it … *yet.*

Once she could, she knew it would be too late.

The bathroom was to the right of that hallway, its own door appearing as a miniature version, a small obsidian monolith framed into the wall. It was just on the cusp of her vision, and though she was afraid to look away, *something* caught her eye.

Three quarters of the way up the side of the door, four pale fingers wrapped around the frame.

Breath caught in Gemma's chest as she watched those digits shift and tense as they pulled something forward, out from the nothingness. Once more, the girl revealed herself. Her face was still wracked with anguish, her eyes still raw, red, and streaming. She was mouthing something, but no words came, just an echoing low wail.

Frozen as she was, Gemma could do little but stare at the horror before her. She wanted to match the phantasm's cries; she wanted to scream and call for Dan. Ideally, leap from the couch and run, either past the creature or into the bedroom, but her body betrayed her, and all she could do was lie there.

Worse, she thought, was that familiarity did nothing to ease her terror. Minutes passed and neither of them had moved, but still the visage before her chilled her soul. There was something innately traumatising about the ghost that could never be acclimatised to. Though really, should such horrors ever be seen as mundane?

Slowly, from behind the spectre, another hand emerged, joining the first on the door frame. It sought leverage at first, before reaching into the living area. Initially, she thought the girl was about to point an accusatory finger. That perhaps this was some sort of revenant seeking justice for a slight she had caused it during life. No, the dead girl was straining against some invisible force, her fingers slowly snatching at the air.

She wants to get ahold of me, was the impression Gemma got from the gesture.

The idea repulsed her. Not only the thought of that pale, papery, and decaying skin upon her own but something spiritually too. There was no good that could come from the living and the dead coming into contact.

With a sudden lurch, the ghost took a single step forwards, her eyes widening as she fought whatever was holding her at bay. *Something will give soon*, Gemma realised. *Whatever is stopping her from approaching will falter, and the dead girl will get me.*

It was that thought that finally caused Gemma's body to pump adrenaline into her system. After what felt like several tortuous hours, she could finally feel her limbs respond to the demands she was making of them. Unfortunately, the paralysis that held her tight was not relinquishing its grasp so easily. Although her legs did begin to kick and thrash, the action was slow and hindered, and all she managed to accomplish was to dislodge a pillow from the couch.

All the while, the dead girl was steadying herself, bracing her weight against one leg as she took another slow step towards her prey.

A slight cracking sound formed in Gemma's throat. It was an attempt at a scream, but all that came was a low, hoarse gurgle. She continued to strain, pushing herself into a sitting position, but the task was still beyond her.

The dead girl took another step as her sobbing got louder, accompanied by the almost deafening howling of metal scraping against metal.

Closing her eyes was all Gemma could do to avoid the advancing horror. Her mind told her she was screaming and that her body was finally moving freely, but she refused to look to verify it. Even when she felt gravity tug her to the cold floor, she sought refuge in the darkness behind her eyelids. Even when she felt the pain shoot through her elbows and feet from kicking and flailing against the hard wood at her back, she kept her eyes closed.

Then she felt fingers wrap around her ankle.

There was no denying it now. Death had come. So, with one final, defiant kick, Gemma planted her heel into the arm of the dead girl and skittered back. She flung herself across the room, not stopping until she crashed into the television stand, toppling the appliance, which cracked open against the window behind it.

Once more, the ghost claimed her, taking her by the shoulders and shaking her gently. In her panic, Gemma failed to register just how big and warm the hands holding her were, nor did she stop screaming, even as the fiend pulled her into its warm embrace. Only when death failed to claim her did she stop resisting and tentatively open her eyes. It was dark, but there was no sign of the dead girl. Her absence had taken the chill and the ever-present screeching with her. All was silent and calm once more as she looked up and into the eyes of Dan, who was shaking his head.

'Gemma,' he said. 'What the fuck?'

8.

'ALL RIGHT, I'VE HAD enough of this shit.'

'What? Me doing—' was all Gemma could get out before being cut off.

'You hear me? This shit right here? I've had enough of it.'

'I don't know—'

Once more, she was stopped in her tracks. This time by the crashing of a till tray being slammed shut. Eva, intentionally avoiding looking at her, marched around from behind the counter and towards the front door, whereupon she cranked the lock and flipped the sign to read *closed.*

'We finishing early?' Gemma asked. 'Guess I'll clean the—'

'Nu-uh,' Eva snapped, still looking away from her. 'Leave that till the morning. We have more pressing shit to do. Sit down.'

Snapping her fingers, Eva pointed to the booth in the corner. Gemma slid into it, and Eva tucked herself in opposite. Obviously, Gemma knew what this was about. As hard as she had tried to hide it, Eva had always known when something disastrous was going on in her life.

Five days had passed since she had smashed the television, and she and Dan had been at one another's throats since. The broken appliance was not the deciding factor of their feud. In fact, that accident had broken Dan's silent stint. He was all over Gemma, making sure everything was all right, fretting over any injuries she may have sustained. Their current rift had only begun once Gemma had explained why, exactly, she had been flailing around on the floor.

Obviously, he refused to believe her, and why would he? His was a world of numbers, calculations, and facts. There was no room to entertain such things as fantasy and magic. Even though he had *seen* the dead girl the night before. He'd *heard* her. He'd *felt* how cold the apartment had gotten, but he would simply refuse to listen when Gemma pleaded her case.

In a way, she could understand. As far back as she could remember, she had always believed there was more to existence than what could be seen and felt. Even now, with those beliefs confirmed in the most heinous way, she had trouble taking it all in. So, if Dan believed there was not enough evidence for his liking, so be it, but that left one question. Where was the trust?

There was a decided effort on Gemma's part to not let her frustration fester into resentment, but she had become overwhelmed with fear and frustration, and her mind would fill with bile and she would go on to curse the man she loved.

Why not just believe her? *After everything I did for him.*

Dan was something of a hypochondriac in the way that only men could be. Every slight sniffle was a full-blown flu, a queasy stomach was food poisoning, a stubbed toe was obviously cause for amputation below the knee. She never coddled him, nor did she play into his delusions, but she would always *believe* him. Inevitably, when the pair broke down the symptoms of Dan's maladies, the truth would be revealed, and the pair would laugh.

Every night, the girl had come to visit Gemma, and every night, she had tried in vain to procure evidence of the hauntings. When pictures and videos were taken with her phone, they had failed to capture the spectre. She had sought other cameras, believing the ghost might be operating on a light spectrum that refused to be caught by digital lenses. Exhausting her wages, she had bought both a disposable camera that used film as well as a Polaroid. Neither worked. Gemma could only speculate as to why, but the only thing that made sense in her mind was that only a spirit could perceive another spirit, and outside of artistic merit, cameras had a distinct lack of soul.

Obviously, the best evidence to convince Dan of the ghoul's existence would be for him to see her again. Clearly this time. Not just as a blurred, naked figure in the mid-distance, but for him to look into those mournful, wet eyes for himself.

Frustratingly, he had been a complete gentleman during their spat and had been sleeping on the couch, leaving Gemma their large bed to herself. He would always be sleeping soundly, ears plugged, and far away from the crying ghoul and her symphony of screaming metal. Far away from Gemma's own wails of despair and horror when confronted with her uninvited guest.

'So what's he done?' Eva asked, crossing her arms.

'Dan?' Gemma asked, deflecting in order to buy time.

'Mm-hmm. I ain't saying his name. What's he done? He fuck someone behind your back?'

'Eva, Jesus.'

'He do it in front of you? Because that's kinda hot.'

'Fucking hell,' Gemma spat with a laugh.

'No, come on, now. Don't joke. Be serious.'

Somewhere deep inside her stomach, a knot of anxiety loosened, if only a little.

'It's not Dan,' she said. 'Not really.'

'Whatcha mean by that?'

'I … Christ, Eva. Where do I even begin?'

'I don't know, girl. It's your story.'

'I've got a situation, and I don't know what to do about it.'

'You pregnant?' Eva said.

'God, no.'

'He got someone *else* pregnant?'

'Eva, come on, now.'

'Someone else get *him* pregnant?'

Letting out a little snort, Gemma shook her head. It felt good to laugh again. Even the smallest of respites made her feel like perhaps all of this could simply resolve itself without any need for intervention. That wouldn't be the case, however, and she knew it. She would have to confide in someone other than Dan to try and resolve this situation. But how on Earth could she articulate the terror she had been subjected to over the last few days?

Sleep had been all but impossible. What scant few hours she had caught were fitful and light, her subconscious always primed and alert, ever vigilant for those telltale heralds of the dead girl's arrival. A sudden drop in temperature or an aching pipe would cause her to snap to attention and prime herself for what was to come.

Between her bouts of trying to record the spirit or attract Dan's attention, she would try and attack the thing. She threw pillows, cups, and mugs. All of which would simply pass through the spectre. Then she tried swinging Dan's bat at the girl, but all she accomplished was taking a chunk of plaster out of the wall. Which gave Dan all the more reason to believe she had lost her mind.

All that was left was to cower and hide until the dead girl faded from view. Although, whatever force had been holding the ghost at bay was clearly waning. She was becoming emboldened, and each passing day, she would advance further into the bedroom than she had the night before. Not by much, just an extra step here and there, but soon, she would be able to cross from the door to the far corner where Gemma would be hiding. Perhaps by the end of the week, maybe sooner, Gemma was certain that would be the end for her.

All she had to do was sum all of those fears and anxieties up in a way her friend who *takes no shit* could digest.

'I need a drink,' was how she decided to sum the feelings up.

'You know something? I need a drink too,' Eva said.

'Want to go to the pub, or—'

'No. We'll go to mine. I'm the boss, bitch. So what I say goes.'

9.

'ONE THING YOU'VE got to understand. Inside these walls, my word is law ...'

Eva spoke through heaving breaths, reaching down and removing her pumps before depositing them beside the front door.

'So, when I tell you to drink, you drink. When I say shots, you down the shots, and when I tell you not to bullshit me about *you know who*, you don't bullshit me, yeah? Besides that, *mi casa, es su casa.* Living room's to the right there. Get some clubland classics on YouTube.'

Gemma slipped off her boots, relinquishing the cherished inches they gave her, as Eva moved from the hallway to a room beneath the stairs. Despite the pair's friendship, this was Gemma's first visit to her boss's home. Much like the cafe, Eva had decorated her cosy semi-detached with warm earthy tones but had also mixed in a peculiar dash of glittering baubles and golden highlights to the furniture. It made her think of it as some sort of hippy boudoir.

There were two two-seat sofas in Eva's living room, so Gemma picked the one that didn't have the remote controls beside it and sat. Books lined the walls on built-in shelves. Gemma was impressed by how well-read Eva was ... until she studied the books a little closer. They were all *soft 'romance'* paperbacks with lurid titles like *A Dark Romance* and *Her Secret Rose*. She laughed and shook her head. It was so perfectly Eva.

The devil herself appeared. In her hands were two enormous balloon glasses, each roiled with bright tropical colours and punctuated with frozen fruit and large straws.

'Girl, get this in you right now.'

'Jesus Christ,' Gemma laughed.

'Just a small one to start. Why is there no music on?'

Twirling on the balls of her feet, Eva scanned the room for the remotes, holding her arms out as a counterbalance. Gemma watched on, spellbound, as Eva continued to wave her giant drink around the room yet not spill a single drop. Absently, Gemma caught her straw in her mouth and drank deep. Instantly, she began to hack and cough.

'What's *in* this?'

'Well, because *you know who* is being an asshole, it's meant to be an *Adios, Motherfucker*, but I didn't have all the ingredients. So, it's mostly gin and Tango. You know, the usual.'

'I thought you wanted to talk to me, not kill me.'

'Well, I only have guests over if they're willing to have a good time. We'll bitch about *you know who* and then I'll remind you about how much of a queen you are, but we're going to have fun first, and we're getting drunk as we do it. All right, girl?'

'You can say Dan's name you—'

Thumping bass cut her off as Eva put her music on. It was a far cry from what Gemma listened to, but she couldn't help laugh as Eva started dancing along to the track, mouthing along to the high-pitched vocals and throwing her hand into the air in faux ecstasy.

Their drinks were emptied before the song had finished, and Eva promptly had their glasses refilled. After this process was repeated a few more times, Gemma began to rave along with her boss, singing along with the clubland covers of classic rock anthems.

Once a more subdued tune came on, Eva lowered the volume and turned to Gemma.

'Come on, then, what's happened? You come into work with a face like a smacked arse and say you're fine, but you're not, and I can't be having that. You know I'm just looking out for you, girl, right? Even if you dress like fucking *Nightmare Before Christmas*, you're still an absolute queen, and *you know who* should be treating you like one.'

'Thank you,' Gemma said before taking a long sip of Eva's concoction as she thought of what to say next.

Talk of ghouls and ghosts had not sat well with Dan. Nor would that kind of talk fly with Eva. Instead, she settled on a half-truth,

'I feel like I'm stuck in a rut and don't know what to do.'

Nodding her head, Eva finished her cocktail as her eyes widened. Her expression read, *I knew it*, but her mouth was too busy to say the words.

'Girl,' she said, once her glass had been emptied. 'What do I always tell you?'

'That you hate the patriarchy.'

'No. Well, yeah … Look, I'm always telling you that you need to believe in yourself more. Don't I always say that?'

'Yeah, you're always looking out for me.'

'So, what? You and *you know who*—' Eva began.

'Dan,' Gemma said, cutting in.

'Fine, fine. So, you and Dan are, what? Growing apart?'

'No, no. Nothing like that.'

'Oh, shit. Is it the cafe? You looking for a new job?'

'No, Eva. I love working there and I love you—'

'Then shit, I don't know what you want from me.'

'This, Eva,' Gemma laughed, holding her drink up. 'This is helping. Honestly, thank you so much.'

'How about this? I've told you how I got the cafe, haven't I?'

'Maybe once.' Gemma laughed.

It was something of a party piece, Eva's recounting of how she had gotten one over on her first husband, aka the first man *who would not be named.* Also known as *Simon the Twat.* He was a property developer who owned dozens of locations across the city, fast food joints, housing blocks, and, most importantly of all, coffee shops. Eva's cafe was actually his first ever business venture. It was also where he would take his mistresses for discreet encounters. Eva had known about it and built up a case for divorce. Simon was worth a small fortune, but Eva wanted only one thing: his first business, the one he committed his adultery in. The way she told it, this crushed Simon so thoroughly that he fled the country. The truth of that was up for debate, but Gemma found it more fun to believe.

'Okay, you know the story,' Eva said. 'Well, I wasn't going to say anything until the paperwork was done and things were straightened out behind the scenes, but things have been going well, so I've been looking at opening another cafe.'

'No way,' Gemma gasped.

'Seriously, girl. I was going to ask you to look after it for me.'

'You're kidding, right?'

'Hell no, I'm not, and don't be giving me any excuses either. Don't be saying you can't do it, because we both know you can. You know your shit, girl. You know *your* shit and you know *my* shit, so why wouldn't you be able to run your own place?'

'God, Eva … I don't know.'

'Yeah, you do. Come on, we need a stronger drink to celebrate. We need to be closer to the booze, and we need shots.'

As they made their way to the kitchen, Gemma's mind roiled with the prospect of running her own cafe. Eva was right; she *did* know how to do it. Eva rarely took holidays, but when she *did* take a break, things ran smoothly under Gemma's watch.

All the same, could she do that full time? It was a huge commitment, and despite Eva's praise and encouragement, Gemma thought it may be best if she remained a simple barista. There was no way to fuck up just brewing coffee and serving sandwiches. Nothing serious, anyway.

Another drink was produced. This one was a sickly green and was somehow even stronger and sweeter than the bizarre orange and purple brew they'd just finished. Eva synced her phone to a smart speaker, and soon, the small kitchen was shuddering along to the thrumming bass. Next came shots. All manner of sweet rainbow liqueurs were pulled from a seemingly endless drinks cupboard as the two danced and shrieked and set the world to rights.

Neither of them took much notice of the time. Nor did Gemma check her phone and the three messages Dan had sent her. Both were lost in their own happy, alcohol-induced worlds. Between that, the pounding music, and the fact Eva was smoking on the back step, Gemma failed to heed the warning signs that indicated their party was about to receive another guest.

'I just don't know,' Gemma screamed over the music.

'I'm tellin' yeh,' Eva slurred.

'No, no. I'm saying I don't know if I can do it.'

'Yeah. I'm tellin' yeh …'

'The second cafe, Eva. I don't know about it. We wouldn't be working together anymore, Eva.'

'Yeah, yeah.'

'You can't hear a word I'm saying, can you.'

'I'm tellin' yeh …'

Waving to catch Eva's attention, she gestured to the speaker. It took her boss a few seconds to register what was being asked, but after fumbling with the controls, the thumping beats of the music stopped. The kitchen, however, was not plunged into silence as it should have been.

'Right, what I was trying to say was if I end up doing this … Oh. Oh God—'

It took a moment for Gemma to process why there was still such a din despite Eva having muted the radio. The upbeat melodies they had been enjoying had been hiding a chorus of mournful howls and the shrieks of metal rending itself.

'Shit, shit, shit.' Gemma began to cry.

'Yeah, exactly.' Eva nodded.

'No, Eva, listen to me … She's here.'

'Who is?'

'*Listen!*'

Scrunching her face, Eva closed her eyes and tilted her head. Even with the theatrics, it took her stepping into the kitchen to acknowledge the intrusion, but once she did, her expression turned to one of fury.

'Who the fuck is in my house?'

Slamming her drink down, Eva flicked her cigarette into the void of the night and marched over to her stove. Beside it stood a large knife block, and from it, she snatched a massive santoku blade. With a furrowed brow, she marched past Gemma and into the main hall, then stopped, spinning on her heels.

'What the fuck?' she cried. The sound was now coming from every part of the house.

'Eva, I've been lying to you,' Gemma said.

'You get the fuck out here right now, or I'll slap the shit out of you,' Eva called out, glancing around the empty lobby.

Paradoxically, Eva's raging outbursts were helping Gemma compose herself. There was a world of difference between being roused from slumber by those dreadful calls and being beside an enraged Eva who was looking to take the horror on face to face.

Perhaps this would exorcise the spirit? She originally thought it would require a couple of priests chanting in Latin and censers filled with incense, but the more furious Eva became, the more convinced she was that the ghost could be naturally driven away by an incredibly angry middle-aged woman.

'Listen, Eva. I was lying about being in a rut. I've been out of it because of *this*. I didn't think you'd believe me. But—'

'Gemma, what the fuck is going on?'

'There's a girl, Eva. She's been following me. She's dead. I mean, she's a ghost, Eva—'

'What the fu—' Eva began, but for once, it was Gemma who cut in.

'Listen to me. Please. I never said anything because Dan doesn't believe me, and I didn't think you'd would either, but she's *here* …'

Before Eva could ask her once more *what the fuck was going on,* the question answered itself. The dead girl was *there*, peering at them from around the corner leading to the kitchen. Gemma had only ever seen the ghoul in the murky hours of early mornings, but here it stood now, fully illuminated. Every sagging loop of dead skin exposed, the rotten nubs of her teeth on full display. Worst of all, those sorrowful, dead eyes had never been more visible, and she could clearly see the tears streaming down her cheeks in rivulets.

There came a moment of stillness as the living and dead made contact of sorts. The last few weeks had felt unreal to her, but never more so than now. She had long since accepted the fact that she was the object of the haunting, but it was still uncanny to see the ghost here, in a stranger's home, in all her ghostly glory. Clearly the *rules* as Gemma knew them—*admittedly from movies and books*—were wrong. The horror before her was not confined to the shadows as it should have been, nor did she have to be alone for it to fully torment her.

As terrified as she was, she was glad the spectre had revealed herself. From where they stood, the dead girl would never make it to them before dissipating. Eva had seen her pursuer now, clear as day, and as drunk as they both were, shared delusions were the wheelhouse of acid and harder drugs, not vodka and tequila. Soon, the ghost would be gone, and she could pour her heart out, and the pair could focus on what to do next.

'Oh, hell no!' Eva cried as she marched *towards* the ghost.

Never in a million years would Gemma have guessed Eva would try to *accost* the spirit.

'No dirty junkie, smack-headed, skinny little bitch is going to …'

Still screaming her curses, Eva bore down upon the decaying figure as Gemma watched on, dumbstruck. Even as Eva raised the heavy blade above her head, the ghoul never once paid its would-be attacker any mind. It kept its dead, hollow eyes locked upon Gemma. It was only when Eva reached out that Gemma snapped out of her reverie and cried out,

'Don't touch her—'

Eva's insults instantly turned to a howl the moment she gripped the girl's shoulder. It was as though the woman had grasped a high voltage electrical line. Her body went slack, though her hand remained affixed to the ghoul. Eva began to convulse and thrash as her scream turned into a wet gurgle. Spittle and foam bubbled from her lips as her eyes rolled and turned white.

Ignoring the woman that now hung from her, the phantasm reached out before taking a step forward.

Instinctively, Gemma wanted to rush to Eva's aid, but she thought she might share her fate if the ghoul were to touch her. Such a matrimony between the worlds of the living and dead was never meant to be. Her coat hung on the rack beside her; behind her, the door.

'Oh God, Eva,' she cried, snatching her jacket from its peg.

The ghost took another step, steadier on its feet and faster than it had moved before. With that movement, it shrugged Eva from its form, and Gemma's boss and friend fell to the floor.

She was dead.

There was nothing more to be done. Gemma turned her back and made a dash for the door, flinging it open and running out into the cold, dark morning.

10.

WITH SHAKING FINGERS, Gemma handed over a pocketful of change to the girl behind the counter and clutched the hot mug of coffee with both hands. She sipped it as she walked, ignoring the scalding heat, cherishing it, almost, as it drove away the chill that had penetrated into her bones. The skies were still a smear of dark purples and greys, but the sun would find her soon, so she positioned herself at the front of the store, beneath the full-length windows, to await the salvation morning would bring.

Glancing around the empty coffee shop, she shook her head. She held a particular disdain for these sorts of large franchise stores. If you had been in one, then you had been in them all. Their uniform colour schemes and seating plans could cause crippling déjà vu at times, and the safe corporate art they had hanging, combined with the sickening royalty-free music, it was just all too revolting.

Perhaps she had been spoiled. Eva's cafe was most definitely how the woman had reached out and expressed herself to the public. She had been through some rough times, and it had made her hard and cold. But the café … that was who Eva really was.

Gemma would never see either of them again, and it was all her fault.

'I'm so sorry,' Gemma croaked before bursting into tears.

Her mourning wails echoed across the room, filling it, drowning out the soft muzak. The few other patrons lowered their heads, refusing to acknowledge the mad woman by the window. The staff lacked that luxury, unfortunately, so they busied themselves and did their best to ignore the crying.

Once Gemma had escaped Eva's house, she had run until her legs failed her. She had collapsed upon an embankment that ran beside a desolate road and lay there upon the cold earth for close to an hour. She was stunned, sick, and nursing a hangover that felt as much spiritual as it was physical. Eventually, she'd staggered to her feet, stumbling back towards the city centre. It was there she found one of the few remaining phone boxes and called the emergency services, not wanting to call them on her mobile lest they trace her. She informed the operator that she was an early morning jogger and had heard screams coming from a neighbour's house, and that the front door was open. To motivate the woman on the other end of the line, she added that she'd glimpsed a body within that home before hanging up. From there, she bought a charger from an all-night convenience store and simply wandered until she happened upon the coffee shop she was now crying in.

Her tear ducts ran dry.

She was reduced to a peculiar retching heave as she checked her phone and plugged it in. Hidden behind a wall of apps, Dan stared back at her. Above his head lay the notification bar which housed all of his unread attempts at communication. She had to call him. Of course she did, but what would she say? What *could* she say?

As she braced herself for what was to come, the sun broke through the grey miasma of clouds and stood at her side. Its light washed through the coffee shop, refracting through the glass and bringing with it a comforting warmth. One that could only be matched by hearing Dan's voice.

'Hey,' he said, answering before the second ring could even complete.

'Hey,' she replied, unable to stop a tired smile spreading across her lips.

'Are you all right?' he asked. 'I presume you were out and wanted some space.'

'Yeah, something like that,' she said.

Then came a pause. Both realising they had just exchanged more words in the past few seconds than they had in days.

Dan broke the silence with a cough. 'I hope you had a good night, and I hope you're feeling better … I love you. I'm sorry.'

'I love you too,' she echoed, then the line went quiet again.

'Well, I should get ready for work,' Dan said. 'See you at home?'

'She's dead,' Gemma said, finally wringing the words from her throat. 'Eva's dead.'

'What? Are you serious?'

'Dan, I'm so sorry. She's dead,' Gemma said, stifling her cries as the coffee shop started to fill up.

'Jesus, what happened? Are you all right? Was it an accident or—'

'It was …' she cut in.

'Gemma?'

'It was *her*, Dan. The girl. She followed me to Eva's house and—'

'This isn't funny, Gemma.'

'I'm not *trying* to be funny,' she snapped. 'That *thing* followed me. I thought that … God, I don't know what I thought. Eva's dead, and it's my fault.'

'Gemma—'

'I didn't know,' she continued over him. 'I didn't know Eva would try and … I don't know why she's following me. I don't know what she wants, and I don't know what to do. But now Eva's dead and—'

'Gemma, stop it!' he snapped, then calmed himself. 'I'm sorry, but please just stop. We can't do this over the phone. I'm going to call in and take a day off, yeah? This must be horrible. Where are you? I'll come to you if you want, and we can—'

With a swipe of her thumb, Gemma cut Dan's ranting off. Instantly, her phone was abuzz with activity as messages and calls and notes came through thick and fast. With her phone set to mute, none of them registered, and the device slipped from her fingers. In the back of her mind, she knew she should have been furious with him, but a numbness had blossomed within her. Be it acceptance, exhaustion, or her mind finally cracking, at that moment, she was incapable of caring and wanted nothing more than to slip into a dreamless oblivion. Crossing her arms on the table, she sought refuge within their embrace and the darkness of her own making.

Between the warmth of the sun on her back and the droning background noise of the shop, Gemma's mind began to slip away. She welcomed the nothingness, hoping it would erase the pain of knowing that Eva was gone. Gone would be the heartache of feeling as though Dan had betrayed her. She could be free.

For a little while, at least.

Half an hour passed, and though her mind never truly slipped into the void, there came some small respite. Unfortunately for her, the noise of the coffee shop continued to dance across her semiconscious mind. The clattering of ceramic mugs, the chatter of morning commuters, the whistling of milk being frothed by the steamers.

When the screaming began, she tried so hard to attribute it to an encroaching dream, but she knew it not to be the case. She knew exactly what the commotion was all about.

Snapping to attention, she focused in on where the noise was coming from. At the back of the building, nestled within a crook behind the counter, lay the bathrooms. Staggering out from them came an older woman in hysterics, her breath visibly steaming from her mouth. The chill had either failed to reach Gemma or was being held at bay by the sunshine.

The dead girl was here.

During the day.

In the middle of a crowded coffee shop.

For a few moments, she tried to argue against the fact, as once more, she tried to argue that this was against *the rules*. *Rules* she had made up. *Rules* that had already been disproven. Yet still, this felt like a greater violation than those committed the night previous. She may have been in a brightly lit house with Eva, but it was still nighttime. She was still vulnerable and within some sort of reach of the ghost. How could she be here, in the brilliant morning sunshine, in a crowded room?

She was no authority on what the dead could or could not do.

The girl then made herself known.

Her pale hands encroached across the gaudily coloured wall that hid the entrance to the restrooms, pulling herself into the open. She ignored the screams of horror, same as she ignored the countless phones that were attempting to entrap her likeness in binary. She had eyes for only one person. Still looking directly at Gemma, the dead girl took a step forward.

Frozen in place, Gemma realised how ridiculous she was being. She should have been running already, putting as much distance between herself and the ghost as she could. How often had she and Dan watched nature documentaries and found themselves frustrated by the passivity some creatures had shown regarding their fates? How oblivious they were to the fact that they were prey.

It was a sickening realisation. That was *her* role in life now … *prey.*

'Jesus Christ. You all right, love?'

A heavy voice rang out beside her, but it was not directed *at* her. A burly man, spattered with a rainbow daubing of paint and plaster, strode across the room, cutting his way through the gawking spectators. His lack of fear came from a place of either incredible bravery or incalculable ignorance—Gemma was unsure which.

Doesn't he know that if you touch a dead person, you die too? she thought. Exhaustion had dulled her wits somewhat, and it took a moment for her to process the fact that no, this stranger was *not* privy to that information.

Leaping to her feet, she began to scream for the crowd to stay away and for the workman to stay back. She was not the only one crying out. Near enough every person was making a raucous din, calling out their disbelief, vocalising their terror, and of course, the ghoul herself was eternally sobbing.

'Don't touch her,' Gemma shrieked again. Thankfully, the words came forth during a slight lull in the maelstrom. Pausing in his tracks, the large man glanced back and was about to respond, but the dead girl continued pushing forward, continuing her slow march towards Gemma. In doing so, her outstretched hand gently brushed the labourer's elbow.

In an instant, the man's body snapped straight, and a whining gasp escaped his throat. His eyes bulged as frothing bile and blood began to gather at his lips and spray into the air in a fine mist.

The already tumultuous shop turned riotous. People began to scatter, fighting to escape the creeping death before them. Gemma continued to scream, advising people to not go near the dead girl, but her voice was lost amongst the din. A woman barrelled past a young couple, trying to make it to the front door, but tripped. All three of them went clattering to the ground, skidding into the legs of the unperturbed ghoul.

Each of them was instantly thrown into a death spasm.

Finally, Gemma was moving. Carried along with the other evacuees, not wanting to look back. Afraid, not only of the glare of the dead girl but also not wanting to witness the deaths she had been responsible for. She knew too well that if she would have been more aware of the ghoul's presence, she could have escaped it sooner. With her absence, the girl would have never claimed four more victims.

The crowd poured from the front door, where they dispersed. The sound of sirens echoed through the streets as passers-by tried and failed to intervene and help. Gemma vanished into the confusion and fled, hoping nobody else would fall foul of her spectral pursuer.

11.

EXHAUSTION SNAPPED AT Gemma's nape and tears pricked her eyes as she wandered the city. As the afternoon slipped away, the shadows cast grew long and dark; eventually, they swallowed her whole. She did not notice this consumption, however, as she wandered in a daze, her mind reeling as she tried to process the events that had led her to this vagrancy.

It wasn't fair, she thought.

A ridiculous thought, but one she simply could not shake.

I've been cheated.

Rules had been broken by this spectre. The dead haunted the dark corners of the world. If not at night, then in areas where light had trouble taking purchase. Their domain should be limited to abandoned hospitals and dusty, deserted homes. Not coffee shops and new apartment blocks, and most of all, they did not snatch away the lives of innocent people with such blasé callousness.

Thinking back to how this had all started, she felt the need to laugh but lacked the energy. It had all been so quaint compared to the nightmare she was living now. Exciting, even … if only for a short while. The creaks, the shadows, the feeling of being watched. *Ghosts were real,* and they behaved exactly as they should. Inhabiting her little council house, shifting through the gloomy rooms that never truly caught the sun. Just the way they were supposed to.

Stopping outside one of the many museums that lay throughout the city, she crashed upon the grand steps that led up to the foyer. Her limbs flopped to either side, and she lay there like a star fish as tourists gave her a wide berth, shaking their heads as they climbed past her bizarre performance.

Of course, that sense of wonder she'd felt was fleeting. As the days went on and the fear within her began to ferment and bubble over, she quickly turned to the internet in search of answers. What she understood now was that the legions of Wiccans, occultists, and ghost hunters online had just as little insight about the realities of the dead as she did. Their advice ranged from burning sage and chanting prayers to simply opening her windows. None of which had helped to halt her steadily worsening situation. There was no stock to be had from myths and legends.

So what *did* she know? What had she experienced that could be of some use?

Pinching the space between her eyes, she tried to fight through the confusion that exhaustion had lumbered her with. If only she knew *why* she had been targeted by the wraith. Perhaps then she could deduce what it wanted.

'It wants you dead, dickhead,' she spat. Only realising a second later the mother who stood beside her, toddlers by her side. She offered an apologetic glance as the woman ushered her children away from the *crazy lady*.

Even the slightest touch from the ghoul would be fatal. *That* she knew for a fact. So long as she kept her wits about her and avoided any dead ends, she was positive she could avoid her pursuer, but for how long?

There had been weeks between the dead girl's first visit. Then it had been days. That morning, there had been only, what? Eight hours or so before she had become manifest. How long until her next appearance? Gemma thought of a sharpened pendulum swinging above her head. Each pass coming sooner than the last as the instrument of her doom ran out of momentum. Eventually, it would come to a standstill and bring with it her death, but for now, all she could do was guess as to when her stalker would make her next appearance. That meant she could get some sort of rest. Perhaps even a nap. The idea delighted her.

Where was the dead girl now? They were tethered in some ethereal way. Yet the ghoul refused to manifest unless she was unobserved, it seemed. Be that by her own doing or some cosmic law that had to be adhered to, she did not know, but it was still solid information she could use to her advantage.

Was she here? Now? Invisible amongst the surging mass of tourists, shoppers, and drinkers? Who else was out there? she wondered. How many other ghosts walked amongst them … lost and desperate to be seen or heard?

Rising to her feet, she began to chuckle. Fatigue and shock were addling her senses. She staggered through the crowds, appearing as if she were drunk. She called out to the invisible dead, challenging them to make contact if they were there.

If they were, then they had the luxury of ignoring her delirious cries. Something the living could only dream of.

12.

CHEERS AND LAUGHTER filled the night air as revellers poured from the pubs and clubs of the city centre. Now they had slaked their thirst, they sought to fulfil their other needs. Most stormed the twenty-four-hour fast-food outlets, desperate for a fix of sodium and deep-fried meats. Others let loose battle cries as they looked for a fight, riding high on cocaine-fuelled adrenaline and bravado. Amidst the chaos, lovers picked their way through the crowds, heading towards the taxi ranks, their appetites being more carnal in nature.

Through ignorance or design, the horde paid little attention to the rough sleepers that morning. The lost and the forgotten, filling the doorways of the city square, nestling under the awnings of the high street stores. Gemma was counted amongst their rank, though she forewent what little shelter from the elements the buildings offered, instead opting to huddle upon a bench that sat in the most exposed part of the plaza.

All day, she had walked. Trudging to and fro throughout the town, lost in her own thoughts or buried in her phone, trying desperately to pluck some solution from either thin air or increasingly infuriating jaunts on the internet. Neither avenue had provided any results, however. Because of her travels, she had managed to avoid the dead girl for the most part, hearing only the faintest of cries carried on the wind as she kept on the move.

Night had come, though, and with it, an exhaustion that could no longer be denied. Gemma's legs ached; her thighs were chafed and burning. She felt her body beginning to crash, so she found the safest place she could think of in a pinch. Somewhere far from any blind corners that could provide the dead girl the privacy she so needed to cross over from her ethereal world.

Though she slept, it was a fitful and unsatisfying slumber. The city was never more alive than it was at night. The dull thundering of nightclubs partnered with the shrieks of joy from the drunks was all-consuming.

Gemma stirred, peering out from under her hood. She held herself tight, the chilling night air biting at her fiercely. With shaking hands, she retrieved her phone from her bra and turned it on in order to check the time. Within seconds, she was bombarded with countless messages. She had been reported missing on social media, and it seemed everyone in the world was trying to get in touch with her now, distant cousins, old workmates, her mother, and, of course, Dan.

More than anything, she wanted to see Dan. She desperately wanted him to pull her to his chest and suffocate the pain and fear out of her. She wanted him to shake her, to wake her up and confirm this had all been some terrible nightmare. Any anger and frustration she had held against her partner had long since cooled. He was right, after all. This whole scenario *was* ridiculous. She found herself comforted by the thought that perhaps she *had* gone a little mad. That would be fine. She would sit and gibber to herself, screaming at the shadows and wailing about the dead girl, so long as she could do it in the company of Dan. Once more, she began to laugh, delirium replacing the fear.

Her hysterics attracted the ire of a gang of young girls who walked by. They were dressed in bright, tight dresses exposing their perfectly tanned and toned limbs. They flicked their shining, freshly blown hair as they turned their made-up faces away from her. She imagined how they perceived her: A filthy, bedraggled lunatic. Wild eyes beaming beneath matted, unwashed hair. A twitching, hooting thing to be avoided at all costs. A harbinger of what could come to pass should their lives veer off course.

Laughter turned to sobs as she thought about Dan's apartment … *their home.* She wanted to shower and to curl up with him and watch whatever boring shite sporting event he wanted to watch. It would be bliss, and she would be happy to do that for the rest of her life.

Moving of its own accord, Gemma's thumb hovered over Dan's name in her phone. Should she call him? He would be there for her within minutes; she knew he would. No matter the time or the location, he would come rushing to her aid and accept her back into his arms. The harsh words they had exchanged would flitter away like forgotten nightmares, and they could start their lives anew.

Nightmarish visions held her thumb in place, however. As she thought back on Eva, she slipped her phone back into her bra. She pictured Dan in Eva's place, his face curled into a torturous rictus, blood and foam boiling on his lips as the embodiment of death wrapped her skeletal fingers around his throat.

For all the times she had longed for him to see the ghost, now it had become imperative he never lay eyes upon the fiend. He would throw himself between her and the ghoul to protect her, she knew he would, and then he would die.

Somewhere behind her, screams filled the early morning air. Not the wailing howls of joy, though, these were cries of terror. She shifted herself on the bench, her aching, freezing limbs fighting against her will. Some fifteen meters away, where two buildings closed in and wove themselves into a side street, the party girls were pointing and crying. The dead girl was the cause of their distress, unsurprisingly. Gemma leapt to her feet and started to run in the opposite direction, knowing that no matter how much of a ruckus she caused, the crowds would refuse to disperse.

She glanced back once as she fled. The girls were being comforted by a gang of young drunk men. Dutch courage and machismo bade the Samaritans to approach the decaying ghoul.

Gemma continued to run, hoping her swift departure would cause the spectre to return to the ether before claiming any more lives. Yet the gurgling howls of dying men told her she had failed that task.

13.

'BLOODY HELL, GEM. Are you all right?'

Stepping back into his studio, Vinny gestured for Gemma to follow. Once she had crossed the threshold, he attempted to slip around her, making for the front door, but Gemma stopped him, snapping, 'Don't!'

'Hey, hey. All right. Whatever you want.'

'Sorry … sorry, Vinny. I just …'

Not long had passed since the incident with the clubbers, so Gemma was confident she had some leeway before her stalker's next visit. It was still dark outside, and every building she passed was in a state of purgatory, vacant and idling. All except Vinny's little shop. The weak, warm light coming from his boarded-over window was a shining beacon in the early morning. Of course, she never would have wanted to put anybody else in danger, but she had to see *someone*.

Someone who had a mind as open as a book with a broken spine. Someone who could offer some sort of solace. Someone who would believe her wild tale. Someone who kept unusual hours.

'Gemstone, you never have to apologise to me,' he said. 'I can't imagine how hard it's been for you.'

'How hard what's been?' she asked.

'Eva, Gem. Being there … when it happened.'

'I … yeah.'

The thought should have come easier, but her mind was addled with exhaustion and pain and shock. *How did Vinny know about Eva*?

'She was a queen, Gemstone,' he said as he moved once more for the front door. 'A bloody good woman. A star. A bright, beautiful bleedin' star. Dunno what we're going to do without her.'

'Vinny, leave the door open, please,' she said, cutting him off. 'Did Dan tell you about her? About Eva?'

'Dan?' he asked, stepping away from the door. 'Oh, yeah, your fella. No, no, no … well, yes. He popped round asking if you were here. He told me you were there when Eva passed, but it was the police who told me first. Bloody vultures.'

'Right. Right …' was all she could mutter.

Taking to a half-squat so the pair could be at eye level, Vinny took her hands into his own.

'Gemma, are you all right?'

Unable to look him in the eye, she glanced around the studio. Surrounded by such religious iconography, she was safe here, surely. She wanted to pray. To God, any God, for forgiveness and help.

'I'm just so lost, and I don't know what to do.'

'Hey, now,' he cooed. 'You'll never be lost with me around, Gem, but … losing somebody. It's a terrible thing. Nothing can prepare you for it. Even if it's an expected loss. You can have years' worth of advance warning, but nothing can ease the pain so soon after—'

'Thanks, Vin. I'll be fine. I am … fine.'

'Yeah. Look at me rambling on, eh? Not even offered you a brew.'

With a grunt, he stood up, and she followed as he made his way towards the back room. Part of her wanted to remain by the front door, but at the same time, this crumb of human contact was nourishing, and she wanted to eat her fill.

Light flooded the murky studio as he opened the back door. There lay a familiar slice of Vinny's personal life laid bare. A simple brick wall and hundreds of pounds' worth of ink hanging from it.

'You don't mind, do you?' she asked, crossing into his inner sanctum. 'Me being back here, I mean.'

'No, Gemstone. You shouldn't be alone, anyway. Hey, remember, *this too shall pass.* Time might not heal all wounds, God only knows that *I* know that, but the pain, the hurt—the worst of it does pass eventually. I'll tell you what, though, tea and Jammie Dodgers help too.'

After so many years of speculation, she was finally privy to Vinny's private life. It was an underwhelming and somewhat sad affair. A single bare bulb hung high above them, illuminating the sparse, cell-like room. A small cot took up one corner, and opposite lay a toilet. A grille lay flush against the far wall with a tap located above it. Vinny *was* living there, it seemed. Only it was more of a prison than a home. Perhaps that was intentional, and he was living a simple, pious life. If there was any humanity to be found in that room, it was a plastic table that held upon it a kettle and a metal tin brimming with various packets of biscuits and teabags.

'So why me, Gemstone?' he asked, flicking the kettle on. 'I'll always be here for you, of course, but why haven't you been talking to your fella? He was worried sick about you.'

'Dan's just … never mind,' she said, then changed the subject. 'So, what did the police want?'

'Usual bollocks, Gemstone. Hounding me for my particulars. Asking me where I was when Eva … well, y'know. I don't know why they were bothering me. It was obvious they were just doing the rounds. Mind you, couldn't tell them I was at home stoned off my tits, though, could I? That's where I was, though.'

'Christ, I haven't smoked in years. I could murder a spliff right now.'

'Sorry, Gem,' he said, throwing two teabags into a pair of mugs and clicking the kettle on. 'This is the strongest shit I'll allow in here. Well, apart from these bad boys.'

Vinny passed over a packet of Jammie Dodgers, and Gemma took them with shaking fingers. She was still freezing, and there was no respite to be found in that back room. The sterile bricks likely neighboured the entry that ran behind the building, offering no insulation.

'You were at home?' Gemma asked through a mouthful of jam-laden treats.

'Yeah. Why? God, you didn't think I lived here, did you?'

Well …'

Beside them, the kettle hissed and sputtered, the heating element causing the dribble of water it lay in to boil almost instantly.

'Dopey bugger,' Vinny said, turning it off and taking it over to the tap in the wall. 'Would help if there was water in the bloody thing, wouldn't it?'

Squeals filled the room as Vinny cranked the tap. High-pitched, metallic shrieks that pierced straight through Gemma to her very soul. She heard them and choked, her heart suddenly fit to burst from the unexpected noise. *She's here. So soon after her last visit too.* And Gemma had only gone and trapped herself in the back of Vinny's shop. *This is it*, she thought. *Time to die.*

Lurching towards the front door of the shop, hoping that by some miracle she could dodge past the spirit's deadly touch, she stopped dead in her tracks. The ghost was nowhere to be found. The open door at the front of the studio was empty, and the howling had abruptly stopped. It was Vinny, she realised. He had turned the tap off.

'Bloody Hell, Gemma. Are you all right?'

'What the *fuck* was that?' she gasped.

'The pipes, Gemstone. They're knackered, ain't they? Why, what's up?'

It was an old building. Pre-war and feeling every year of its age. The walls, the floors, the ceilings, they all whined and creaked in their own harmonious ways, imperceptible once you had spent more than a few days listening to their songs. Even *their* pipes in the café, they screamed in agony when they were used, but not *quite* like the ones in this back room, not in the way that resonated the way *his* pipes did.

Not just the pipes either, she realised. She could *feel* it now, the coldness of the room. The loneliness. The utter *hopelessness* in that drab little back space. Somehow, it *felt* like the dead girl. It was a ridiculous notion but true all the same. A small part of her, perhaps her soul itself, could feel the connection.

Placing the kettle back upon its stand, Vinny's face dropped any pretence. Gone were his usual smirks and jittering ticks. He held out a hand. *Expecting what?* For her to take it?

'Gemma,' he said, taking a step forward.

Instinctively, she matched his pace, backing away towards the open front door.

'Gemma, I don't mean to sound horrible, but you look awful. Come here. You'll be all right here.'

'No,' she spat.

'If you're going to be sick, there's a toilet here. I won't look. This is a safe space, Gemstone.'

'Don't call me that,' she snapped.

He appeared to her as a ghoul. Worse even than the spectre that had been tormenting her. His skin loose and hanging from its frame; his flesh warped and smudged from years of abuse. His eyes too. She could see now, with his playful facade dropped, they were cold and lifeless.

Shaking her head, she backed away, clattering into his leather tattooing chair and falling to her knees. He made no attempt to follow, however. He simply lowered his arm and remained on the cusp of the back room, watching as she ran from the last bastion she had.

14.

HATRED PROPELLED HER.

Marching through the streets, delirious and enraged, she swore and spat as she marched.

Vinny! What has he done? There was no question now, *he* was the source of this. But how? And why? Gemma thought of the girl. About seeing her face again, hearing her sobs and the howls of the pipes. It made her stomach churn and her already frozen body ripple anew with goose flesh, but she decided she would confront the ghoul. She would have answers, one way or another.

Picking her way through the lurching early morning traffic, she made her way towards the docks. Countless abandoned warehouses littered the streets there, the empty cobbled roads a cross-hatching from a time before city planning had streamlined everything. Finding a fair-sized entry, Gemma collapsed in a heap, resting herself against the wall at her back. It was cold and damp, but she was beyond caring.

It was maddening, the waiting. She had spent so long dreading the appearance of the dead girl, cherishing every second that passed without that foul spectre haunting her; yet now she wanted to confront the horror, it was nowhere to be found.

With nothing but time on her hands, she tried to piece together the puzzle that now lay before her, but even knowing that Vinny was to blame for everything, she had trouble putting all the pieces together. There were gaping holes across the board, and soon, her frustrations were boiling over into fury. Vinny had inadvertently killed so many people by laying this curse upon her. He had killed her best friend, and to think they had both *loved* him too.

'You fucker …' she spat, then shouted, 'Why'd you do it, you old bastard?'

The only answer given was that of an echoing *ASTARD* …

Her mind was ablaze now. Eva's memory was alive and burning, illuminating the darkness that shrouded her thoughts. Why *were* the police interrogating Vinny about Eva's death? She had just accepted it so willingly in the studio, but it made no sense. The other girl who had died had been a client of his, but Eva was just the owner of a neighbouring business. Why would her death raise any flags with the authorities?

Unless this had happened before and there was a connection, besides Vinny, that had triggered some alarm with the detectives. The cause of death, perhaps?

'Those other girls,' Gemma whispered, cementing the thought.

Though Amber Benson had been the most recent and the most well-known case, there had been a spate of deaths across the city over the past couple of years. Young women, all in fine health, passing away without warning. It had garnered a little media attention but was ultimately washed aside amongst the usual deluge of celebrity gossip and football news.

Opening her phone, Gemma cursed when she saw how little battery life she had left. Ignoring the messages and alerts in her notification bar, she opened up a web browser. She had to battle her way past the usual deluge of advertisements, but eventually, she found a website that had a comprehensive list of the peculiar phenomenon.

Amber Benson. Katie Sunderland. Ashley Mathers. Fiona Schwarz.

These girls and more. All found dead, their hearts having failed them in catastrophic ways. All reportedly suffering from bouts of mental illness beforehand too.

Shame washed over her as she opened up her social media app and punched in the names of those recently deceased. The idea alone felt ghoulish, but the true fiendishness of what she was doing only hit home once the first profile loaded and she came face to face with the spirit of Amber Benson.

Her profile picture had been memorialised and encircled by flowers. Amber would remain in the memories of those who cared for her as she did in that snapshot, dancing and smiling, her summer dress spinning and revealing the stark contrast between its bright fabric and the heavily tattooed legs it had once covered. As a sign of respect, whoever had access to Amber's profile had locked it, preventing any further snooping on Gemma's part. Instead, she said a silent prayer and moved onto the next girl.

Much like herself and Amber, Katie Sunderland's body was a testament to ink. The girl's profile page was awash with messages of grief and pledges that her spirit and soul would never be forgotten. Though Gemma had never known Katie, she felt compelled to skirt over those memorials, hoping to get some sense of who the victim was, before beginning to scavenge through her private pictures.

Luckily, Katie's profile was an open book. Luckier still, the woman had organised all of her photographs into separate folders. One of them being titled *Ink*.

Swiping through the pictures, Gemma scanned the woman's tattoos as they flew past. Portraits of heavy metal icons, frozen in eternal screams where they had been punctured into human flesh, flickered before her. Then came the horror icons: Pinhead, Chucky, Ghostface, and more. The work was fantastic and eye-catching, which was distracting her from what she should have *really* been checking for, which was the filler ink *around* the main pieces. With that in mind, she began again and quickly found what she had been searching for. Upon seeing it, she let out a shrill yell that filled the entryway.

A deep, red rune lined the back of Katie's thigh. It was exactly the same design Vinny had inscribed upon her forearm.

'God,' was all she managed to choke out.

This was it. The connection she had been looking for, though it offered cold comfort.

Next, she brought up Ashley's profile. There was no reverence for the departed this time, and Gemma swiped straight to the girl's pictures. Once again, with quarry in mind, she barely had to dig through the countless pictures to find more evidence of Vinny's handiwork. There it was, exposed for all to see. Upon Ashley's shoulder lay that same cursed tattoo.

Three more times, she sought the sigil. Three more times, she found it, bound to the flesh of innocent women.

Gazing down at her arm, she felt sick. The mark was hidden beneath the leather sleeve of her jacket. But just *knowing* it was there made her feel queasy. However, there were still more questions than answers. *Why* Vinny had done this to her. And *how*? Had she wronged him? Was this some sort of punishment?

He was always vocal about how much he hated people who had no respect for the art of tattooing. How much he loathed people's frivolous choices to daub their bodies with ink just because they could. That made the most sense to her, and finally, one part of the puzzle had clicked. Somehow, he had conjured an ethereal assassin to take out those he found *distasteful*.

Another hour, Gemma spent in the alley. Her phone dead. Her only company the charcoal sky above and a valley of bricks to her sides. She paced the entry, conjuring a plan. She would have answers. If not from the dead girl, then from the conjurer himself.

Echoing cries and the whine of Vinny's aching pipes came bounding down the alley. Gemma turned towards her would-be killer but found all the fury and hatred she had inside quelled by the distant, mournful visage of the dead girl. She stood at the far end of the passageway, looking and pointing, but even from that distance, her aura was flooding Gemma's soul with horror and remorse.

Gemma's plan, such as it was, was to stand her ground and point an accusatory finger at the ghoul and *demand* answers, but now, face to face once again, all she longed to do was flee.

'I-I know Vinny sent you,' Gemma called out, her voice cracking. 'I know you're here because of this.'

With that, she pulled up the sleeve of her jacket, exposing the tattoo. Had she expected a reaction from the spirit? The girl's lost, red eyes did not even flicker at the sight of the ink. She kept her gaze solely locked upon her prey.

'What did he do? To you, I mean? Are you his … slave or something?'

Again, no reaction. Not to the question, anyway. But the dead girl did slip effortlessly from the wall she had been holding on to and began her approach. The first time she had done so, so many days ago, her actions had been slow and forced, as though something was holding her back, but now, the ghoul stumbled forwards with no such restraint. She was appearing more often. Moving faster each time. Soon, there would be no escape.

'Maybe I can help?' Gemma offered.

Arms outstretched, the ghost continued its advance. Its cries became mournful shrieks despite her gaping mouth barely moving. With every slapping footfall, she gained momentum, as though she were tumbling down a ravine.

'Just tell me why!'

Gemma's screams were drowned out by those of the dead girl. The horror was moving at a fair clip now, her bony form appearing as a marionette as she bore down upon her.

Turning, Gemma began to run. She would get answers, but first, she needed something that would help make Vinny talk.

Death would not take her before she understood why.

That, she vowed.

15.

STANDING BEFORE HER apartment complex, Gemma looked up and took in the staggering mass of concrete and steel before her. A sickening wave of vertigo proceeded to swallow her whole as she realised their home could well end up her tomb. All the same, there was nowhere else to go. Somewhere up above, sat upon her pile of unopened boxes, lay Dan's utility knife. Vinny might have looked like a reanimated skeleton, but Gemma dared not try and take him on without something a little stronger than keys in her fist.

Other options had crossed Gemma's mind before she'd decided upon returning home. There were multiple stores in town that sold craft, garden, and kitchen knives, but looking how she did, she was certain none of them would sell her anything more dangerous than a wax pencil. Sleeping rough and running nonstop for God knows how many hours had left her resembling a feral beast.

She would have to brave the tower if she wanted answers.

Passing through the glass door, into the foyer, she approached the lifts as per her routine, then stopped. There was no telling how long she had before the dead girl would make another appearance, so she would have to be smart. Locking herself within a steel coffin was anything but. Instead, she made a move for the stairwell.

After what felt like an eternity, she fell through the fire escape and into the twelfth-floor corridor. Heaving, she sucked down lungsful of air and coughed up a throatful of bile. Spitting and swearing, she cursed herself for not being in better shape. All the same, she braced herself against the wall and rose on shaking legs, pushing on.

With a twist of her key, she slipped into the apartment and felt as though she would cry. For so long, she had fought against the idea of living here. Moving in. Settling down. Only now did she see this cosy little slice of normalcy as *home*.

Nostalgia warmed her heart, despite having only been away for a couple of days. She longed to spend another morning hungover in Dan's arms on the couch. She wanted to spend another night lounging in bed, doom scrolling on her phone. She wanted to unpack her things and *live*.

She would. Vinny would have the answers she sought. He would undo his curse. She would live. All she needed was the …

Some small part of Gemma had recognised the apartment as looking a little different to the last time she had seen it, but only now did the alteration truly register. The pile of boxes that had stood unopened and unorganised in the far corner had vanished. Along with it, the blade she sought.

'Shit,' she hissed. 'Fuck it.'

Bounding over to the kitchen, she snatched at the knives in the wooden block that sat beside the oven. They were huge, menacing things and sure to put the fear of God into anyone. Unfortunately, that was also why they were so unsuitable. Concealing them would be nigh impossible without doing herself some serious harm.

Flinging open the drawers, she emptied them upon the hardwood floor, casting various useless utensils aside. Dan would have a fit when once he got home that night and saw her handiwork, but he would understand. Once all this was over, she would make him understand.

Swearing again, she scratched uselessly at the bottom of the final drawer. The box cutter was nowhere to be seen. Standing up, she looked across the apartment to the passage that led to their bedroom and shuddered.

'Oh God.'

Approaching the hallway, she could barely make out the door that resided at its end. She took a step forward and was consumed by the darkness. A chill swallowed her. Though, luckily, it was not the icy presence of the dead girl. It was the cold realisation that *this* was where her ordeal had truly started all those nights ago when the ghost had forced her way into the world. An irrational fear slowed her, cramped her limbs.

This was when she would return. Gemma was now certain of it. Now, as she crept forward, inching towards the bedroom. *This* was when the dead girl would pounce, throwing open the door and crashing upon her like a tsunami of rot. *She's just been toying with her prey*, she thought. *Like a cat batting a mouse from paw to paw.* The spectral assassin was just waiting for her to return to where it all began so she could make her prey's death more poetic.

'You can fuck off,' Gemma spat, fighting back tears. 'You can fuck off. Vinny can fuck off. You can all fuck off.'

Rallying herself with curses, she propelled herself forward. Kicking herself free from the wood beneath her feet, bounding towards the door. If the dead girl *was* waiting for her in there, then *fuck her*, she would meet her head on, and she would die trying to scratch the bitch's eyes out.

Flinging the bedroom door open, she was greeted with a once sparse room that was now filled to the brim with open boxes and strewn with her personal belongings. There was no confrontation here, and she sighed a breath of relief, thankful she still had some say in what her ultimate fate would be.

Nestled between the pillows on their bed sat a plump, warped black and white bear—the mascot from one of her favourite video games. The wall opposite that housed the bland skyline painting Dan was so fond of was now far more colourful, as it was now plastered with old pop-punk posters. The built-in wardrobe was open, crammed full of her clothes, hanging neatly, all uniform black.

Laughter escaped her lips as tears pricked her eyes. She had been dreaming of unpacking and settling in, and Dan had been here this whole time, making those dream come true. Confident she would return and stay with him, certain they would be able to put these terrible days behind them.

The knife was upon the windowsill, illuminated by the unobstructed sun, appearing as a gift from the Heavens themselves. Claiming her prize, she held it for a moment, appreciating how heavy it felt in her hand. It was cast from metal, and the blade slid open and locked with a satisfying click.

She secured the weapon, pocketed it, and left the bedroom, the path back into the apartment appearing far less ominous now that she was armed and with purpose. However, she was barely halfway down the hallway when she heard a voice call her out.

'Gemma?'

She let out a shriek, and within seconds, the path before her was blocked. Filled by Dan's tall and gangly frame.

'Oh God. Oh my God,' he said, smiling and laughing. 'You're all right. Thank God …'

Extending his arms, he closed in on her, trapping her within the tight passageway.

'Dan, what are you doing here?'

'I've been looking for you. I mean … not here. I wasn't looking for you in the flat. I've just—I took emergency leave. I've been out looking for you. I popped home for my wallet and—'

'I'm fine, Dan. Please move.'

'Where have you been, love?' he asked, stepping forward.

'Move, Dan,' she said.

'Gemma?'

'Dan, I love you. I love you more than anything else I can think of, but please *get out of the fucking way.*'

'I've been talking to your mum, Gem. We've been calling. Looking for you. We're not mad or … or angry. We just—'

'Dan! For the love of God, *move*. If she comes back, we're both dead. *Eva is dead.* People are *dead* and—'

'Hey, hey,' he cut in. 'I'm not saying you need a doctor, but—
'

Words were not enough, Gemma realised. She pulled out the knife and unsheathed its cruel blade. She held it before her and took a step forward.

'Move,' she ordered.

'Whoa, whoa,' he gasped, holding his hands up. 'There's no need for that. Come on, now. We can do whatever you want. *I'll* do whatever you want. Just—'

'I *want* you to get out of the way, Dan. Just *believe* me. I love you, but I have to go. I can't be near you right now.'

'Okay. That's fine,' he said, matching her by stepping forward himself. 'I'll get out of the way, but please. Give me that before anyone gets hurt.'

'Do you hear that?'

Somewhere down the hall echoed the creaking wail of high tensile steel as the lifts kicked into life. Gemma knew they did not herald the girl. Her calls were so unique they were burned into her very soul. But it was close. The sound was near enough to make her stomach spasm and try to empty itself again. How much longer would she have before the real thing came for her? Her *and* Dan.

'Back off,' she screamed and swung her arm at Dan.

It was intended as a threat, but the blade caught him, skipping across the underside of his outstretched fingers, opening them with ease. Blood and screams escaped Dan's body. The former misting the air with crimson, the latter filling the apartment with curses. He reeled backwards as Gemma drove her shoulder into his side, sending him toppling. He snatched out, trying to steady himself, but only succeeded in leaving a long, red streak across the wall.

Bounding for the front door, she turned as he called out for her to stop. There was no hint of malice or anger in his voice, just concern and confusion.

'I'm sorry,' she cried out as she ran. 'I love you.'

16.

WITH HER HANDS buried deep in her pockets, Gemma hurried through the streets, back towards Vinny's tattoo parlour. Her knuckles strained, and it felt as though her fingers were bruising, such was the ferocity with which she held the knife. She had daymares of it slipping from the world, vanishing into another time or dimension should she relinquish her grip on it for even a second. It was a fantastical notion, but as the last few days had proven, fantasy and reality were closer bedfellows than she had ever thought possible.

Passing through the surging masses, she wondered if any of them could have ever imagined that death walked among them. Not that they need see the dead girl in order to understand that Gemma was trouble. While the threat she towed was invisible, Gemma herself was not. *Drugs*, she would hear people say with a tut as she passed by, her body twitching and juddering with each step.

So sad we can't look after our mentally unwell, they would say as she snapped her head to and fro. Checking her blind spots, yipping to herself. *Stay away from the bad lady*, parents warned their children. She couldn't blame them. Dirt and grime caked her body, and she was enshrouded by a rancid miasma.

Arriving at Vinny's, she was relieved to see the street was empty and the light on in his studio. She had been worried he might have fled the city now that his schemes had been uncovered. Worse still, the police might have pieced together that he *had* been responsible for the peculiar deaths across the city. What would she have done then with him behind bars?

There was also the possibility that the police were actively looking for *her*. After all, she was already on record as a *missing person* and *in distress*, and now she had just carved a chunk out of her boyfriend's hand and was wandering the streets with the same deadly weapon. Thumbing the blade from its sheath, she prepared herself as she approached the door. She knew if the police *were* looking for her, this would be one of the first places they'd check. If there had been even a sliver of hesitation within her, it had been completely wiped away now.

'That you, Gemstone?' came Vinny's voice as she opened his front door.

He was in the back room. *The dead girl's room.*

'Don't call me that,' Gemma replied.

Without any fuss, Vinny stepped out from where he had been working at his little table, wiping his hands clean. It took a few moments for him to register the weapon she held before her.

'I knew you'd come ba—whoa, whoa. Easy, Gemstone, let's just—'

'Don't call me that,' she said again. 'I've always hated it.'

She noted that both Vinny and Dan had held their hands up in submission upon seeing her armed. Both their faces had fallen in the same shocked and bewildered way too. She surged with confidence at that fact and took a step forward, jabbing the knife in Vinny's direction.

'Move,' she said, forcing him back. 'To the back room. Go.'

Without offering any resistance, Vinny complied with her request. She glanced at how he had been occupying himself in the cold brick cell. A soldering iron lay beside shards of metal and wires. He had been setting needles.

'There's no need for the knife, Gem,' he said.

'What have you done to me?' she asked.

'What do you mean?'

'Don't play stupid, Vinny.'

'What do *you* think I've done to you?'

Although he was clearly trying to talk her round in circles, there was no malice to his voice, nor was he goading, as though he'd gotten away with some master plan.

'You've killed me, Vinny. That's what you've done,' she spat. 'Me and all those other girls. Eva and loads of other people too. That *thing* you put on my arm, that you put on *their* arms, and that fucking ghost you sent to kill us.'

'Oh. That,' was all he said.

'And why? Why, Vinny? Because we had weird shit tattoos? Because we didn't love the art of tattooing as much as you? You think that justifies murdering people?'

'What do you mean?'

There was a sudden shift in his demeanour. For a person with a knife aimed at his heart, Vinny had remained incredibly composed, but that question shook him. Now, he looked genuinely befuddled.

'The ghost girl, Vinny,' she said. 'I know the police have been hounding you because you tattooed those girls with the same shit you put on me, and then you sent an assassin to kill us all.'

'Jesus. That's not what this is, Gemma,' he said.

'Well, what *is* it then? Enlighten me.'

Placing his hands behind his back, he moved himself into the corner, as far away from Gemma as he could.

'Okay, look. What I'm going to say will sound weird, but it's not a trick. I'd never want to hurt you, so I'll just stand over here quietly. I want you to do something for me, though. Have a look on my table there.'

'What?' she asked.

Keeping the knife pointed in Vinny's direction, she edged closer toward the mountains of soldering equipment on the table.

'What am I looking at?'

'The book, Gemma. Just … be careful with it, please. It's old. It's fragile … a bit like me.'

'Fuck off with the jokes,' she snapped. 'I'm not in the mood.'

Lost beneath a sea of looping wires and rags, there lay a book, bound in ancient, cracked leather. The spine was a nothing but a burst mess of fibres; it looked as though it might turn to dust at the merest touch.

Angling herself so she could keep Vinny in her eyeline, she used her spare hand to free the tome from its bonds and opened it up. The pages were the colour of strong coffee, the ink upon them faded to the point of being barely legible. What she *could* see was beyond her comprehension, as the language was one she had never seen before. It was accompanied by images. Pictures of complex symbols and shapes that aligned into complex patterns and spirals.

'What is it?' she asked, absorbed by the pages. 'What are they?'

'You know what they are,' he said, staying true to his word and not moving, despite her distraction. 'They're sigils, Gem. I've found they're most potent when applied as tattoos. They're ancient, forgotten, flash designs. You don't know what any of this shit is, do you? Like, you're a cool chick and into all your Wicca and stuff, but you don't know what this *really* is, do you?'

'No,' she said.

'It's magic, Gemma,' he said with a smile broad enough to split his face. 'Real fucking magic. Ancient, archaic, chaotic *magic.* Used to run in some weird circles back in the day. Literally, sometimes, when required. Couldn't do that these days, mind. Me and my little clique got up to all sorts, Gemma. Been all over the bloody place, picking up what we could. Then we'd get on the mushrooms and micro-dots and do a bit of light levitation, bit of conjuring, the odd possession, but that was all party tricks, really. We were too young and too stupid to do anything grand. We didn't want to put in any real work. We were just having a laugh, y'know.'

'Magic, Vinny. Seriously?'

'Yeah, seriously,' he said with a scoff. 'You hear *magic,* and you think of what? Gandalf? Dungeons and Dragons? Happy Potter waving a wand around and shouting *alakazam* or some bollocks? Nah, Gemma. This stuff? The real stuff … it takes hours, days, *weeks* sometimes. The incantations for the simplest spells alone … the rituals, the totems. The *sacrifices,* Gemma. It would make your head spin.'

Taking a slow, measured step forward, Vinny pointed at the book and nodded his head.

'Here you are,' he said, 'more proof.'

Allowing Vinny to pick up the tome, Gemma held her knife steady as she tried to come to terms with what she was hearing. Naturally, she thought him mad, as there was no such thing as *magic*, but by that same token, she had just spent the last few days cursing Dan for not believing *her* when she'd tried to broaden his perception of reality. So magic was real, then? It was a notion she would simply have to believe until this ordeal was done with.

'Look at this,' he said, thumbing open a page of the book.

Gemma already knew what he was about to reveal. Upon the dark, coarse page lay the sigil that had been drawn upon her arm.

'There's power here,' he said, gently turning the pages. 'They used to carve these into stones back in the day. Channel the magic that way with sexual energy or blood or whatever, but braver men would risk their skin, literally, to really give their spells some kick.'

As he rambled on, Gemma's mind began to spin. Pieces of a puzzle she'd never even known to be there began to lock into place. Vinny had been so meticulous during their ill-fated tattoo sessions. Usually, he would have music on and the pair would chat and joke, but on that day, he had demanded absolute silence, citing his need for utmost concentration.

The sigil had to be replicated *exactly* for it to work. She understood that now. And that would extend to the ink too, she presumed. Vinny had foregone a transfer because perhaps it would dilute the ink. The murky, red ink …

'Blood …' Gemma whispered to herself.

Turning her head, she took in the rainbow cascade that made up the far wall of the room. Immense wire racks held every colour of ink imaginable. Scanning the section that held the red bottles, she hoped against hope that nothing would be out of place. However, there, hidden in plain sight, was the thing she hoped to not find. Glass amongst the plastic. A container twice the size of all the others. It was etched with wards and runes, the neck stoppered with wax.

It was a bottle of blood.

'You've tattooed us with the blood of a dead girl,' she managed to choke out. 'You killed her and put her blood into the ink.'

'No. Gemma, for God's sake—'

'I'm going to be sick. You've put someone's blood in me.'

'I didn't put her blood in the ink, Gemma. She *is* the ink.'

'You're a fucking lunatic; you know that?' Gemma said, not truly hearing what he was trying to say.

'I loved her, Gemma,' Vinny shouted over her, closing his eyes and holding the book tight as he spoke. Then his voice calmed to a near whisper. 'You have no idea how much I loved her, Gemma.

Bloody hell … *I* didn't even know how much I loved her … not until it was too late. I only thought I knew what love was, until—'

Vinny's knuckles turned white as his fingers dug into the book. The pages let out an agonised groan as flakes of parchment flittered to the ground. It was a small, fleeting reaction, but Gemma readied herself, lest he snap.

'Cancer, it was. Wasn't much of her that wasn't riddled by the end. She was a fighter, Gem. A real bloody fighter, but they stopped trying once it got too far. Gave us some painkillers and told us to get on with it. Just … *fuck off and die*. That's what they meant, the bastards.'

'So what did you do?' she asked, lowering her voice, matching his tone.

'I saved her, Gem.'

'The dead girl?'

'She's not dead, and her name was Zoe,' he said.

'Zoe …'

Chaos erupted upon the utterance of the dead girl's name. Gemma had inadvertently summoned her through some unknown rite of incantation—names are powerful words, after all. The walls began to shudder as a freezing chill swept in from the open door, and somewhere in the neighbouring room, a woman began to cry.

'We'd left the magic behind, Zoe and me. Left it behind when we moved up here. Like I said, it was mostly parlour tricks anyway. But when she got sick, I got back in touch with my old mates. They'd been getting really serious with it and wanted to help. I started studying. Properly this time. Digging as deep as I could, pulling every favour for just a little bit more knowledge, y'know?'

'So you got her blood so she could *live on* or something?'

'I told you before, that's not her blood. It's *her*. It's *Zoe.*'

'What? What does that mean?'

'If I'd have started studying earlier, I might have been able to cure her, but the best I could do was *save* her. There's a crossover between magic and alchemy, and I managed to distil her into something more concentrated. More pure. *Vitae,* it's called. Zoe, as I knew her, is gone, but it's still her. She's still with me. With *us.*'

With that last word, he pointed to her arm. She doubted it was magic, but the gesture brought with it a wave of nausea. Retching, she shrugged off her jacket and let it fall where it may so she could gaze upon her tattoo. It was bad enough when she thought she'd been inked with a stranger's blood, but the thought of having the *essence* of another person within her—it was violating in a way she never thought possible.

'So you did magic on her,' Gemma said.

'I did what I had to do,' was his reply.

'In here …'

How long had it taken? The ritual, the magic he'd woven to reduce Zoe into something that would fill a glass jar. He had said himself that for even the simplest results, it could take hours. So how long would it have taken for something so grand? How long had Zoe been confined here, within this cold and miserable cell, as Vinny lit candles, chanted Latin, or whatever else was required? Zoe could have been here for months. Bound in the cold with nothing but her own cries and the wail of pipes for company. Was it any wonder, then, that her psychic projection that had been haunting Gemma had brought with it those same self-horrors.

'She's coming for me, Vinny,' Gemma said. 'It's all right, though, she'll kill you before she kills me. I'll make sure of it.'

'No, she won't,' Vinny said.

Taking the hem of his ragged t-shirt between his fingers, Vinny raised the fabric and exposed his stomach. Like the rest of his skin, it was a near-incomprehensible tapestry of faded ink. All bar one, which ran from below his sternum to his belly button. It was another sigil, long and elegant, all curves and curls. Unlike hers, it was a bright and vibrant blue.

'A ward,' Vinny explained. 'There are all kinds of things out there we can't see, Gem. Weird bits and bobs floating around in the ether. Not just ghosts. Mostly harmless, but better safe than sorry, eh? Take some doing to get past this. You'll be all right too.'

'Why? Because of your ward, or sigil, or whatever it is?'

'No, Gem. Because of *yours*. I got it right this time. You have to trust me.'

'Eva is *dead* because of this, Vinny. Other people are *dead*. Innocent people. Strangers I don't even know. They got between me and her, and she *killed* them.'

'Accidents,' he said.

'*Accidents?'* she cried out.

Outside, in the studio, Zoe's cries grew in strength. She brought with her an even fiercer cold and an echoing warble of metal straining against itself. She was already manifest, Gemma could feel it, but she was being held at bay for now. Be it Vinny's ward or the cell itself, she was being repulsed as much as she was being summoned. Whatever magic was coursing through their little part of the universe, Gemma felt attuned to it now, somehow.

'Eva was a star, Gemma,' Vinny said. 'I'm heartbroken she's dead. Believe me, I am. I'm not a monster, but the living and dead aren't meant to coexist like that. Those other people, I'm sorry about them too.'

'And the girls?' Gemma said with a snarl. 'The others you put Zoe into. Are you sorry about killing them? And me? Are you sorry she's going to kill me?'

'Accidents again,' he pleaded. 'Those other girls, I really liked them. I thought they were cool, Gemma. Like you. That's why I picked them. I didn't mind all their other daft tattoos. They reminded me of Zoe, in one way or another. I thought they'd be a good match. But I didn't get the sigil right with them. This is advanced stuff. Advanced, *advanced* stuff, and I'm still learning, but I've got it right this time, I swear.'

'A match for what?' Gemma asked. 'Are you trying to have your old girlfriend possess me?'

'You'd still be you, Gem. But also … a bit of her too. One or the other would become sort of a tulpa, I guess … if you know what that is.'

Closing her eyes, she took a moment to try and compose herself but failed. Fury burned hot in her veins as she thought about the violation, the abuse, and the sheer *gall* of it all. Even if he *was* right and when Zoe eventually lay her hands upon her … then what? She would have to share her consciousness with some invading spirit? Horrifyingly, that was the best-case scenario.

Because, worse still, if the sigil Vinny had cursed her with was imperfect and Zoe killed her outright, he would never stop. Her death would be ruled an accident, and sure, he'd be under intense scrutiny from the police, but they could never convict him. They could never begin to imagine what his plan was. Eventually, he would find more victims and subject them to his sick attempt at playing God.

There was only one question left. 'How do we stop this?'

'We don't,' he said, nodding to her tattoo. 'She's part of you now.'

'You're an evil bastard, Vinny. She's in pain. You know that, right?'

'Not for much longer,' he said, looking past her. 'Hello, Zoe.'

Snatching a quick look behind her, she caught sight of the dead girl. She was crouched behind Vinny's large tattooing station in the dark, her pale face catching the dim light of the cell and making it appear as though it were floating in a void. For the first time, she was able to look into Zoe's red, weeping eyes and feel something other than terror. Now, all she could feel was an overwhelming sense of grief and sympathy. A bone-white hand appeared from the nothingness in the other room and reached out for her.

'Go to her,' Vinny said.

'You can fuck right off,' Gemma's replied.

'It won't even hurt,' he pleaded. 'Think about your karma, Gemma. Imagine how much good you'd be doing, bringing a life back into the world. Bringing someone back from the dead. Someone so incredible and beautiful. Gemstone, please—'

'I said don't *fucking* call me that!'

With a scream, Gemma turned from Vinny and snatched at the wire racks beside her. She hooked her free fingers into the frames and leapt into the air, tugging at them as hard as she could. She was petite and light of mass, but the wires holding the inks in place came loose regardless. Large puffs of dust exploded from the wall as the anchors that held the shelves popped from the ancient brickwork.

Vinny roared, his howls joining those of Gemma and Zoe. A rainbow fell upon the floor of the cell. Most containers simply bounced away, but many plastic pots burst, splashing their viscous contents across the brick walls. Most importantly, though, the glass vial that contained the living vitae of Zoe shattered against the concrete.

'Zoe,' Vinny howled, diving to the floor.

A deluge of liquid mixed in kaleidoscope swirls as it sluiced towards the drain. What remained of Zoe travelled with it, slipping away through the metal grille. Her essence was joined by Vinny's as he spilt his own blood trying to save her. Diving into the colourful quagmire, he pawed at the floor, hoping to halt Zoe's escape. His fingers split easily upon the long shards of glass that coasted along with the ink. He was blind to the pain, however. The fear of losing the love of his life for a second time had consumed him entirely.

Thunder pounded within Gemma's chest and adrenaline caused her breath to catch in her throat as Zoe was finally upon her. The gaunt, skeletal figure of the dead girl stood in the doorway of the cell, blocking her escape.

'It … it's okay, Zoe.' Vinny was on his knees now, looking up at the ghost. 'It'll be all right. I've done it right this time. We'll be all right …'

If ghosts were real and magic was real, then Gemma decided to believe that God was real too, and wherever God was, she was smiling favourably upon her in that moment, because Zoe was no longer looking at her. Instead, the dead girl was staring at Vinny. More specifically, the small pool of liquid he had cupped in his ragged, bleeding hands. He held the murky collection of ink and vitae up for the ghost to inspect.

'Enough,' he managed to gasp. 'If this doesn't work, I think I've got enough for another go. I can save this. I can save you …'

Shuffling forward on bloody knees, Vinny attempted to approach Zoe, but the phantasm recoiled. The ward on his stomach pushed her away. Gemma found cold enjoyment in that. How even in death, Vinny repulsed the one woman he longed to be with.

Just how long could their little act play out for? How much time did Gemma have? The pendulum had stopped swinging and had come to a standstill over her head. There was no chance of escaping Zoe now, nor was it likely her spirit would dissipate anytime soon. Looking down at the tattoo on her inner forearm, she wondered: was there *anything* she could do to prevent her imminent death?

How deep are tattoos?

During those brief few weeks when she had envisioned herself being a tattoo artist under Vinny's tutelage, she had done *some* research. It had been for naught, like all of the other things she had planned to do with her life but avoided or skirted on the edge of *doing*. But this? This was the one time she had no choice *but* to commit.

Tattoo needles punch ink just a few millimetres into the skin.

Not ink, in this case … Zoe's vitae.

Bringing the utility knife to her forearm, Gemma let out a pre-emptive scream before plunging the tip of the blade into her flesh, just below the tattoo. Blood welled from the gash as she dragged the box cutter up her forearm. The room began to spin as pain consumed her, and soon, the sigil was lost beneath a crimson tide.

Despite the agony raking its way up her arm, despite the nausea welling in her gut, despite her mind wanting to shut down to end the horror, Gemma continued. After the first incision was complete, the knife refused to leave her body. She had plunged too deep and had to give the box cutter a sharp tug. Her flesh relinquished the blade with what felt like a *pop*, and immediately, she drove it home again. This time, on the other side of the tattoo.

Falling to her knees, her vision greying, she angled the incision so that she would only have to carve into herself three times. A neat, rectangular scar would have been preferable, but a skewed triangle would be fine, so long as she lived long enough to see it. Every heartbeat brought with it an explosive throb of agony, but even though her world was now a hazy blur of pain, she could still see Vinny before her, dumping Zoe's remaining vitae into the steel box where he stored his biscuits. She knew this could not be allowed to continue. She could never allow anyone else to fall prey to him. Nor could she allow Zoe to continue living her torturous spectral half-life.

Through a red haze of pain, Gemma looked down. The tattoo was now hanging free from her arm by a small tag of flesh. She gripped it as tight as she could, the skin wet and slick and constantly trying to slip free from her grasp. Holding it fast, she let out a throaty roar before yanking on it as hard as she could. The pain was a blinding flash that shook her from head to toe, snapping her alert. The sigil, and Zoe, were now free from her body.

That should have been it, her nightmare over.

But she was far from done.

Her actions had not gone unnoticed by Vinny, who was carefully placing his filthy biscuit tin on the table. He held the container between his wrists, his fingers now useless. The damage done to his hands was immense, and even if his digits were repaired, it would be unlikely he would have the finesse to tattoo with the accuracy required to mark someone with Zoe's sigil again. She knew it wouldn't stop him from attempting to resurrect his old lover. He *would* ruin more lives if she didn't act.

'Bloody Hell, Gemma,' he stuttered, stepping away from the table. 'What have you done? What have you *done?* Zoe, I'm sorry ...'

Still unable to approach the ageing tattooist, the ghoulish Zoe turned her attention back to Gemma. Only now Zoe's eyes were affixed to the flap of skin she clutched within her fist. One touch from the dead girl would still be fatal, so she had to be careful. She pressed herself up against the back wall and edged her way towards Vinny.

'Gem, what are you doing?' he gasped. 'Gemstone?'

'I told you not to call me that,' she hissed.

Pouncing, Gemma tackled him, and the pair tumbled into the old plastic table. Soldering equipment, needles, and the tin that held Zoe's remains flew across the room. The dead girl's vitae was swiftly lost to the drains, along with so much ink. There was little fight left in the old tattooist. His ruined hands slapped at Gemma as she positioned herself atop him, straddling his chest. Her fist easily slipped past his flailing arms and found his face. She slipped her fingers and the flesh they held towards his mouth.

Slick with both of their blood, Gemma found it easy to force the skin between his lips. His screams turned to coughing gags, and he gnashed and bit, tearing at her fingers. Those agonies simply replaced the ones that were already wracking her body, and were easily ignored. Steadfastly, she refused to relent, forcing the sacrament deeper into his mouth and then, in turn, his throat.

From within Vinny, Gemma felt the muscles in his neck contract as he took her gift down into his gullet. She ripped her hand free from his face, leaving between his teeth long strips of skin from her fingers. She fell back, splashing across the wet floor, painting herself as she kicked away from her ex-friend.

'Fuckin' ... fuckin' ...' was all he was able to say as he coughed and hacked, bringing up great wads of blood that sprayed across his face.

Above them, Zoe loomed, watching on. Her eyes remained cold and without hope, but now their attention was solely upon Vinny. She reached out towards him and took a slow step forward.

'Zoe … Zoe …' he whined.

Whatever protection the rune on his belly had offered was now forfeit. It was still doing its best to repel Zoe's spirit, but the magic that called for her and her vitae to be reunited was far too strong to be denied. His attempts to escape the dead girl only found himself backed into a corner, splayed across the same filthy mattress where Zoe had spent her last agonising moments alive.

'I love you,' were his last words as her fingers made contact with his chest.

He smiled. Elated to be touched once more by the woman he loved. The moment lasted just a fraction of a second before he began to convulse and shake. His skin turned red; thick veins bulged across his forehead. He choked on his own body's rebellion as Zoe's agonising embrace continued. His lips peeled back, revealing raw gums, as a high-pitched whine sang from his throat. His head snapped to the side as his eyes protruded, huge and white, his own vitae bubbling beneath the lids as he cried bloody tears.

Time seemed to slow as Gemma watched Vinny die. His sigil dragged the process out, extending his misery. Zoe's hand had vanished into the tattooist's torso, and she toppled forward, following it. Her descent was slow and gradual. Eventually, her body met his, and they became one, her spirit merging with his flesh. What little there was left of Vinny began to spasm. Eventually, there was nothing left to be seen of Zoe, and neither was there anything left of Vinny.

With some effort, Gemma retrieved her phone from her pocket, only to discover it had been crushed during their fight. She allowed it to fall to the ground, where it joined the rest of the debris, as she looked around for something to stem the blood that was oozing from her ruined arm. Using tissues and rags, she tried her best to plug the hole, but the ragged bites that pocked her good hand prevented her from binding it as well as it should have been.

Zoe was gone. Yet Gemma remained chilled to the bone. It was a cruel fact, but perhaps it was too late for her. If she were to die, what would come next? Magic was real. Ghosts were real. She had accepted that God, too, was real. So it stood to reason that there would be some sort of Heaven awaiting her once she passed. Whatever came next, the last thing she wanted was to end up like Zoe. Haunting people whilst constantly reliving her final moments in that miserable little room.

Gemma managed to haul herself to her feet.

When she died, she would do it outside. In the city she loved.

She had haunted those streets before, countless times, and would be more than happy to haunt them again, forever.

If that was to be her fate … then so be it.

17.

FRUSTRATION AND ANGER bubbled to the surface as Dan checked his phone. Every slight rustle, every quiver in his pocket made him think it was vibrating, and each time, his heart would leap into his mouth, thinking it was Gemma. So when a call finally *did* come and it was just his mother asking how his search was going, he responded with a stern, '*eff all.*'

Shaking himself loose, he decided that, seeing as his phone was in his hand, he may as well check his socials. Unfortunately, nothing had come to light in the ten minutes since he'd last checked. A maelstrom of thoughts and emotions roiled within him as he wandered the streets, scouring known areas where Gemma might be. His fingers still ached and felt clammy and stiff beneath the thick, homemade bandage they were wrapped within. He loved Gemma's wild streak. She was the riotous Yin to his steady Yang, and in their balance, they'd found harmony. They had fought before, but for her to attack him, it was beyond the pale.

Laughing, he held back a cry as he thought about how she would mock him for thinking of them as a Yin-Yang. She always made light of him being into spiritualism and esoteric ideas if and when the need suited, despite claiming to be a staunch atheist.

That was why he needed to find her. Needed to make sure she got the help required to ensure whatever sickness had consumed her was treated. He would do anything. They could live apart again. He would move back down South if needs be. They could *take a break* if it would help. It felt as though there was a part of his soul missing, knowing he could lose her.

There he was, borrowing theology again for his own petty needs.

He was on the move. Doing his rounds. Checking all the usual places she was likely to be. Next on his check list was Eva's cafe. Even before he reached the little side street, Dan could hear a commotion. Breaking into a jog, he rounded the corner and discovered the source. Workmen were crowded around someone lying on the floor. Their high-visibility jackets were piled under her head and being used as a makeshift blanket. One was frantically jabbering to someone on his phone.

'Gemma?' Dan cried out, racing towards the men.

Before they could say anything, the girl they had been protecting was struggling to sit up, calling out his name with a weak voice. They soothed her and gave the briefest of introduction before allowing Dan to take their place. Holding back a cry, his heart lurched when he saw her. She was bone white, somehow paler than she usually was. Her clothes and face were caked in drying blood and spattered with every colour known to man.

'Keep pressure on the wound,' a man with the phone to his ear said. 'Ambulance is on the way.'

Gemma's lips split into a smile, though it never reached her eyes. She winced slightly as Dan held her arm tight, feeling his own wounds ache and bleed.

'Hey,' she managed to say.

'Gemma, what the fuck happened?' Dan asked.

She began to laugh. Her head lolled, and she slurred her words. The blood loss had the peculiar effect of making her seem drunk.

'What?' he said.

'You. Swearing.'

'Oh, yeah. You're going to be fine, Gem,' he said, cooing.

'I know, as will Zoe.'

'Who?'

'Forget it,' she said, her eyes closing.

'Gemma?' As he spoke, he shook her, keeping her awake.

'Dan, I want to go home,' she said, waking up, if just a little. 'I want to live with you … I want to live … with you … for the rest of my life. But, Dan … I really hate that apartment.'

'We'll move out, then,' he said. 'As soon as we can. We can live wherever you want. Decorate however you want. We can have as many pillows on the couch as you want.'

'You're going to regret saying that,' she said with a snort.

Smiling, her eyes began to close as the sound of sirens filled the street. He shook her, rousing her from the darkness once more as paramedics rushed to their side. They took the pair into the back of their ambulance.

~~~~

Theirs had been a rocky journey and was far from over, but for now, they were safe. Vinny's body would be found, and though the truth would never be known to the public, a whole new world had been opened up to Gemma.

Whatever she chose to do with her life now, going forward with Dan, it would be one filled with wonder and magic and the knowledge that death is not the end. Because more than their choices, and more than the ink on her skin, theirs was a true and everlasting love.

They would be with one another together.

For now and forever.
~~~~

NEEDLE FALLS

DE McCluskey

For Lauren …
Who is ALSO the luckiest girl in the whole world.

1.

THE DARKNESS SMELLED of smoked cheese.

Her father had a smoker in the backyard when she was a child, and whenever they'd had a cookout, he would smoke a huge slab of cheddar for a few days so he and his beer-guzzling buddies could enjoy a fat Cuban and some fine smoked cheese.

It was all so American.

She tried to think of them as good times. *What do they call them?* she asked herself. *The good old days?* Well, they hadn't been that good for her. Her father had left. Her mom had told her he'd run off with a whore and no longer gave a fuck about either of them. She had never believed this. Not her dad. He loved her fiercely. He always told her that if she ever found herself in trouble, of any kind, then she was to tell him, to call on him, and he'd sort it for her, no matter what it was.

That's what daddies were for.

Something told her there was no way he would be able to help her in the predicament she found herself in now. She didn't think anyone could help her. She supposed it was her own fault; she must have brought the sadness on herself.

When her daddy left, or disappeared, life had taken a turn, an upside-down one, which, considering her current situation, was clearly ironic.

Her mother, who had never been the maternal type anyway, had taken on a string of lovers. Some of them at the same time. As a child, she had been subjected to parties in their house with men and women she didn't know, and didn't want to know. There was a lot of drinking, there was a lot of drug taking, and there was a lot of fucking. Some of the men had taken an interest in her, even though she had been barely thirteen years old at the time. Her mother had encouraged it, telling her she was doing a service to the house, as they *all* had to pay their way these days—there were bills to pay after all, and they didn't just give food away for free at the store.

When she hit sixteen, she got out of there as fast as she could. The pain of living with an abusive slut of a mother and her many boyfriends had been too much. In fact, the only thing she'd found that helped with the pain and agony of her situation was to self-harm. The stinging of the slices at the top of her legs and arms overpowered the ugly, dull throb from between her legs that would be a constant from three-day weekends of forced sexual abuse. It helped with the constant vile taste in her mouth too.

In another twist of irony to her current position, and she didn't mean the fact that she was somehow suspended in the air, in a room she didn't recognise, she meant being here in Needle Falls. She'd had the idea to join her many scars together, to decorate her body, to make it as repulsive as she could so the men her mother pimped her out to wouldn't want to fuck her. She was far too young for official tattoos, but there was nothing stopping her from making her own.

Multiple piercings, hot needles piercing her skin, filled with dark ink, poisoned her flesh. She didn't mind, as sometimes the men would look at the scars and the vile words she'd etched into herself and wouldn't want to fuck her.

Others weren't bothered by it, and there were some, mostly of the sicker variety, who were excited about it.

They were the worst ones. They were the ones who got off on the pain, the suffering, and, of course, the blood.

Which brought her to where she was now, to her current predicament.

When she'd run away, she inevitably ended up with the wrong sort. What was a sixteen-year-old who had only known nonconsensual sex and self-harm going to do? She was never going to fall in with the *right* crowd, spend her days in a sorority, surrounded by popular and beautiful bitches.

That was never in her stars. She found herself in a small circle of drug abusers, devil worshippers, and general misfits.

They were her tribe.

Despite their failings in societal norms, these people looked after her. They listened, they helped her on her journey through the darkness into, well more darkness, but at least it was a darkness she welcomed.

Her life became a haven of consensual sex, drug taking, and drinking. In short, she'd turned into her mother.

The self-harm continued.

Once you started, it was difficult to give up on. It became a habit, but as she was old enough now to get tattoos, she sought them out, swapping one addiction for another. She wanted her body to be one, huge tattoo. She wanted ink to hide her shame, her pain, and the mental torment of everything that had been her life.

That was what brought her to Needle Falls in the first place.

That was how she found herself in this room with searing, hot, or were they burning cold, tubes inserted into her that were slowly draining her blood.

With her vision dimming and whatever drugs she'd been given wearing off, as wave after wave of unfathomable agony crashed over her like breakers on a beach and the cloyingly thick stink of smoked cheese filled her nose, she watched him. He was kneeling before her. His arms were raised into the air as his mouth formed silent words.

All she could hear was her life draining away—a roar like a lion, antagonised and feeling the need to exert its dominance.

All she could feel was the exodus of existence from her burning, pierced, heavily inked body like water flushing from a faucet.

His eyes were open, and he was looking at her. They didn't look like the eyes of a human. They glowed in the dimness of whatever room she'd woken in. He was a big man; his nakedness proved this. He obviously took care of his physical fitness, and the tattoos that covered his chest, stomach, neck, and arms spoke of occultist symbols and the dark arts. He wasn't alone. There were others in the room with her, others who were naked and heavily tattooed. They were watching her too.

~~~~
~~~~

The sacred pot was full. He couldn't allow his precious harvest to spill. He needed every drop of the sacred scarlet. There was ink to be made. There were followers he needed to mark. His mission was far from over, and she had been an excellent, almost willing, sacrifice.

It was almost done. This harvest was fantastic.

The Great Lord Glimm would indeed be happy.

~~~~

Her eyes looked into his. Vicious cramps tore through her, torturing her internal organs as she drained of the lubrication they required to function, the oil keeping her engine moving. In her delirium she could hear them scream. She, however, refused to.

She wouldn't give him the satisfaction. It was like how she never cried when her mother's *boyfriends* hurt her. Oh, she had at the beginning, but back then, she couldn't comprehend what was happening to her. When she knew, when she finally understood, she became strong, and she refused to give them what they wanted. They took from her much more than she could ever regain, but she would not give them the satisfaction of her tears.

Fuck him, she cursed as she watched. He was flickering in slow motion, removing the buckets from beneath her. They were filled with thick, dark liquid that she knew was her blood. *Fuck you,* she spat, in her head, as her bodily functions were slowing. *Fuck you to HELL.*

The stink of charred flesh, her charred flesh, was what was causing the smoked cheese effect. She had been told cooked human was supposed to smell like barbecued pork. All the books she'd read about supposed cannibals and their *long pig* exploits must have been a crock of shit. Searing flesh—or her searing flesh, at least—smelt like ten-year-old cheddar being treated in a hickory smoker.

Lying bastards ...

Sweet death, come and claim what is yours, she thought.

These were the last thoughts of Amelia Cross, as something in the darkness, something huge, maybe bigger than life itself kneeled before her. She smiled internally. She should never have come to Needle Falls, but then, she had never been one to make good decisions.
~~~~

2.

CARSON HAD BEEN searching for her for a while. Every lead, of which there were many, had led him to this small town in upstate New York. It wasn't one of those you see depicted in the beautiful, picturesque films on TV. The ones filled with pleasant, friendly, down-to-earth people, the type who never lock their doors at night and meet up in the village square ever December twenty-fourth for the ceremonious *lighting of the Christmas tree* ceremony.

This one was rougher than that.

As he drove through the town, he marvelled that it might have probably been a beautiful place to live, once upon a time. Nowadays, it looked like a struggling community. It may have once been prosperous, but sadly those days could only be seen in the town's collective rearview mirror. Most of the shops on—the originally named—Main Street were either boarded up with faded FOR RENT signs on them or they were fast food joints, vaping shops, or hairdressers. Gone were the boutiques that would have adorned this street along with the fancy bistros and wine bars.

Economic decline had not just nipped at this town; it had taken a bite from it and then come back for more.

As his rental Prius moved almost silently through the town, he drew a number of looks from some of the locals who had taken the time to notice him. To him, they looked sad. They looked as if they longed to be anywhere other than where they found themselves today. The American dream had turned into a nightmare here, sour and bitter. He was going to have a tough time getting these people to open up, especially regarding the reason why he was here.

He passed a sign that read Needle Falls, declaring itself as America's Sweetheart Location. The faded colours and the rotting wood of the sign told him that these particular sweethearts had moved away, far away, a long time ago.

It was a beautiful name, and the scenery he'd driven through to get here had been pretty spectacular. He took a wild guess that the town had gotten its name from the many pine and spruce trees that grew in this location all year round, and he bet this place would be gorgeous around Christmastime.

Not a bad little opening for my journal, he thought as he checked his satnav. It informed him his destination was a little more than a half mile further down Main Street. He'd booked a local bed and breakfast on the outskirts of downtown. He wanted to be in the thick of it, to taste the crust of the apple pie that small-town life offered, to reacquaint himself with how these people lived.

He'd been a small-town boy himself, back in another lifetime, before he'd had the audacity to get himself an education, leave, and never go back.

He liked to tell himself he didn't miss it.

But the truth of the matter was, he did.

He missed the friendliness. He missed knowing everyone he passed on the sidewalk. He missed the community spirit. What he didn't miss was the familiarity breeding a contempt he couldn't live under anymore. He didn't miss the competitiveness and the bullying, and he didn't miss the pecking order they were forced to endure, even from school, where the king and queen of the prom ruled the roost. If you didn't conform, you were outcast from all social aspects of society.

Carson hadn't conformed.

He'd been a goth kid. He listened to the wrong kind of music, and he liked to wear makeup. Mostly, he thought his ostracization began when it became clear he was attracted to the wrong sex. He was everything a bigoted small town hated, personified. When he left, he knew they were as glad to see the back of him as he was to see the back of them. The fact he was out of their lives made their sad existence that little bit more bearable.

For them.

He had been more than happy to offer them that service.

They were relieved they didn't have to deal with the fag-kid, the weirdo, the corruptor of the younger generation with his *gay shit.*

He grinned as he approached a coffee shop on the main road. There were two big guys standing outside, talking and laughing at the back of a flatbed. They were dressed in flannel shirts, jeans, and engineer's boots. A total cliché of *good ole boys* if he had ever seen one. Both snapped to attention as a thin man wearing glasses and an expensive suit approached them. He said something, and both men jumped into the cab and drove away, leaving the thin man to climb into his expensive car parked a few yards away.

This made Carson laugh. He would have put good money on both those guys beat that skinny guy's ass, every single day when they were in school. Now, they were working *for* him in a declining economy.

The irony was perfect.

He pulled his Prius over to the space on the curb that the flatbed had vacated. Even though he was still half a mile from his destination, he fancied himself a coffee. He'd been driving for five hours straight, and his eyes were stinging; also, by the description given to him, this place could be the one Amelia wrote to him about.

As he got out of his car, he stretched and took in a deep breath of small-town air. The moment he did, an eighteen-wheeler drove past, and all he ended up with was a lungful of diesel discharge.

He coughed, shook his head, and entered the coffee shop.

3.

AS THE DOOR opened, a bell rang, alerting the old man behind the counter to the new customer. He offered a warm smile and looked genuinely happy to have someone else in his place, even though the shop was already pretty busy. He leaned on the counter and grinned, spreading his greying moustache all the way across his face.

'What'll it be?' he asked. His accent was thick, upper state New York, and it took her a few moments to understand what he'd said.

'Huh?' Amelia asked as she removed the bag hanging over her shoulder. She was a small-framed girl with short blonde hair, shaved at the back in a very masculine style. She had been accused on more than a few times of trying to hide her femininity. She had a lot to hide it from. 'Oh, erm, coffee, please, black.'

'Sugar?' the man asked as he turned away, slinging the towel he was holding over his shoulder.

'Three, please,' she answered almost as sweetly as her coffee would be.

'Take a load off, and I'll bring it over.'

She looked around the room. There were few seats, and what were available were on the same tables as judgemental-looking people, who were eyeing her suspiciously. There was one table by the rest rooms that was empty, so she took that, passing the snooty looks from the other patrons with a shy smile.

'Here you go, darlin', black, extra sweet,' the man with the thick moustache said, surprising her with how fast the coffee had been.

'Oh, thank you,' she said, not quite looking him in the eye.

He stood over her for a moment, looking down at her. She glanced up from her steaming cup as he loomed with his arms crossed.

He was a big man, and if he hadn't had a genuine smile on his face, this situation could have been somewhat intimidating.

She offered him a twitchy smile. It was timid at best.

'You're going to struggle to pay for that, aren't you?' he asked, there was no malice in his voice.

She looked away and nodded.

He sat down, uninvited on the other chair at the small table. Everyone in the café pretended they weren't interested, but she knew they were lying to themselves.

'So, is this what you do? You use small establishments and play on their generosity?'

She put her cup down and stood. Her hand was on the strap of her bag, ready to bolt out of the shop, and maybe even out of town, in a heartbeat. She'd been through too much to be subjected to the judgement of people from a small town, who knew nothing about her struggles.

A thick, heavily tattooed arm shot out and caught her. His grip was strong, but it wasn't cruel. She knew cruel, this wasn't it. Still, she flinched at the big man's actions. Her legs were nothing but jelly within her dirty jeans, and her stomach was ready to eject the couple of sips of coffee she had just enjoyed. It was all she'd had all day.

'Calm down,' he whispered. 'Listen, my name is Malic, short for Malachi, if you can believe that. What kind of parent calls their kid Malachi?'

The smile plastered on his face soothed her.

'You can go if you want, but you look to me like you've nowhere to go to.' His eyebrows raised as he spoke.

She sighed a long rush of air through her nostrils.

'Sit. Finish your coffee, and maybe, just maybe, there's some pie left over from yesterday I was about to throw out. What do you say? You look like you could use some pie?'

'Not if it's mouldy,' she mumbled. She wanted to sound wise-ass and sassy, like the character of Chandler Bing from one of her favourite TV shows, but all she managed was whispery, mouselike, pathetic.

He laughed and released his grip on her arm. 'Sit back down, get yourself comfortable, and I'll get you that pie.'

She liked this man. She'd had trust issues with men from an early age, but there was something about this one she thought she could trust.

'Good girl,' he said as she relaxed. There were so many ways that phrase could have sounded condescending, creepy even, but somehow, it didn't. Coming from him, it sounded genuine, reassuring.

She dropped back into the seat, wrapping her hands around her coffee, pulling it towards her and holding it to her chest as if it were a shield rather than a strong caffeinated drink. She watched Malic slip behind the counter and remove a slice of pie from beneath a glass lid. He put it on a plate, grabbed a fork, and returned to her table.

All of this garnered attention from the other patrons, but he didn't seem to care. 'So, you have me at a disadvantage here,' he said, pushing the pie across the table. She took the offering greedily and stuffed almost half of it into her mouth in one bite.

'Huh?' she offered him in return.

'A disadvantage. You know my name, but I don't know yours.'

She looked at him over her demolished pie. 'Kirsty,' she said a little too fast, spraying crumbs over the table. 'Kirsty Range.'

Malic grinned and nodded. She could tell he hadn't bought it.

'OK, Kirsty Range, do you have somewhere to stay tonight?'

She just blinked at him.

He nodded. He looked like he'd seen her before, a lot of times.

'There's a B&B up the road a bit. Martha will take you in for two days maximum, but then you'll have to pay your way. Are you OK with that?'

She looked at him again, searching his face for an agenda, for what was in this for him. She wondered what services she'd have to perform for him or his buddies. What depths of degradation would she have to stoop to garner this level of generosity. She couldn't see any agenda in his features, and over the year or so that she'd been on the road, she'd become quite adept at reading people and their motives, but that didn't mean there wasn't one.

For now, for some reason, this man, Malic, seemed genuine.

She could do with some good luck.

Fuck, could I do with some good luck.

4.

'YOU LOOK LIKE a man in need of something strong, black, and caffeinated,' an older female voice cackled across the almost empty room. 'Why don't you sit yourself down and I'll bring you one over. How do you like it, child? Black with lots of sugar is my guess.'

Carson grinned as he selected a table and sat down with a weary moan. 'Almost, but with a dash of cream, that will do me fine.'

It felt a little strange to hear the sound of his own voice. He didn't think he'd spoken to anyone since checking into his motel last night. That would have been over twenty-four hours and maybe six-hundred miles ago. He shifted his bag to the floor and removed his laptop. As he logged on, the older woman made her way to his table. Her shaking hands spilled more of his coffee than he was likely to drink, but he didn't care; he appreciated the kindness of strangers. She didn't have to provide table service. Most places didn't these days.

'Just by looking at you, I'll guess you're not from these parts.' She smiled as she put the cup and saucer onto his table. The saucer was full of dark beige, but fantastic smelling, liquid.

'You got me. I'm from Illinois, Pontiac, Illinois. Well, from that area, anyways.'

'You runnin'?' she asked.

He thought it was an odd question to ask a stranger, and he cocked his head towards her.

Her grin widened. 'Most people passing through here are running. Listen, I don't mind who I serve coffee and pie to, just as long as they don't go running out of my shop without paying.' This tickled her, and she started to laugh at her own joke.

Carson looked around him. He was the only customer, but he could have sworn there'd been someone else sitting at one of the tables when he'd walked in. He hadn't been taking too much notice, but he hadn't heard the door ring, letting whoever it was out. He shrugged, putting it down to fatigue.

'I'm good for the coffee, just about, what with the cost of gas these days.' He laughed back. 'I might even be able to stretch to one of those slices of pie you mentioned, but only if I'm too late for a bacon and egg muffin?'

The old woman's eyes beamed. 'One bacon and egg on English coming right up, and a slice of pie.' She danced off back towards the counter, leaving him to his coffee and his laptop.

'Do you have Wi-Fi?' he shouted.

The old woman popped her head back from inside the kitchen area. 'What did you say, hun?'

'Wi-Fi? Do you have any?'

'Oh, I don't think so. I could look in the back for you,' she said, raising her eyebrows to show she was joking.

He got the jape.

'The password is on the wall over there,' she said, pointing to a small chalk board hanging over the till.

He selected the correct SSID and logged on. He opened up his emails and pulled up the ones he'd been sent from Amelia.

This was the right town, and he was almost sure this was the coffee shop she'd sent him the email from. He was on the right trail.

The old lady came back with his bacon and egg muffin.

'Can I ask you a question?' he asked as she walked off. 'How long have you worked here?' he finished, not giving her the chance to deny him.

The old woman turned and chuffed. 'Forever, sweetheart, forever.'

'So, you'll remember a girl called Amelia Cross?'

The old woman stopped and looked at him. It was a look of genuine confusion, but he also had an idea that she was looking *into* him, deep within him. Eventually, her eyes rolled in their sockets as if she were trying to remember something. 'Amelia Cross.' Her screwed-closed mouth moved to the side of her face as she shook her head. 'I don't think I remember an Amelia Cross. Was she a local?'

'No, she was passing through, but she wrote me, told me she'd gotten a job at a coffee shop. Is there another coffee place here?'

'Not in Needles. There is in Proville, a good ten miles down the County Road. There was a Starbucks here for a while, doing their best to put us out of business. What they didn't take into consideration is loyalty. Our customers won't go anywhere else, that's for sure.'

'If this is the only place, then it must have been here. It would have been about a year ago.'

The old woman reeled, just a little but enough for Carson to notice. He noted it for consideration later.

She sighed while shaking her head. 'No one called Amelia. We get our fair share of waifs and strays passing through though. Malic is a sucker for a sob story,' she said with a laugh.

'Malic?'

'My husband. I'll give you his number. He's at the wholesalers today, but he'll answer sure enough. Tell him I give you the number; otherwise, he might be a bit cranky.'

'Unless I tell him a sob story,' Carson cracked.

'Exactly,' the old woman laughed as she leaned down onto the table, pulling the pen and pad from her apron.

Carson noticed, as her sleeves rode up, that her arms were heavily tattooed. He thought it a little odd from a woman of her age, which he guessed might have been touching seventy, maybe a little beyond. *A child of the sixties,* he thought with a grin, thinking about the wild things this woman might have gotten up to in her youth. *Their generation puts ours to shame,* he thought absently.

'Give him a ring and tell him Moon gave you the number.'

'Moon? As in Moon Child or something like that?'

The old woman laughed again. 'No. My name's Luna. Malic has always called me that. If you use that name, he'll know it's from me.'

'Well, thank you,' he said, waving the little slip of paper. 'I'll give him a call just as soon as I've finished this delicious breakfast.'

'You take your time and enjoy it,' Luna said heading back to the counter. A few customers walked through the door, each looking at him. Their eyes flickered between him, Luna and back to him again.

Carson was too busy enjoying his meal to notice.

5.

'I'M SO GRATEFUL for this,' Amelia said as Luna helped her tie a pristine apron around the back.

'Think nothing of it. We need all the help we can get. This is the only coffee shop in town, so we tend to get quite a bit of business. Honestly, I wish I'd thought of doing this years ago. I might not have gone into the Navy then,' Malic said as he prepared the pans and griddle for another long day of frying.

'Is that where you got your tattoos?' Amelia asked, pointing to his exposed lower arms.

He looked at her and grinned. The absence of an answer was answer enough for her.

'Did you get yours from the Navy?' he asked, pointing to her own decorated arms.

She smiled as she made a small but obvious attempt to cover them. She didn't like people noticing the scars carved into her flesh or the tattoos covering them.

He raised his eyebrows, and she got the hint.

'Have you worked in a coffee shop before?' Luna asked turning her around and straightening the collar of her white blouse. 'It gets easier once you've served your three hundredth customer. It'll be like second nature to you.'

Amelia's eyes widened.

Luna began to laugh. 'I'm kidding; it's more like four hundred. All you need to do is greet the customers as they enter. You start with *hello,* but as you get to know them, and mostly they're a good bunch, you'll get to know their sense of humour, and you'll also get to know if they're in a good mood or not.'

'Then take their orders,' Malic jumped in. 'If it's food, you can't cook them the food, you need a certificate for that. Take their order, their table number, and hand the slip to me or Moon. If it's coffee or other drinks, that's up to you. You good with that?'

'Raring to go,' she said, fixing her apron.

'Good.'

'Listen, thank you for everything you two have done for me. The B&B is lovely, and Martha has been great with me.'

Amelia dropped her head a little, and Luna put her hands on her shoulders. She looked up at her husband, meeting his eyes for a few moments. 'There's no need to thank us. Just do a good job and we won't have to fire you.'

Amelia laughed, diffusing the emotion of the situation.

'Here we go,' Malic announced when the bell rang, announcing her first customer. 'Be gentle with her,' he said to the man who had just walked in. 'She's a virgin.'

Amelia looked at Malic, shooting him an amused look.

'What?' He grinned, raising his hands in the air and walking backwards towards the grill area of the café.

'I'm sorry about him. I think he's a little tapped in the head,' she apologised to the young man.

'He's more than a little,' Luna added as she disappeared into the kitchen, joining her husband.

'I'm sorry about them both,' she offered, fixing her hair behind the back of her ear.

The man was smiling at her. 'Virgin, eh?' he asked.

It set alarm bells ringing in her stomach, but as she looked at him she saw he was almost as embarrassed about what Malic had said as she was disturbed about it. She relaxed and looked away for a moment, wishing the redness of her face would go away.

'I'm sorry,' the customer offered. 'I was just—'

'I know,' she interrupted. 'I'm sorry. I was just reacting wrong. I know you didn't mean anything by it. What can I get you?'

'Well, I came in to see Malic, but as it's your first day, and I seem to be your first customer, then I'll have a …' He studied the large board behind the counter. 'Hmm. I'll take a latte, please, but could you put some hazelnut in it? Can I also have that to go?'

Instantly, there was a sheen of sweat on the palms of her hands. 'I've never made a latte before,' she whispered.

The young man laughed. 'Listen, I can order something else if you want, something easier.'

She shook her head. 'No, I've got to learn. It's a life skill.'

The man was laughing. 'It really is. My name is Kevin. I don't think I've seen you around these parts before.'

'Hang on while I attempt to multitask,' she said, turning her back to him.

'I'll just go and speak to Malic while you do that. I'll be back to give you my critique on your barista skills.'

'Good. I thought you were just going to stand there and watch me. I don't think I could have dealt with that level of scrutiny.'

He chuffed as he walked past her.

She watched as Malic appeared and gestured for Kevin to go into the back, then struggled with her attack strategy towards the dreaded coffee machine. She heard the excited welcome Malic offered the young man, and by the time she had gotten the coffee into the compactor, she found herself trying to listen to their conversation. She couldn't, as whatever they were talking about was drowned out by the hissing of the coffee maker's pipes.

She poured the coffee into a paper cup and then added the hot milk she'd frothed and was just wiping the spout—Luna had told her this was one of the most important things to do—as Kevin walked out of the back room. Suddenly, she felt a little self-conscious of the way she was wiping.

'Is that for me?' he asked.

She blushed, before she realised he was talking about the coffee and not her treatment of the pipes. She nodded as she pumped the hazelnut syrup into the cup. 'Three fifty,' she said.

He offered her his card, and she looked at the name on it. Kevin Prince. *Well, hello, Kevin Prince,* she thought.

She beeped the card on the machine, and it registered the sale. 'Enjoy your coffee and have a nice day.'

'You too, Kirsty,' he said. He winked at her as he took the card, the coffee, and his leave of the shop.

She looked towards the back room and saw both Malic and Luna peeking out of the window at her. The moment she saw them, they both pretended to be doing something else.

She was already blushing, but now it was that little bit deeper.

6.

THE COFFEE AND pie were better than they had any right to be, probably because they were homemade and not straight out of Costco or some other mass-produced place. The food had filled a hole, and the coffee had made him alert enough to go and find the B&B he was supposed to be staying at.

He took his cup and plate back to the counter, offering smiles to the customers who had come in, as he did.

'All finished?' Luna asked as he approached.

'Delicious,' he said. 'Could you tell me where this little B&B is? The woman's name is …' He looked at the slip of paper in his hands. 'Martha,' he finished.

'You're staying at Martha's?' Luna beamed. 'That is just the nicest little B&B in the whole of the county. Tell her you had some of my pie, and she'll be delighted. It's just two blocks down the way,' she said, indicating that he carry on a little further the way he had been headed. 'Springmore Street. You can't miss it.'

'Thank you so much.'

'You make sure you make it back here for more pie before you leave. Do you hear me?'

'You can count on it. It was delicious.'

The B&B was less than five minutes away in the car. He had a feeling it might have been quicker if he'd walked, but he had his suitcases and computers with him, so he didn't want to risk it. Parking was easy anyway.

An older woman, one he could only assume was Martha, was on the stoop. She was wearing a large grin that looked open and warm. *Is everyone so fucking friendly in this town?* he thought, thinking back to all the Christmas films he'd watched over the years. The ones where the high-powered executive got sucked into the small-town gene pool, fell in love with the fire chief, gave up her six-figure salary to live on a reindeer farm in Schittstix, Nebraska.

'Mr Hess?' she shouted as he climbed out of the car. He looked up at the sound of his name and waved. She waved back energetically. 'Moon told me you were on your way. Did you enjoy her pie?'

Carson's face smiled, but it was only a mask for the cringe it was trying to hide. This was playing out like a really shitty film.

It unnerved him a little.

'Delicious,' he replied.

'Do you want me to give you a hand with those bags?' she asked.

He looked her up and down. She must have been one hundred and ten pounds soaking wet. 'No, I'm good, thanks,' he replied, dragging his sports bag from the back seat of the rental.

'Right this way,' she said before excitedly turning into the house and disappearing into a gloom he couldn't quite see through.

For just a moment, he thought he saw someone standing in the hallway. It was just a silhouette, and it was only there for a moment before it disappeared. A shiver crawled up his spine. The figure had looked female, even though it had only been there for a moment. He then remembered the figure in the coffee shop, the one he'd thought had been another customer, but wasn't.

Was that female too?

He wasn't enjoying this train of thought, so he pushed it to the back of his mind. He was here to find Amelia, to bring her home, back into the loving embrace of her aunt, his mother. The woman who had been the sister of her father. They needed her for the court case against her mother. She was the swing witness, the one who could put that evil crackhead bitch away for good.

He *had* to find her.

He pushed on through the hall. For some reason, he held his breath when he passed the spot where he'd seen the silhouette. There was no reason to; it just felt right.

'I've set the best room in the house up for you. You're my only customer this week,' Martha uttered excitedly.

'Thank you. I really could do with getting in there and just relaxing. The journey has been crazy long. I'm so tired.'

'That's no problem. Would you like me to fix you something to eat? Or maybe, later, you could join me for dinner. I really do enjoy company when I'm eating.'

'That would be lovely. Thank you.' He wasn't hungry right then, but that didn't mean he wouldn't be in a couple of hours.

'Should we say about seven o'clock?'

He looked at his watch. It was almost half past five; that gave him an hour and a half to relax. 'Perfect,' he said with a smile.

'Well, if there's anything else you need, just holler.'

'Actually, there is a little something you could help me with.'

She turned to look at him. As she did, the neck of her blouse shifted just a little. A shadow beneath the garment caught his eye. He only glimpsed it for a moment, but he could have sworn it was a tattoo. He wasn't one to judge people on their appearance, or how they lived their lives, but he thought it a little odd that the woman in coffee shop had tattoos too.

'Yes, dear?' she asked.

'I'm looking for a girl,' he began.

'Oh, I'm flattered, I really am. But a big, good-looking boy like you shouldn't have any problems in that department.'

Carson laughed. 'No, it's nothing like that. She's my cousin. I got an email from her saying she was in this town. She didn't want anyone coming to look for her; she had a rough upbringing and kind of fell off the radar. We really need to know where she is.'

'Do you have a name?' Martha asked.

'Amelia, Amelia Cross.'

The old woman pouted and shook her head. 'The name doesn't ring any bells. I could go and look in my resident book if you wanted. If she stayed here, I'll have her signature for sure.'

'Thank you. At least it'll be one less place to look.'

'How long ago do you think it was?'

'Maybe a year. Around this time.'

For the second time in as many hours, he noticed the same odd look fall over an older lady's face when he mentioned Amelia had been here a year ago.

'Well, you go and rest, and I'll take a look and see if there is any news on your Allison.'

'Amelia,' Carson corrected her.

'Pardon?'

Her name was Amelia. You said Allison.'

'Did I?' she asked with a smile that became a little laugh. 'Age comes to us all,' she said absently. 'Enjoy your rest.'

As she turned away, he looked at her neck, hoping to get a better look at what it was underneath her blouse. He felt his face flush as he thought about what he was doing. *Trying to see under an old lady's shirt, eh, Carson? Maybe we'll make a man of you yet,* his father said in his head.

Ignoring his bigoted father, he watched Martha leave. Her long, grey hair was pinned up in a way that women of a certain age favoured. It allowed him to see the nape of her neck. It *was* inked. It looked like a design as opposed to a picture, but he couldn't see what it was.

Pushing it from his mind, he unpacked and lay down on the bed, hoping to catch a few winks before it was time to eat.

7.

'A SWEET GIRL like you shouldn't be sitting home alone on a Saturday night,' Martha said, warming her hands by the fire. It had been unseasonably cold today, and she had no hesitation in turning the central heating on. 'The coffee shop isn't open tomorrow. Why not take yourself down to The Pickle? I'm sure there's a live rock band or some other ruckus that you young uns like, happening there. Don't be sitting in on my account.'

'Am I cramping your style?' Amelia asked.

Martha's thin eyebrows knitted together. 'Of course you are. I have a hot date coming over, and we were going to do some serious necking on the couch.'

Amelia laughed out loud.

'You've been here two weeks now, and I still haven't seen you socialising with anyone. Any boys *or* girls. Are you one of those girls who likes other girls?'

Amelia laughed again. 'Sometimes, I wish I was.'

'Well, even if you were, I don't mind any of that malarkey. I'm a modern woman, you know.'

Amelia nodded. 'I can tell, what with all those tattoos. Are they tribal, or was it a sixties thing? I've noticed Malic and Luna have a lot of them too. Were you guys at Woodstock or something?'

On the mention of the tattoos, Martha pulled her sleeves down a little. 'Oh, it was just a childish thing, dear.'

She was lying; Amelia could see that. But she couldn't judge her, as everyone knew her as Kirsty Range and that was a huge fat lie, so a little white one about tattoos didn't bother her.

'I see you have decoration too.' Martha surprised her by bringing up her ink. 'I'll share if you do,' she offered with a sly wink.

Amelia wasn't ready to tell anyone about her disfigurement just yet, maybe ever, but she suddenly realised how rude it was of her to bring it up in the first place. Some people got them to show off like peacocks, others for deeply personal reasons.

She was guessing it was the latter for her host.

So here we are, two heavily tattooed women, neither willing to share our stories. She could live with that.

'Go on. Slap on a bit of makeup and go dancing. You never know who you might meet tonight. This time in fifteen years, you could be standing in your very own house, with your very own husband, and your very own children, thinking, *I almost didn't go out that night.'*

This made Amelia smile.

'You really want me to go out, don't you?'

The old lady nodded. 'I don't want you to miss out on anything. You're young; you should be living your life to the fullest. Go on. I can lend you some dollars if you need it. You can pay me back whenever you have it.'

Amelia grinned. There was a twinkle in her eye and a strange feeling in her belly. *Maybe I* should *go out tonight,* she thought. 'OK, then,' she said rolling her eyes. 'I'll go to The Pickle.'

The old woman clapped her hands and whooped. 'Good for you, girlie. You've been working too dammed hard not to let your hair down a little.'

'I really have. Now, if you would just tell me where this Pickle is, and why it's called The Pickle, then I'll be off and leave you to whatever debauchery a woman of your wise years gets up to.'

'Oh, I'll be in bed as soon as you leave.'

'Alone?' Amelia asked.

'Oooh, you are wicked girl,' Martha hissed playfully flapping her away.

~~~~

Within an hour, Amelia was washed, changed, and already had a lining of vodka and coke in her stomach, courtesy of Martha and her
~~~~

strangely overfilled liquor cabinet. It turned out The Pickle was only a five-minute walk back into town. It was on the next block along from the coffee shop, and as it was a nice night, she decided to walk.

She was glad she did. The air was sweet, the smell of the pines and the coming fall filled her lungs, and she felt good about life for the first time in such a long time. *Maybe this is where I'm destined to stay,* she thought, absently rubbing her arms. Her fingertips tracing the lines of scars hiding beneath the ink.

The Pickle seemed to be the only joint in town. It was a two-story building on Main Street, and she was amazed she'd never noticed it before. It looked busy, as she kind of expected it to, what with it being Saturday night.

She stood outside and looked in.

She'd never felt so much like an outsider as she did right then. There were people sitting in the windows, all of them having fun. Music was playing, and laughter was echoing out into the street. She could envision everyone knowing each other and dancing the night away. A scene from an old film her father had enjoyed and allowed her to watch with him before her life turned to shit—two Americans walked into an old English pub, and everyone stopped talking and turned to look at them. She didn't know why, but she remembered a man throwing a dart and missing the board.

This had been a mistake. She didn't belong here. She *was* an outsider, an intruder into their world. She didn't fit in here. Taking in a shuddering sniff, she hugged herself and turned away.

'Kirsty?'

She began to walk off.

'Kirsty …'

She was starting to feel the cold biting her, and she wished she'd brought a coat.

'Hey, Kirsty. Where are you going?'

She hoped she wasn't going to disturb whatever Martha's plans were for tonight. The last thing she wanted to do was walk in on her and some old dude getting it on. This caused her to crack a smile.

'Kirsty!'

She felt a hand on her shoulder and froze.

'I've been shouting you,' the man's voice from behind her laughed. He sounded a little out of breath.

She turned. Her mind's eye flashed the faces of all the men her mother had allowed to touch her, to do things to her that no grown man should ever do to a child. She was just about to break away, to run as fast as she could from her abuser, when the face changed once more.

It was the smiling, pleasant face of one of her customers.

One of her favourite customers.

One of the customers Luna had told her had only started coming in regularly since she'd been working there.

'Kevin,' she gasped, a smile breaking on her lips.

'I've been shouting for you. You must have been in little world of your own.'

She'd forgotten. It was a slip she couldn't afford. In this town, she wasn't Amelia. To these people, she was Kirsty Range. *I have to remember that ... Kirsty,* she scolded herself.

'Where are you going? Aren't you coming in?'

'I ...' she started, not knowing exactly know how to finish the sentence.

'Come on,' Kevin said, linking his arm inside hers.

She didn't really need that much coercion.

~~~~

She was glad she hadn't gone home. The night had been great. Kevin was a gracious companion, and he hardly allowed her to buy a drink all night. On the two occasions she did, she made sure they were expensive ones, as she believed in paying her own way.

There was a live band on stage. Kevin knew all the members, he knew all the bar staff, and he knew a good few of the patrons too. He seemed to be a natural people magnet. She was introduced to a lot of people, more than she'd ever known in her whole life, and her head was spinning, not only from the socialisation, which she'd never been comfortable with, but from all the booze too.

She'd watched Kevin drink the same number of drinks as her, but it didn't seem to have any effect on him. As the night wore on, she was feeling more than a little tipsy and thought it prudent to leave. She
~~~~

didn't want to overstretch her welcome in Martha's B&B by being drunk and having a hangover tomorrow.

'I'll walk you home if you want,' Kevin offered.

'No, no. You stay here with your friends. I'll probably see you on Monday when you come in for coffee.'

He was laughing and put his hand on his heart. 'No, listen. I insist. I give you my word as a gentleman that I won't try to kiss you or anything embarrassing like that. Watch this.' He walked over to a group of people she recognised from the coffee shop and who she had been having a good time with tonight. 'Kirsty is looking to go home, so I said I'd walk her. I wanted you to know, just so she knows I can't run away with her and take advantage of her drunken state.'

'No, it's nothing like that,' she protested, just a little slurry. 'I told him to stay—'

'I'm coming. It's either that or I walk behind you the whole way to make sure you stay safe. This way is a little less creepy. Deal?' His smile was so charming, so disarming, that she couldn't say no. 'I'll get my coat, and you can wear it. It gets a bit chilly out there this time of year.'

Reluctantly, but thankfully, she slipped into his long coat, and they left the bar, together.

'Hey, what's the deal with all the tattoos in this town?' she asked as they passed the coffee shop. On habit she looked in through the windows.

'What you mean?' he answered, grinning.

'Everyone seems to be covered in tattoos. Almost everyone at the bar had them, including the bartenders and the waitresses. All your friends had them. The band all had them.'

'I noticed that you have them.'

His reply was evasive, overtly so. She laughed. 'Mine mean something, every one of them. Do you think they mean something to everyone at the bar?' Then she remembered Malic's and Luna's, and even Martha's.

Kevin shrugged. 'How would I know?' he replied, still grinning.

She wasn't a fan of his eyes at that moment. They were the eyes of a cat who was about to pounce on a poor unsuspecting mouse.

Shrugging off the feeling, putting it down to too much booze, she continued on towards the house.

'The thing is, you don't have any.' She slurred this a little, much to the amusement of Kevin, who was now slightly behind her.

'Any what?'

She turned and looked at him. His face was sporting the wide smile she found so endearing. 'Any tattoos. Not that I can see, anyway,' she continued with a cheeky grin. 'Have you got any in any secret places you don't want anyone to see?' The instant she asked that question, she regretted it. She hated it when anyone asked about her ink, and everyone else in this town seemed to not want to answer questions about theirs either.

Kevin screwed his mouth closed and shook his head. 'Not one,' he said, shrugging. 'It's not because I'm against them or anything. I was just never attracted to the idea of them. Yours look beautiful, though,' he said.

Without thinking much about it, she touched her neck, almost as if to hide what was there. She turned and was shocked to find they were at the door to the B&B. 'Well, this is me,' she said, slipping his coat off and handing it back to him.

'Yup, Martha's place,' he replied, looking up at the house.

She looked at it herself. As she did, one of the drapes in an upstairs window twitched. She smiled as she imagined Martha either spying on her with Kevin or looking out in horror at seeing her arriving home and her lover still being there, caught like lovestruck teenagers.

'I'll see you around, then?' she offered, thinking she might still be stood here until Thursday before he made a move to ask her out.

He licked his lips.

Here it is, she thought, delaying entering the house.

'S-so, I was thinking …' he stuttered.

'What?' she asked, as if she didn't know what was coming.

'Tomorrow, can I take you out for a coffee or something?'

She grinned, sobering up rapidly. 'I work in a coffee house. I don't know if I want to be around more coffee on my day off,' she said. There was sass in her voice like she hadn't heard from herself in … *how long? Too long,* she answered her own question.

'So, how about a walk in the pines?' he asked, looking a little more nervous than when he began.

'How about I call you? See how you feel about it in the morning when the booze has worn off.'

'I know exactly how I'll feel,' he replied. 'Alcohol has no effect on me.' He shrugged again. 'I'll feel this exact same way in the morning, even if I went back and drank a gallon of whiskey.'

She laughed. 'Give me your number,' she said, removing her phone from her bag.

They swapped numbers and said goodnight. He fumbled a small kiss on her cold cheek, and she watched him walk off.

I like it here, she thought.

Needle Falls!

8.

SHE WAS FREEZING. Mostly because she was naked, but she thought it was more than that. She was cold on the inside. Her bones felt like icicles sharp enough to pierce her skin. Their frozen tips ripping her insides, flushing iced water through her vital organs.

The pain was on a different level.

Am I cold, or is that my flesh burning?

This was more than a question; it was an all-consuming thought. Even they were painful.

There was a nasty smell. It was one she knew, one she recognised from somewhere. Right now, she couldn't recall it, but she thought it might come back to her later.

Do I even have a later?

She wanted to open her eyes, but moving her eyelids hurt too much to allow her to do it. She was bound, or paralyzed, maybe both. She was unable to move, not even to wriggle her toes or fingers. Something other than the cold was rushing around her body. It felt like liquid. It was probably something vitally important. She had an idea it was rushing out of her as opposed to through her.

There was someone else in the room.

They were in close proximity.

She could smell them, whoever it was, but it might have been a fevered dream, or even the overwhelming stench of earth, of soil, plants, trees … pines! The feeling of not being alone was proved right when she heard the voice. It sounded male, but she couldn't really tell, as whatever was being said was whispered. She concentrated—it hurt her brain, her entire body, maybe more than her body. She was attempting to listen to what was being said. It shocked her, even in her confused, muddled state, but she was sure there was a chorus repeating.

None of it made any sense.

'Hickula, tragantie a billinctus, shakker, toogorey.'

The reply was hushed, but it *was* there.

'Hickula, tragantie a billinctus, shakker, toogorey.'

It was the same phrase, repeated.

'Hickula, tragantie a billinctus, shakker, toogorey.'

Her body wanted to shake, uncontrollably, but there was nothing she could do about it. How her thoughts were so lucid when all she knew was agony—and that *fucking* chanting—she couldn't comprehend, but they were. She couldn't even move her eyes. She tried to move her mouth, to release the scream building up inside her, but her lips just wouldn't work.

Suddenly, there was light.

It was too much for her, and she tried to blink it away, only her eyelids rebelled against her.

'Hickula, tragantie a billinctus, shakker, toogorey.'

The chant was getting louder, as was the response. She had never heard anything so horrible, so terrible, in her life, and she'd been privy to a lot of horrible things in her few, short years.

'Hickula, tragantie a billinctus, shakker, toogorey.'

'Lord Glimm, hear our prayer, accept this offering for the twelve.'

It *was* a male voice, and it hurt her ears.

The liquid sloshing around her continued, and the cold was unrelentingly freezing her innards. Then there was a draining sensation, as if the liquid was pouring from her, gushing like a pig in a slaughter house.

That was when she realised she was suspended. Over what? She couldn't tell.

The bright fuzz faded as her agonised eyes got used to the torture of the light. They were blurred, as if they were failing, but she could make out figures. There were a lot of them.

She also could see tubes coming from her were feeding into containers beneath her.

It was dark.

It was blood.

It was her blood.

How am I still alive?

'The Great Lord Glimm accepts your suffering,' was the reply. She didn't know if she had said her thought out loud, and this was a reply.

Why me? She continued.

'The Great Lord Glimm accepts your suffering,' was the only answer. The voice was familiar to her, but she couldn't place it, much like the smell.

She knew she was dying.

It was happening slowly, lucidly. It wasn't fair. It was wrong, and it was tragic. Her dying wish was that things could have been different, better even.

The main silhouette turned towards her. He—at least she thought it was a he—was wearing a mask. It was a stag. Its antlers were impressive, but they looked cumbersome. He looked at her, leaning in close. He reached up to remove the mask, revealing arms beneath his robe that were plain and pale. They were devoid of tattoos.

The mask was removed just as her eyesight failed her.

The last thing she heard before her world went dark was the man in the mask …

'Hickula, tragantie a billinctus, shakker, toogorey,' he whispered.

9.

AMELIA WOKE IN her bed, covered in sweat and finding it difficult to catch her breath. She couldn't take in the air she required from the claustrophobic darkness of her room. This caused panic to bloom inside her, for a few moments, until she realised it had all been a horrible dream.

The nightmare had been horrible.

It had also been troubling.

Kevin had been keeping her somewhere. She was unable to move, unable to get away from him and the cold, or the hot, she couldn't remember, dark space he held her in.

He kept telling her something. She couldn't recall what it was, as the dream was fast fading, leaving her feeling more than a little silly.

It was only a dream.

Then the whole thing was gone. It was nothing but a dark blur on her conscious. She looked at the clock. It was three fifteen am, and still dark. She shook her head once her breathing was back in check, flipped her pillow over from the damp side, and closed her eyes.

10.

THE MEAL WITH Martha was delicious. He'd forgotten just how good home-cooked food could be. He'd eaten his fill, yet she'd insisted he have desert. When he found out it was homemade apple pie with a handsome dollop of ice cream for good measure, he was helpless to resist.

'If I lived here permanently, I'd be the size of a cow in no time.'

'Nonsense, you're a growing man. You need calories inside you; otherwise, you'll start to fade away.'

'Did you look at the books to see if Amelia had stayed here?' he asked, wiping crust crumbs from the stubble of his three-day-old beard.

'I did. There's no record of an Amelia Cross staying here at all last year. Maybe she stayed in one of the motels on the edge of town.'

Carson bit the inside of his cheek. 'I don't think so. I'm almost sure she said she was staying in a gorgeous little B&B in the centre of town. Are there any others in the area?'

Martha laughed. 'Not any gorgeous ones,' she said. 'I've got the monopoly on that. Do you remember what time of year it was? I don't mind asking around for you.'

'It would have been around this time. I remember it because she mentioned the way the pines smelled in the fall. She'd never been one to sit back and take in her surroundings, so when she mentioned it, it kind of stuck.'

'I'll ask around for you tomorrow when I'm out and about. We'll see if anyone knows of anything that can help. You say she worked in a coffee shop; Malic might know something.'

Carson pushed his plate away from him. It was empty with the exception of a little melted ice cream and a few crumbles of crust on the side. 'That was fantastic. I'd say it was the best meal I've eaten in a long time.'

'Well, that is praise indeed. Now, you run along and do whatever you're going to do, and I'll get on with the washing up.'

'Do you want me to help?' he offered.

She shook her head. 'It's my kitchen, and I like it all to myself, but thank you for the offer. It is much appreciated. Now, off you go.'

'I think I'll go for a walk. It's a nice night.'

She nodded. 'You should. Just don't go out of town if you don't know the landscape. You can get lost in those pine woods, and no one would ever find you. It wouldn't be the first time it's happened.'

'I'll be careful,' he said as he eased himself up and away from the table. 'I'll take a walk into town and see what Needle Falls has to offer a guy like me.'

'You be careful,' she said, turning towards him, her face losing most of the jolliness it had only moments ago.

'I will,' he said, slipping into his coat.

As he left the kitchen, and the house by the side door, Martha watched him go. She watched him walk down the path towards the gate and turn left. When he was out of sight she reached for her mobile phone and selected a number. 'He's left,' she said into the device. 'Yeah, he went left, towards town.'

~~~~

The evening was indeed beautiful, and the fresh smell of the pines brought about that early fall excitement he'd felt every year heading into what his friends liked to call *the spooky season.* He adored all the horror tropes, but most of all, he loved Christmas, and that was the feeling he was getting here.

It was a Christmas feeling.

Downtown wasn't quite deserted. A few places were still open. The coffee shop was one of them, but as he looked in on his way past, he saw the old man putting the chairs on the top of the tables.

There were two restaurants that looked busy, and he could hear the thrum of either live rock music or a loud jukebox. *That must be The Pickle,* he thought.
~~~~

He walked over to it to see what all the fuss was about. The building was a two-story affair with balconies on both levels. There were French windows that were open, allowing the people sitting at the tables on the balconies to still be part of the atmosphere inside. The tables were full, and the music from inside screamed live band.

Carson loved live music.

He decided to go and take a peek, to soak up a little of the atmosphere and maybe get himself a beer, or even two, in the process.

The instant he stepped inside, he knew the place.

It was the same bar in every small town. In his hometown, it had been called Garry's Bar and Grill. No one knew why it had been called that, as no one could ever remember anyone called Garry owning or even working at the place. It smelt of spilled beer and too much cologne. The only difference between The Pickle and Garry's was this place was brighter, mainly due to the French windows, and it was airier due to the two-level split.

The stage took up all of his, and most of the other patrons', attention. It was a decent size, and there was currently a five-piece rock—or maybe country, it was difficult to tell these days—band playing. Lead singer with an acoustic guitar, drums, bass, guitarist, and a female fiddle player giving it the country edge.

They were kicking up a storm.

There was a pool table in the back of the room, and the bar was a large square in the centre. Most of the seats around it were occupied, as were the majority of the tables, but there were still a few spaces available. He eased himself onto one of the stools and leaned over, careful not to soak his sleeves in the spilled drinks.

'Can I get an IPA draft, please?' he asked the big guy behind the bar. He was a bear of a man with a heavy beard. He was just the type of guy Carson liked, but he wasn't getting any vibes as he poured the drink, so he didn't pursue any banter.

He turned and watched the band.

They were really good. The singer had the crowd eating from the palm of his hand, and they all loved it, whooping and dancing along to the tunes.

He felt a little bit out of touch with the evening as he observed the people. He knew they all know each other. They would have all been in school together, or worked together, or were even neighbours.

He understood what being an outsider in a small town was like. There was a lot of laughing, a lot of hugging, and a lot of banter going back and forth.

He was a little envious of their friendships, as it brought back his exclusion from most of the social gatherings back home. He'd never really been accepted anywhere, not until he got to the big city.

All of this was brought home to him with a bang when he was barged in the back by a well-built guy wearing jeans and a Stetson hat. He knocked into Carson, spilling his drink down the front of his shirt.

'Hey,' he shouted, putting his half empty glass back on the bar and turning towards the big man.

The big man ignored him, so without thinking about what he was doing, he tapped the guy on the shoulder.

It was when he turned, Carson realised his mistake.

The guy was good looking but in a rough way. Like he had been in too many fights trying to knock his good looks out of him.

'What?' he asked. He never spat it, nor did he growl it. It was just a simple one-word question. 'What?'

Carson shook his head. 'Nothing,' he said, making a show of wiping the front of his shirt.

The man's eyes looked away for a moment before coming back to rest on him. 'There must have been something you wanted for you to tap me on the shoulder. So, I'll ask you again. What?'

Carson could feel adrenaline coursing through his body. His ears were pounding as blood pumped through them. He was aware of the others around him, making him hyperaware that he was the new kid in town, and people in small towns liked to look after their own. They were never quick to defend the new kid, especially since he'd been the aggressor in this situation. 'Seriously, it's nothing,' he almost whispered.

As if sensing his unease, and maybe even tasting fear in the air, the big man turned all the way around and looked at him. 'I'm going to ask you one more time, fag. What the fuck did you want?'

On hearing the word *fag,* Carson's stomach flipped. He'd been on the receiving end of too many ass-kickings to be ignorant of how this was about to go down. His fingers were tingling, and the thumping of blood pumping through his ears had turned into a roar. He always thought that if he could control the surges that happened to him before a fight, he might actually be better at it. He looked at his aggressor and the two men that were standing around him, who'd appeared from nowhere, ready to step in if this *fag* surprised everyone and took a shot.

He was alone in town, and that loneliness had never felt as prevalent as it did right now. He had literally no one to fall back on.

He resigned himself to the pain he'd feel soon enough. The man before him was big, and his shirt sleeves were rolled up in the redneck way to show off his muscles, but it was his tattoos that caught Carson's eye. They were up and down both his arms. This was nothing new in this day and age, but usually if a person was sporting a *sleeve*, then they would be pictures, images of what that person was into, of how they wanted to define themselves.

Carson's were just words.

Up and down both his thick arms, in the same font, and in the same dark-coloured ink.

He didn't know why he was focusing on this when he was just about to get his ass handed to him on a plate, but something about them called to him. He looked at the other two thugs behind the man. They had the same ink; one of them had the words up his neck, almost to his chin.

That was when the world began to spin around him.

The intense feeling in his jaw and the violence to his body took him by surprise. As he reeled, all he saw was the grins of the other two as the first guy, the biggest guy, spun him around.

Carson knew the floor was calling his name. He could almost hear it as everything had an odd focus and a slowing down of time. The guy's brow was ruffled, and his eyes and mouth were filled with rage.

Carson closed his eyes. He knew the drill. Fall to the floor, let them take their cheap shots at the queer who'd so offended their sensibilities, and hope beyond all hope that someone would step in and drag them off him before his bones started to break.

As if on cue, the floor rose up to meet him.

It slammed into his face.

Lucky enough, he had the foresight to turn his head to stop his nose from getting mashed on the filthy patched woodwork. His head bounced, and he reeled in the promise of bruises tomorrow.

A new voice spoke up then.

My saviour?

At first, it was muffled, but he put that down to the shock his system was experiencing as he tensed himself for the next and inevitable volley of attacks.

They never came.

He dared open an eye and look up towards his aggressors. There were four of them now. A newcomer was standing in between him and the other three, stopping them from continuing what they'd started. His desperate mind grasped, trying to make some kind of sense of what was happening, but it looked like the new guy, only a skinny kid, much like himself, was telling the *good ole boys* to leave him alone.

The part that was astounding him, more than anything else, was that they were listening.

All three of them were backing down.

Never one to look a gift horse in the mouth, he wasted no time in scurrying away, out of the reach of the boys, to give him some much-needed seconds for when they inevitably pushed past the newcomer and returned their attentions on to him.

Only it never happened.

The biggest of the three, the one who had banged into him in the first place, starting all of this nonsense, just wiped his mouth. He grinned down at him before walking away, much to the astonishment of Carson, whose back was now leaning against the bar. His trousers were soaking up the spilled ale that amassed in such places. The looks he was offered by the departing characters were enough to tell him that he wouldn't be coming back into this shithole anytime soon.

'Kevin,' the newcomer offered, along with his hand to help him up from the floor.

'What?' Carson asked, accepting the extended hand and pulling himself up onto his shaky feet.

'Kevin, that's my name.'

'Oh. Well, thanks for stepping in there, Kevin. I thought my ass was done for.'

The man—not much older than a boy, really—grinned. As he did, Carson saw that he was wrong. This was a man, just a very boyish looking one. He felt himself begin to blush a little. He shook his head, rubbing at his jawline as he did.

'I'm sorry about the town bullies,' Kevin continued, indicating a seat at a table far enough away from the band, who had continued to play all the way through his humiliation. 'Every town has them.'

Carson sat at the table, still nursing his jaw. 'That they do,' he mumbled, remembering the beatings he'd taken at school at the hands of boys like those three.

'Can I get you a drink? Think of it as a kind of apology for your poor welcome into Needle Falls.'

Carson looked at the grinning man facing him. He chuffed. 'Something cold to ease the pain in my jaw, maybe.'

'Coming right up.'

As Kevin walked away, he watched him go. He was only slight, yet the way the three boys had moved on at his insistence had impressed him. He got served at the bar almost instantly and returned with two iced glasses of frothing beer. Carson knew the drink would be just what the doctor ordered.

'How did you know I was new in town?' he asked after he'd taken a swig from the cold brew, enjoying the numbing effect on his aching jaw.

Kevin laughed and shrugged. 'You look new.'

Carson rubbed his jaw again, wincing as the pain returned momentarily. 'I don't feel new.'

'Well, believe me, when you've been in this town for a while, everything new stands out. Not everyone is like Billy and his two little friends. They're OK guys, if you know how to handle them.'

'Well, you sure seemed to know how to do that. I thought they were going to tear you to pieces.'

Kevin looked to where the three boys were currently harassing a group of young women and exhaled slowly. 'You just need to know how to talk to them. It's a good thing I speak native Neanderthal.'

'Well, thank you, Ugg. I thought I was about to spend the night in the ER rather than Martha's.'

Kevin was laughing at the name he had just called him. He stopped for a moment and offered him a look before taking a large gulp of his cold brew. 'So, I was right. You are the new guy Martha's been telling everyone about. You're looking for your cousin, aren't you?'

Carson laughed. 'Well, news really does travel fast around these parts, doesn't it?'

'You'd think it was Christmas the way Martha is telling everyone about you.'

He scratched his head, marvelling at the way his head didn't hurt. This guy really had saved him from a proper beating. 'Really?'

Kevin nodded. 'Seriously. There's not many people come here, especially to stay, so when someone new turns up, the locals tend to get a bit excited. New DNA for the pot.'

This made Carson laugh. He liked this guy. Dare he even think there was something of a *connection* with him? He decided to do something big-city-like and let a little something slip. 'Well, I don't think they'll be getting much DNA from this guy.'

Kevin's brow ruffled as he looked at him. 'How so?' he asked, tilting his head.

'I'm not really the sort of guy who spreads his DNA to a new generation, if you get my drift.'

Kevin continued looking at him, his eyes asking the questions his mouth wasn't.

Carson rolled his eyes a little. 'Gay,' he whispered. 'That's why those guys were beating on me.'

Kevin laughed. He leaned in and looked him in the eyes. The questions and the humour were gone, having been replaced by something else; a devilish smile breaking on his lips. 'Let you into a secret?' he whispered.

Carson's heart was pounding, only this time, it wasn't giving him danger alerts. It was quite the opposite.

The rest of the night was filled with drinking, laughing, and if Carson had his signals correct, flirting.

11.

THE DREAM UNNERVED her, causing sleep to evade her for the rest of the night, or at least until the small hours when it was almost a useless tool. She had to be up in a couple of hours, to cover an extra early shift due to Malic and Moon attending an appointment they couldn't miss. They hadn't told her what the appointment was, but she figured it was none of her business and never asked.

Martha, who was usually up at the crack of dawn—if she ever slept in the first place—was nowhere to be seen either. There was a note on the table informing her there were muffins in the oven and for her to help herself. Amelia shrugged, opened the oven door, and revelled in the smell of the freshly baked goodies. She selected two, poured herself a fresh orange juice, and sat at the table picking at the treats. Her thoughts drifted to Kevin. A smile crept over her face. She looked at her arms and the thin welts that the images of playful dragons and flowers covered. Then she thought about his arms. These days, it didn't seem normal for someone to not have at least one piece of body art ... *At least in this town,* she thought with a grin, imagining Malic and Moon sitting in a tattooist's chair and getting their ink done.

Suddenly, a cold shiver ran through her.

The dream from last night slapped her. She was suddenly covered in sweat at the stark image of those tubes draining her. About the cramped room and the fact, it was Kevin keeping her there.

Jesus, Amelia. You have one fucked-up psyche. Some people show you kindness, and you repay it with scorn and bad dreams. Absently, she rubbed her hand up her arm, feeling the memories of her scarred youth. As she popped the last of the first muffin into her mouth, she picked up her phone. She looked through her contacts, of which there were exactly five. Malic, Martha, Kevin, a therapist who'd insisted she take her number in case of emergencies, and her cousin, Carson.

She decided to email Carson. He was the only person from her past she knew she could trust. Probably the only one who would give a shit if she was OK, or even alive.

She sent him a short message, telling him about Needle Falls and where she was working, but she omitted the part about Kevin. He didn't need to know *everything*.

When that was done, she ate the second muffin and left the house. It took her a moment to realise how silent the street was. She didn't notice at first due to having her EarPods in, wanting to drain away the stresses of the morning with some loud rock music, so when she pressed the button to cross the road, it surprised her there were no cars on either side of the road and she could just skip right over. It prompted her to pause the music on her phone and listen to the sounds of the town.

There were hardly any noises at all. There was wind, birds, an aeroplane, but there were no cars, no people walking, no signs of normal life at all.

It was eerie.

She tried to pass it off as being early in the morning, but the sudden feeling of claustrophobia, the same one she'd had in her dream, descended over her. This was different than in her sleep. This had a physical aspect to it instead of it being in her head, or in her psyche. With her heart racing, she stepped away from the pedestrian crossing and almost threw herself against the wall of the building behind her. The feel of the cool brickwork on her back was soothing, reassuring. It told her that not everything in her world was suddenly questionable, yet it didn't do anything for the sickening churning occurring in her stomach. She suddenly wanted, no, needed to go to the toilet. Cold sweat lined her forehead as the cramps in her stomach doubled, then trebled. She was sure she was going to either vomit or maybe disgrace herself from the other end.

Then it passed almost as quickly as it appeared.

Her stomach settled, and the sweat evaporated. She could feel the warmth of colour seeping back in her cheeks.

A single car, a flatbed, rolled along the road. The driver, a big man with a battered Stetson and a gruff-looking beard, glared at her as he passed. She realised that she must have looked a mess, holding on to the building behind her as if it were her only anchor to this world. This, of course, was exactly what it was.

The driver slowed. He looked like he was going to ask her something, maybe enquire how she was. Was she OK? She sure hadn't felt OK.

She waved. The man tipped his head before driving on, leaving her alone on the streets of this deserted, alien town.

~~~~

The shadows in the room were long, nothing more than silhouettes, dark on dark in the almost pitch black. The only illumination came from the huge table in the centre of the room, and they were only from a number of pinpricks, twelve in total, offering almost nothing.

There was movement.

Through the lack of light, the moans, the stink of sweat and sex, the sounds of flesh slapping against flesh were loud enough to wake the Gods … which was, after all, what was happening here.

A lone figure stood atop the table. The light from the twelve pinpricks illuminated his thick, lush velvet cloak. It also cast an eerie glow on the headset he was sporting. The cruel, lethal antlers stood grand in the poor light as they twisted and turned, watching, presiding over the debauchery happening before it.

Beneath the cloak, the lone figure was naked.

This was the only indication he was male.

He was aroused, and his pale, unblemished flesh glowed in the odd lighting like false teeth in a disco. His unmarked skin was in complete contrast to the dark, tattooed bodies that writhed at his feet. There were hundreds of them in the dark room, squirming and rutting like rats huddling together in the cold darkness for safety and warmth. Only these bodies had a more *carnal* agenda than merely keeping warm. The stink from their cavorting was heavy, and it was moist.

It was exactly what was required.
~~~~

The man in the cloak was holding one hand in the air. His other was furiously beating a rhythm up and down his extraordinarily long and proportionately thick erection. The people on the floor were shadows, almost hidden from the light, but as the human eyes compensated for the darkness, he grinned at the blood and the ink that covered their bodies. He had personally inked the flesh of each of these bodies. The young and the old alike. He had groomed them, and they were almost ready for the ultimate sacrifice, the one The Great Lord Glimm demanded of them.

He commanded blood, death, ink. In return, he would grant them everything they could possibly want.

But first, she must die.

She must be drained.

She must be used.

As the ambience in room lifted toward a climax of moaning and shouting, as the warmth of the wet stink of humans fucking filled his nostrils, he allowed himself to go too.

As semen flew from the tip of his cock, he whispered a name.

'Amelia!'

~~~~

The coffee shop, which usually had at least one customer waiting for it to open—on some mornings, there would be a queue—was as deserted as the rest of the town. Amelia looked down the street, hoping to see the flatbed truck again, or at least another car. There was nothing, not even a stray pedestrian. Another shiver tore through her, reminding her she needed to pee before opening up.

A single sound carried on the wind. It was the sound of children. They sounded like they were screaming.

She stepped away from the doorway and listened.

It *was* children.

They were screaming, laughing, and shouting too. The sounds were coming from the school, the one that was five blocks away. Presumably, she'd never heard it before because of the usual sounds of traffic. She grinned a wry smile, turned, and opened up the café.
~~~~

12.

THE GIRL DIED with a curse on her lips.

He didn't care. She was a tool, an important tool, but a tool, nonetheless.

His guests had clothed and moved on, back to their lives, back to the grind of small-town mediocrity. They'd be back. They would need the mark on their flesh, the mark of Glimm. The mark that the Great Lord himself would see, would read, and identify them as his own. He had done his research into the influence of The Glimm and the power their God held. Yes, he had read about the failures too, about how vengeful he could be if the offerings were not to his liking, but he disregarded all of that. He was doing things correctly, the way the Great Lord wanted him to.

This girl was not the final piece in the jigsaw, but she was important. There had been many before her, and the good people of this town, of his town, bore the marks of this work, of his research, of his long and hard labours on their skin.

She was the catalyst to bring the final piece to them.

The final piece was a number, but it was written that they had to come of their own volition. They couldn't be coerced in any way. They had to give themselves freely to The Glimm, and she would, she had already, lured them here.

The fluids that had drained from the poor girl's heavily tattooed body lay in urns around him. Urns he had procured over the years of work inking and marking the stinking rich and famous. He had once been celebrated far and wide for his skills and an artist of some desire. He had used this fame, and indeed the infamy, for his own needs and found himself here, in Needle Falls. It was a far cry from the life he'd once lived, but ever since the scandal with the Hollywood star and the infant's blood he had used to create a work of art, Kevin knew this place would be suffice for his final work.

With promises of exotic sex, debauchery like they had never imagined, and most of all immortality, the hungry and bored residents of this slowpoke town were easily seduced. Now, he had his twelve, had everything he needed to complete his work, and that suited him fine.

13.

CARSON WOKE. HE didn't want to move his head. He smacked his tongue against the roof of his mouth, where it stuck. The taste on the back of his throat was the worst. He could taste grease, something fatty, mixed in with stale alcohol. As hangovers went, this wasn't his worst, not by a longshot, but every hangover was unique, and this one was as uncomfortable as all the others.

Eventually, he braved moving his head and was pleasantly surprised to find it didn't fall off. He groaned as his brain took a microsecond longer to catch up with his head and the resulting dizziness woke the demon in his stomach.

He didn't know if he was hungry or if he wanted to vomit. He hoped it was the former.

Using all of his willpower, he sat up. His eyes were still closed, as he didn't want the spinning room to anger his stomach monster any more than it already was.

It didn't, and he braved a look.

He was a little disappointed that he was in his own room. He rather fancied waking up in Kevin's room, but then he guessed how he might look right then and decided he didn't want to inflict that upon anyone else, especially a potential suitor. *Who'd have thought I'd come chasing Amelia and find someone else?* He smiled at this question, and laying his head back on his pillow, he smiled at what he could remember about last night.

Kevin had told him he'd been waiting for him.

'Is that cheese or is it romance?' he asked himself, pleased that his stomach seemed to be telling him he was hungry, not sick.

As he eased himself out of the bed, a memory took him, making his heart flutter a little. There was a kiss. It had been a long one. He remembered it had shocked him. He'd been getting vibes from Kevin all night, and had readily given them back, but the kiss while they were walking home took him by surprise. Kevin had pushed him against a wall, pulled himself close, invading his personal space, and the next thing he knew, a tongue had been pushed into his mouth.

He pushed back, just enough, responding to the amorous attack.

Kevin had cast away any worry of being caught or even being set upon by the big *good ole boys* from the bar. He had just kissed him as if it were the most natural thing in the world.

Then another memory flashed into his head.

This one—it wasn't worrying, but it was odd.

It was what he'd said after he'd pulled away.

The kiss had come to its natural conclusion and hit that awkward moment where you pull back and look at the other person before one of you started to laugh. Only Kevin hadn't laughed. He'd just rubbed a finger along his lips and licked it, as if tasting him. He was just looking at him. His eyes intense, dark, maybe even far away. Carson thought he might have been using poetic licence here, as he had been rather drunk at the time.

Or maybe he wasn't.

Kevin was smiling when he said something weird. 'You're the one she brought!'

Thinking about how he'd said it, about the actual words used, sent a cold shiver up his spine. He didn't know why, but the memory kind of disturbed him.

He got out of the bed, attempting to shake off the ill feeling worming its way into him, and ran the shower. As the warm water cascaded over him, the odd feeling wouldn't pass, and even when he was dressed and ready for the day ahead of him, the feeling persisted.

Martha was cooking a full breakfast, and his stomach growled with the aromas wafting towards him as he made his way downstairs. He pushed the odd thoughts to the back of his head and concentrated on the day ahead of him. He'd come to this town on a mission. His agenda was to be cold and distant to everyone he met, find out about Amelia, before getting the hell out of Dodge to sort out the legal mess happening back home. He hadn't counted on everyone being so nice and so welcoming. *Well, with the exception of John Wayne and his pals in the bar.*

He grinned, thinking about how Kevin had stepped in.

'Good night last night?'

The voice jumped him out of his thoughts, and he turned to see Martha setting a plate of bacon on the table next to a stack of hot buttered toast.

'Uh?'

She was grinning too. 'Last night. Was it good?'

'Oh, yeah,' he agreed as he sat, and Martha placed a cup of hot coffee before him. At that moment, he thought he could have married the older woman. Everything was exactly how he needed it right then.

'Did you meet anyone?' she asked.

There was an inflection in her voice that he thought of as teasing. Her smile was lopsided, and his brow ruffled. He pouted at her.

She laughed. 'Well?'

He shrugged. This woman was so disarming, nothing at all like his cold, judgmental mother.

Maybe someone like me can *thrive in a small town like this,* he thought.

As he bit into the breakfast muffin, she sat facing him. 'So, did you?' she persisted.

'What is this? The Spanish Inquisition?' He laughed while he chewed.

'You just look happy this morning, that's all.'

'Well, if you *must* know, there might have been a certain *someone* I met. We had a few drinks, and we had a good night.'

Martha sat back and clapped her hands together. 'I knew it,' she almost squealed.

Carson felt the fingers of heat clawing at his cheeks.

'So, are you seeing this person again?'

'What's happening here?' He laughed again. 'Are you trying to marry me off, woman?'

'I'd do no such thing,' she said, putting her hand to her chest, the twinkle in her eye belying the shock. 'You're a nice person, and I'd like to see you stay here for a bit.'

Carson continued to eat as Martha stood and began fussing with something on one of the counters. 'Besides,' she mumbled, barely loud enough for him to hear. 'You're the one *she* brought to us.'

Carson hadn't been listening, but he caught the gist of it.

His stomach lurched.

'What?' he asked, struggling to keep the shake out of his voice.

'Nothing, dear. I was just asking what you were going to be doing today, what with it being Saturday and all.'

Had she asked about his plans? He didn't think she had. He thought she'd mentioned something about *her* bringing him here. Martha turned towards him. Her smile was genuine, and nothing had seemingly changed in her demeanour. *I must have heard her wrong,* he thought as he continued to eat. *I'm putting too much emphasis on what Kevin said last night. If Kevin even did say anything last night.*

His appetite left him for a moment as he watched the pleasant old lady leave the kitchen. He watched her picking up her things and moving her knickknacks around. Normal, everyday activities, but something was different about her now. It wasn't sinister per se, it was a million miles from that, but something about it felt … unnatural.

~~~~

Unable to shake the odd feeling he'd woken with, even though he knew he should be on a high because of the events of last night, he took his leave from the house, much to the excitement of Martha.

'Are you going to meet up with someone?' she asked.

He looked at her and exhaled through his nostrils. 'Have you been speaking to someone?' He could hear the annoyance in his own voice and didn't like it, but he had a strange feeling, as if he were being played with. The questions coming at him were beginning to wear thin.

She shook her head. 'No, I just like you and want you to be happy. We need you here.'

Once again, he felt it was an odd thing to say. He cocked his head towards her. 'You *need* me? What do you mean, need me?'
~~~~

Martha smiled her sweet smile and raised her pencilled-on eyebrows. 'Oh, nothing sinister, dear. It's just that this little town could do with a little, you know, flamboyance.'

Carson couldn't do anything but laugh as she'd said it, and he was still laughing now. Apparently, he was flamboyant. He wanted nothing to do with flamboyant. He'd been too flamboyant in The Pickle last night and look what had almost happened there. *Almost but not quite,* he told himself as he pushed open the door to the coffee shop. He wasn't really in the mood for more coffee, but he wanted to ask around about Amelia a little more.

This seemed like the obvious place to start.

As the bell jingled, announcing his arrival, the many customers already inside looked to see who it was. More than a few turned away when they saw it was him. A few others looks lingered, even as he found a table and sat down.

'I'll be with you in a minute.' The attractive older woman, Luna, smiled at him. He put her age as at least sixty and guessed that back in the day, she'd been a mighty beauty.

He nodded.

'Are you still looking for this Amelia girl?' Luna asked as she came over with the coffee jug to fill the cup she placed before him.

'Yeah. She was definitely here. She's a huge coffee drinker, so she must have come in here at some point.'

'Do you have any pictures of her?' she asked, finishing pouring.

He removed his phone and opened the photo app. 'Only these from a few years ago. She was always changing her hair colour. She might have had a few more tattoos by the time she landed here too.'

He watched as Luna subconsciously pulled at the sleeves of the top she was wearing, covering the ink on her arms.

He turned his phone so she could see the picture. It was of a young blonde girl laughing into the camera. It was a sweet picture, but each time he looked at it, all he could see was the pain behind the laughter, the tears in her eyes ready to fall at any given moment.

'Amelia Cross, you say?'

'Yeah, although I'm wondering now if she was using another name. Was there anyone new in the town around then? Anyone you might have noticed?'

Luna was still looking at the picture. Her eyes were wide, and they were telling stories that her mouth didn't want to speak. Her lips were quivering, and Carson was sure he could see a shake in her hand.

'Moon,' the voice boomed from behind the counter. It was a loud, good-natured voice. 'Are you looking at pictures of men in their swimming trunks again?'

Malic loomed over from behind, casting his shadow over the table. It was the first time Carson had noticed just how big this man was. His sleeves were rolled up his arms, showing off the tattoos that covered them. Carson's eyes were drawn to them. There were no pictures; it was just words. Sentences up and down his forearms. They looked like the ones he had seen on Moon's arms and, now that he thought about it, the same as were on Martha's neck too.

He tried to think about the men in the bar last night. *They were covered in ink as well,* he thought. He tried to remember what their tattoos looked like, but he couldn't—his focus hadn't been on their arms at the time.

'Who's this?' Malic asked, looking over his wife's shoulder at the picture.

'It's the girl he's been looking for. The one he was asking about yesterday.'

'Amanda?' Malic asked.

'Amelia,' Carson corrected him.

'You know, she does look familiar,' Malic mused as he stared at the phone.

This caught Carson's attention. 'So, you think you *might* have seen her?'

Malic bit the inside of his cheek as he continued to study the picture. His eyes shot to his wife, only for a moment, but in his excitement of this revelation, Carson missed it.

Luna licked her lips.

'Listen, I don't want you to get your hopes up, as this was a while ago. If I remember right, she was here and then she wasn't. She skipped town pretty quickly. However, there might be someone who could help you.'

'Really?'

The big man nodded. 'Yeah. I'll have a word with him. See if he knows anything.'

Carson's eyes were wide. He'd expected an arduous day, trudging around the town, asking questions, hoping to bump into a certain someone and to not bump into a certain other three people. He took back his phone and looked at the picture of Amelia smiling into the camera again before putting it away.

'Her name wasn't Amelia, though,' Malic continued. 'It was Kirsty, or Krystin, or something like that. It does look like her though.'

Carson thanked the couple and continued drinking his coffee. After he finished, he left the café, offering them a wave in thanks as the door closed behind him.

~~~~

'Call Kevin and get him over here. I think it's time he met our latest resident,' Malic said as they watched Carson cross the road.

The other customers in the café were watching him go too, all of them with interest.

What Carson failed to notice while looking at Malic and Luna's tattoos was the fact that everyone else in the café were sporting the exact same designs up and down their arms.

When Carson disappeared from their view, they all returned to their business at hand, all of them with contented smiles on their faces.
~~~~

14.

THE GIRL WAS dead. He no longer cared about her. She was nothing, merely a vessel to get what he needed, what they all needed. Her body hung in the background, forgotten. Her flesh was pale, the tubes protruding from her had run dry. The only important thing about her, was the fact that the ornate urns beneath her were filled.

The aroma of exotic perfume filled the room. It masked the sweet, thick reek of sex that had permeated the room as the girl died.

Kevin's normally pale skin was awash with dark blood. Bloody hands were running up and down his naked torso, coating him, painting him in the girl's life blood. His arms were raised, and the stag antlers he wore were pointing proudly into the air. His mouth was moving as silent prayers passed between his lips. His eyes were open, but they were almost fully white, as his face was in rapture.

The hands were delving hungrily into the urns, fighting for the privilege of coating his body in the warm gore that filled them.

When he was covered, the men and women—some of them old, some of them young, but all of their bodies coated in tattoos—fell to their knees, bowing their heads in reverence at the man before them.

The twelve lights in the table were dim as the blood dripping from him ran through the grooves carved into the ornate platform. They cast a pinkish-purple light over him as his body shivered. Urns were placed at the twelve outlets for the blood to drip, collecting the valued, viscous liquid.

The lights dimmed even further when the washing of Kevin's body was complete. A hushed reverence filled the room. His eyes closed as something touched him. It didn't have the warmth of human hands; it didn't have the wetness of the blood; it didn't have the sublime eroticism of the anonymous touching and caressing of his followers, of his fellow travellers.

This was something different.

It was otherworldly.

It felt odd, like what he would expect a sensual caress from a lizard might feel like. It was a strange thought, but it was one that stuck with him. It wasn't the first time he'd experienced this phenomenon, but it was the strongest sensation he'd felt.

The expectant silence from the congregation—all of them covered in blood and sweat from their physical, sexual exploits—was consuming, he felt himself sway to some rhythm he couldn't quite hear.

Hickula, tragantie a billinctus, shakker, toogorey.

The chant was coming from somewhere in the large room. With his eyes closed and the odd beat thrumming through his entire being, he didn't care where it came from.

He was just glad it was there.

Hickula, tragantie a billinctus, shakker, toogorey.

He knew the words.

He knew the sensation.

He recognised the touch.

They were in the presence of The Great Lord Glimm.

He had come to promise them greatness. He had come to offer something greater than what they had now, something greater than what he had once had.

It was immortality for him.

Hickula, tragantie a billinctus, shakker, toogorey.

He didn't care what the others wanted. This had always been about him. They were tools too. Sycophantic tools. They were the means to his ends. If they got a little excitement in their lives, if he gave them a glimpse into something their drab little existences had never been able to visualise, then so be it. He was happy for them. He needed was their flesh, their seed, and their corruption. The Great Lord Glimm would give him everything he wanted, everything he needed.

He would be truly immortal.

As the inhuman caress continued, as it washed the blood from him, as it ran through the channels in the table, as it dripped into the urns, mixing with the rest of the poor girl's blood, he laughed.

Once the blood that had been washed, cleansed by the deity that had chosen him and which he in turn had chosen, filled the waiting urns, it turned black.

It was the unholy miracle he had been expecting.

The blood of the sacrifice was now ink.

Ink that would scar, colour, and mark the flesh of his willing congregation. They would line up to be blessed by it. This would be the penultimate marking. This sacrifice would bring the last they required.

He required.

He could finally rise. He would stand next to the gods he had adored, worshipped his entire life. This would be his final step.

His grin grew into a smile.

The smile turned into a laugh.

Everything was happening as it should.

~~~~

Darkness had consumed her.

Pain and agony from the torture she had been subjected to washed over her like a dousing in cold water to rouse her from sleep. Every sense, every nerve tingled with a freezing suffering that she could never have imagined.

Fuck you, she cursed. *Fuck this world and everyone in it. Fuck them, fuck them, fuck them all.*

She couldn't move, or twitch, or adjust herself in any way. She thought she must have been dead, or if not, she was as good as. Lost in a sea of darkness and agony, a voice penetrated the abyss she was staring down. It was rich and as dark as the velvet darkness surrounding her. It brought memories of thick, luxurious hot chocolate complete with marshmallows, brought to her by her father.

It surprised her in its completeness.

'AMELIA CROSS, ARE YOU READY?'

She wanted to flinch from that voice. It wasn't a nice voice despite the chocolatey resonance. Its tones spoke of volume, of mass, of a physicality that seemed impossible. It told of time, immeasurable to her, maybe even to the world as she knew it.
~~~~

'FOLLOW ME, AND YOU SHALL BE UPHELD IN MORE THAN THIS WORLD HAS SHOWN YOU.'

She held her breath. She wanted to laugh at this, as there was no breath to hold. She wanted to reach out, metaphorically at least, into the nothingness around her. She knew it would only be a symbolic gesture, as she had no hands to reach out with, but the compulsion to do so was strong.

The pain, the torture of a million wounds, the agony of a life past raced through her as something in the darkness touched her.

The touch wasn't human.

It was far from it.

It felt like pain. The sensation peaked, and as she cried out in rapture, it ebbed.

Everything, both physical and mental, escaped her in that moment. She envisioned a river running down a steep mountain.

All she was left with was a dark, cold, bleak expanse.

'MY CHILD.'

The voice was loud. It was the embodiment of the cold, and the heat. It was the furthest distance she could imagine from anything resembling humanity.

'MY CHILD,' it spoke again.

It could have been a dream, a fevered rattle, a dying synapsis in her brain spasming, or it could have been something else.

'OPEN YOUR EYES.'

Her eyes opened.

They didn't see what she expected. Her existence was filled with colour. A glowing darkness. A paradox not lost on her but embraced. Everything was there in a glorious darkness that felt alive.

'DO YOU SEE IT, MY CHILD?'

'I see it.' The whisper didn't come from her but rather was emitted from the nowhere and everywhere where she now resided.

'DO YOU SEE WHAT NEEDS TO BE DONE?'

'I see it.'

'GOOD. OUR TIME IS NEAR. BE READY, MY CHILD!'

'I am ready!'

15.

SOMEONE WAS SITTING at a table in the café. The sight of him, sitting in silence, watching her with his bright blue eyes, unnerved her. It excited her at the same time. 'Kevin,' she uttered as she stepped back a little. 'What are you doing here?' She looked around the room. 'How did you even get in?'

Kevin didn't reply.

'Do Malic and Moon know you're here?'

Still, Kevin didn't reply.

'Do you want coffee?' she asked. A strange feeling was coursing through her as she looked at the silent man. Yes, he was handsome, and yes, she was attracted to him, but the dream she'd experienced had put her off him—a little, anyway.

'Have you been avoiding me, Kirsty?' he asked. His voice was low. It didn't sound threatening, but her well-tuned ears caught anger in it. Maybe anger was a little too strong a word, but he was definitely pissed off.

'What? Of course not,' she laughed.

'I haven't seen you at The Pickle the last few nights.'

'I've been staying home. I'm trying to save money,' she lied. She had been avoiding him, just like she'd been avoiding life for the last few years. It was the reason she'd found herself in this little town in the first place. It was the reason she was Kirsty and not Amelia.

'You don't need to spend money to enjoy yourself. Besides, I'd have paid for your drinks.'

She stiffened at this. Her mother had drunk, her mother had been a kept woman, and it was what had ultimately led to her father's leaving. She would not be her mother. She refused to live that life. She shook her head and busied herself unpegging her apron from the door and wrapping it around her. 'Do Malic and Moon know you're here?' she asked again.

'I have access,' he said with a nod.

The way he was talking, the things he was saying, gave her ugly feelings in her stomach. Her skin itched, and she was suddenly cold. It felt like all the drawings, all the designs on her flesh stung, all at once. It was a sensation she'd never experienced before. Suddenly she was fourteen again, experienced enough to know what the bastards wanted from her, but stubborn enough to know she would give them the satisfaction of her screaming. She refused to let him to know the effect he was having on her, so she turned away, lifted the flap and entered behind the counter.

That was when she screamed.

There were people behind her.

She hadn't heard anyone coming in. She didn't hear the shuffling of their feet as they had entered. She hadn't felt their presence, hadn't experienced that strange sixth sense people get when someone stands behind them.

Another thing that shocked her, even more than the fact that somewhere between six and ten people had snuck up on her, was that they were all naked.

All of them.

There were men and women, of all ages.

Her eyes were drawn to the nakedness before their faces. It was something she had never expected. It unnerved her more than scared her, although once the scream subsided, her body was instantly wracked in tremors.

She had flashbacks to the parties her mother subjected her to. To the naked people, all of them leering at her. Her mother, also naked, counting cash in the kitchen as the men ogled her, touched her, roughed her up.

The fourth shock that morning was, she recognised these people.

Malic and Luna were there, as was Martha. The rest of them were customers from the café, people she served every day. Passing them coffee and pastries, sharing a smile and a pleasantry, maybe even a joke or two. She never once thought she would—nor had any desire to—see any of them naked.

Their bodies, old and young, were covered from head to toe in tattoos. Some had faded like older ink had a tendency to do; others looked fresh. However, the oddest thing about this was that they all were sporting the exact same designs. They were words. Amelia's unfocused eye couldn't fathom what they said. Her eyes just saw the letters, the sentences as blurs, yet there was an understanding that even if she could read the words, they wouldn't have made any sense to her.

Everyone was still as statues. Their faces vacant, their eyes elsewhere, staring into a distance that couldn't have been any further than the back wall of the café, but looked an eternity further than that. Faces that had usually been so animated, offering her kindness, smiles. The lines at the corner of their eyes deep from smiling, their pleasant natures etched into their features. All of that was gone.

'Malic?' she gasped as her eyes focused on his face. He was at the front of the motley bunch. There were a few other men at the back. Men she recognised from The Pickle. They had looked her up and down, as if thinking about hitting on her, but had ultimately, and thankfully, left her alone.

That was the time she had met …

Kevin!

'Have you met my …' Kevin's voice, coming from somewhere behind her, sounding fuzzy, foggy, as if he were speaking from inside a huge ball of cotton wool, paused. '… friends?' he concluded eventually.

She turned. Maybe it was a little too fast for her brain to keep up with her, as a sudden wave of dizziness washed over her. She stumbled, putting her hands on the counter behind her to stop herself from embracing the floor. 'What?' she gasped.

Kevin hadn't moved. He was still at the same table she'd found him at. The only thing that had changed was his grin. It had gone from unnerving to creepy. It encompassed his whole face, so much so that in her daze, she was having trouble seeing any of his other features.

'What's going on here?' she gasped, her throat feeling like it was constricting, adding to the waves of nauseating dizziness. A flashback to one of the times her mother, the psychopath that she was, had grabbed her tightly around the throat, accusing her of sleeping with her own father, hit her.

She had been nine when that happened.

But suddenly, she *was* that nine-year-old, dressed in a SpongeBob Squarepants nightgown, the glass of water she'd come down for on the floor. The glass hadn't broken, but the water had seeped into her slippers, just like the fear had slipped into her heart and soul. It was cold, the only indication that her bladder hadn't opened. She often wondered what might have happened if her father hadn't come into the kitchen when he did.

That had been the start of the slippery slope that eventually brought her to this quaint little town.

Or at least she'd thought it quaint, fifteen minutes ago.

Right now, with Kevin looking at her and the group of naked, tattooed townsfolk behind her, it was far from *quaint*.

It was something right out of a fucked-up version of *The Twilight Zone*.

'What is this?' she gasped again.

Kevin stood. His eyes never left her as he walked slowly towards her. His grin never wavered, but she could see that it wasn't overtaking his features. It was just a normal, everyday, creepy grin. 'You were brought to us for a reason, Amelia.'

She stopped breathing as her real name was used. She tried to swallow, but her mouth was now as arid, as dry as a desert. 'I … I …'

Kevin shook his head. His smile reflected in his eyes. 'Don't,' he urged. 'Don't struggle. Don't try to make sense out of this. It'll seem random to you, and in many ways it is, but you need to know there *is* a bigger picture. You're very much a part of that picture. You're integral. You were brought to us, Amelia. You know that, don't you?'

She took a step backwards, her backside pressing against the counter. She continued to press herself against it, willing it to allow her to pass through it. There was nowhere for her to go. The naked people were blocking her exit to the street, and she knew the back door was locked. There would be no way of getting to it, fumbling with the keys, and opening it in in time to make a clean escape.

'Kevin, what are you doing? What are you saying?' There was a chuckle in her voice, but it was too high-pitched and panic-gilded to resemble anything remotely stable. 'How did you know—'

'That your name is Amelia?' he finished for her. 'It wasn't hard to find out. A quick search here, a look on the internet there, and of course, we had the added help of The Great Lord Glimm.'

'Who?' she asked, sparing another a glance back at the naked group, who hadn't moved during this whole exchange.

Kevin pouted. 'You'll find out. You've been selected, Amelia. You're the penultimate part in an intricate jigsaw. A puzzle I've been unravelling for years now.'

'I am?' she asked, slowly edging her way towards the back of the counter. She could see the back door. Even though she knew it would be locked, it didn't stop her from thinking it might be her only way out of this situation.

'Yes, you are. The Great Lord Glimm foresaw your arrival, and my life's work …'—he gestured towards the naked crowd behind him— '…our life's work is about to come to fruition.'

'So, what does it have to do with me?'

Kevin's grin was back. 'I'm a tattooist, an artist of some renown. I need to ink these good people with the words *he* gave us.'

'Hickula, tragantie a billinctus, shakker, toogorey,' the crowd whispered as if on cue.

Amelia turned to look at them.

'The Twelve, destiny calls, fulfil, encapsulate, embrace!' they continued.

Amelia saw this as her chance, and bolted from the counter, out of the door to the back of the counter, and into the kitchen. She reached the door in record time and tugged at it, clawing at the handle. It wouldn't budge. It felt as if it were welded to the frame.

She turned and looked at the door she had just escaped through. Malic was stood in the frame. His naked body was bathed in sunlight from the window at the side. Words were all over his body, including his penis, around his nipples, and his belly button. They glistened in the reflective sunlight.

'Where are you going, Amelia?' he asked. His voice had no inflection. It was devoid of life, all his personality gone, replaced with a parody of a voice she'd heard in movies a million times over, of slaves, or zombies, or someone under the influence of someone evil.

The last example seemed fitting.

'I'm leaving,' she whispered, unable to catch her breath as her boss stood before her, naked and threatening.

'You're not going anywhere.' The second voice came from behind him. It was Luna's. 'You're needed here.'

'Well, I don't want to be here.'

'That's as may be,' a third voice said. It was a young man she'd seen hanging around The Pickle. She'd thought him rather attractive in his Stetson and checked shirt when she'd seen him; now, though, standing behind her friends, or who she had thought of as friends, naked as the day he was born and covered in inked writing, he couldn't have looked anything further from attractive.

He looked dangerous, threatening.

'Kevin,' she tried to shout, hoping her burgeoning relationship with him might do something to help her in this oddest of situations. The chuckle that came from behind the naked people was all she needed as an answer to her plea.

No help was forthcoming.

'Amelia.' It was Kevin. His condescending tone caused her stomach to flip. She rattled at the door behind her again. He shrugged as he advanced. 'You simply have nowhere to go. Why fight this? You're part of something much bigger than you. You have an important role to play; that must be obvious by now.'

'All that's obvious is that you and everyone else in this fucking town are part of some weird cult.' Her throat hurt, forcing all the words out, as her tubes were so constricted.

The naked people in the doorway, barring her way, just looked at her, their faces vacant, their heavily tattooed bodies static. A laugh from behind them chilled her once again.

'You're right,' Kevin said, his tone mocking, with just enough sick humour to petrify her even more than she already was. 'But you're also wrong too.'

As she saw him pushing through the naked townsfolk, she saw he was now naked too. His pale, unblemished skin was a deep contrast to the flesh that was on show from the others. There was not one tattoo on his body, nor did it look like he had seen much sun in the last few years. He was pure white, almost blue. Her eyes were drawn to his penis—it was either semi-hard or was longer and thicker than it had any right to be on such a skinny man. She swallowed as he stood before her, her hands still on the latch of the door, still hoping to make her escape from this madness.

Living with her psycho mom, she had been privy to quite a few crazy scenarios, but nothing like this.

'You're wrong only in the fact that you say this is weird.' He laughed. His eyes hadn't gotten the memo about the humour his voice portrayed, as they remained trained on her, blazing and intense with a mad, crazed burn. He shook his head. 'We're not weird, Amelia. We're just trying to make life better for ourselves, for our families, and our descendants. You're a big part of that. We need you. Look at yourself. Look deep into yourself and think about the part you can play, have been playing, in this big, bad world. Does *anyone* truly love you? Have you ever felt accepted by anyone, anywhere? Look at all those marks on your arm that you've so bravely tried to cover with cheap body art. Do you think you're fooling anyone? I see your pain, Amelia. I see how deeply you've been hurt. The people you loved. Your mother …'

She winced as he mentioned her Achilles heel. Her mother *had* hurt her, in too many ways, but how did he know that?

'Your father …'

She swallowed. 'You're wrong,' she hissed. 'My father never once touched me. He was a good—'

'Did he ever once try to stop the abuse?'

As she glared, she bit at the insides of her cheeks.

'Did he? Or did he run away? Did he promise he'd be back for you? Tell me, Amelia. Did he *ever* come back?'

'He did. He did come back for me.' Tears were stinging her eyes.

'Did he, now? And tell me, how did that work out for you?'

She closed her eyes, and the threatening tears fell, tickling her skin. *How does he know all of this?* As she opened her eyes again, all she could see was his huge *shit-eating* grin.

'I know because I know,' he whispered.

Her brow creased as she listened. She shook her head.

He nodded his.

Without thinking, she bent down and picked up a small table next to the wall.

Satisfaction swelled in her as Kevin's grin faltered, just a little, when she swung it towards the large window next to the door. It smashed the glass with ease, shattering it into a hundred lethal slivers.

None of the townsfolk behind Kevin even flinched.

She grabbed the window frame, not caring about how deeply the shards cut her hands and clambered out. The fresh air of the day hit her like a heavy blanket, and her knees threatened to buckle beneath her. She willed them not to. It would have made a mockery of her brave escape. The air was sweet, but she thought it might just have been relief to be free of the café. Without thinking to where, she began to run.

She couldn't go to Martha's to get her things, as Martha was currently naked in the café, one of the many zombies Kevin had in his thrall. Over the road, she saw an SUV that was painted in the black and white of the local police department. She didn't know him, she'd never had any dealing with him, but if there was anyone who might be able to help her out, it had to be him.

He was currently sitting in the front seat, eating something out of a paper bag. It looked like a sandwich or something similar.

He jumped as she banged on his window.

Turning, offering a quick glance towards the smashed window next to the back door to the café and Malic and Luna's house, she relaxed as she realised no one was following her. This gave her hope. The police officer turned his big frame and looked at her. He was all smiles as he wound his window down. He looked towards the smashed window and saw the blood all over her hands.

'What's going on here?' he asked, his voice deep and slow.

'Please help me,' she gasped. 'Please, they're trying to kill me. They're all naked and trying to kill me. They say I'm special or something. You need to help me.'

Her words were gushing from her, making her plea sound like one long, sentence of complete mumbo-jumbo.

The man in the police uniform put his sandwich down and struggled to open his door. He unbuckled his seatbelt and opened the door. Amelia gasped in relief as he struggled out of the vehicle. 'Who's trying to kill you, little lady?' he asked.

She slowed her breathing and turned to point at the broken window. 'They're in there. There's a whole bunch of them. They're naked, and … and they all have these strange tattoos. I think Ke—' She stopped talking abruptly as she looked at the tall, wide police officer. He was slowly unbuttoning his shirt, revealing the tattooed words all over his chest.

It was only then she noticed the ink up and down his arms.

She turned, looking back at the café. Kevin was now in the street. He was naked except for a hat that sported a pair of impressive stag antlers. The others were streaming out of the back door.

She turned to the police officer. His shirt was off now, and he was working at removing his shoes.

Her mouth was dry, and her head was whirring. The street was spinning around before her.

As the cop began removing his pants she thought she screamed, although she couldn't be sure.

~~~~

It was cold. No, it was more than that. It was freezing, yet she was hot. Too hot. Maybe she was burning, she had no way of knowing.

She opened an eye. It took a moment for the blur of her environment to become focused. When it did, she wished it hadn't bothered.

She was in a room. It was dark, yet she had the impression it was spacious. There were designs on the walls, intricate markings that looked like patterns but also looked like depictions of wicked acts. They were carved into the plaster and the wood panelling.

She wasn't alone.

Kevin was standing to the side of her. He was naked and sporting a silly looking hat that appeared to be either the skull of a great beast with antlers or something he'd bought at a novelty shop. She guessed it was the former. She wanted to move away from him. She wanted nothing to do with him or with the freaks of this godforsaken town. She wanted to get as far away as she could and start
~~~~

again somewhere new. However, when she tried to move, she quickly found out she wasn't going anywhere. She was shackled. There was no way of telling how she was shackled, as she couldn't move any of her limbs; her head wouldn't move either, it was fixed into place. She could see Kevin and the others, *all* the others from the café, the ones she had trusted, the ones she had tentatively thought of as friends.

It had all been a sham.

'What the fuck is happening?' she shouted, or she might have if she had any voice to shout with. There was nothing obstructing her mouth, no rag stuffed inside stealing her breath and her words, yet nothing would come forth. Panic blossomed within her, a panic that should have been there minutes earlier when she realised the predicament she was in, but here it was, late to the party.

She could feel a heavy rhythm in her bones and in her teeth. It was akin to an underlying chant. She moved her eyes towards the naked throng, who were all staring at her. Their faces were one, in rapture at the situation. She knew then that they had groomed her for this very thing. They'd all been nice to her for just one reason.

Kevin joined in with the chanting, his voice rising above the others as he looked at her.

That was when she saw his hands.

She had always enjoyed horror films. Perhaps it had been a cathartic exercise for her, a strange break from the horror of her own life, long enough to revel in the horror of some fictional character's demise. Either way, she had been a fan of many of the slasher genres, even some of the cheesier films further down the franchise roads. There had been one she loved more than all the others. It was the man with the burned face and the glove with the knives as fingers. He'd scared her more than the others because of the way he'd wormed himself into his victim's dreams. That had always been the worst part for her. Her dreams were too personal, probably the only private part of her entire life. Everything else had been public domain. Her psycho mother had made sure of that. Her dreams had been her own, and no one could infiltrate them if she didn't allow them to.

Now, as the worst nightmare of her entire life was playing out before her, Kevin was doing exactly that. He was infiltrating her nightmares.

On his hand was a glove.

It had been specially designed for this event. The tips of the four fingers were needles.

She'd seen such needles before on programmes about veterinarians. They were the ones used to penetrate into the heavy muscle of horses. They were long, and they were thick. She could see the sharpened tips glinting in the strange light, and the horror of the situation piled on—her inability to move, coupled with the odd room and the townsfolk standing, watching, now this.

'This is required,' Kevin said as he regarded the needles on his glove. 'We need the essence of an innocent, one who has given themselves willingly.'

'I'm not here willingly,' she wanted to shout, to scream, to yell until she tasted her own blood on the back of her throat and her eyes ached. Alas, no sound emanated from her. No rant, no declaration of her anger or her unwillingness to be in this situation.

The thrum of the chant escalated, and the throng of naked townsfolk began to sway.

'Hickula, tragantie a billinctus, shakker, toogorey,' they chanted in unison. 'Hickula, tragantie a billinctus, shakker, toogorey,'

'Twelve, destiny calls, fulfil, encapsulate, embrace!' Kevin answered the chant. This caused them to raise the volume again.

'Hickula, tragantie a billinctus, shakker, toogorey,' they shouted.

'Twelve, destiny calls, fulfil, encapsulate, embrace!' Kevin replied again, matching them for volume.

Then he turned towards her.

His face was intimidating. His eyes had a cold blaze. His teeth were too white, in complete contrast to the darkened room.

'Twelve, destiny calls, fulfil, encapsulate, embrace!' he whispered as he stared at her. She didn't know if it was just her fear, her all-encompassing terror of this situation, but she thought she could see someone standing directly behind him. Just for a moment, there were two Kevins, the regular psychopath she had been on a date with, and had kissed, and even considered doing more with, and a different version of him. One that was much bigger, more fearsome.

One that looked more than human.

Maybe it was Godlike.

'Twelve, destiny calls, fulfil, encapsulate, embrace!'

'Hickula, tragantie a billinctus, shakker, toogorey,' the rest of them chanted.

Kevin began to encroach upon her. It wasn't a straight walk; it was akin to a lion stalking its prey, one he knew was defenceless, weakened, easy meat. He waved his needles in the air, wagging his fingers back and forth. She didn't want to give him the satisfaction of seeing how much he was terrifying her right now. That was personal; it was for her only. She'd done this for most of her life—what was one more time right now? Her eyes caught the urns beneath her. Her fevered mind told her what they were for, but she couldn't think about that right now.

That way lay dragons, very real dragons.

The chanting continued. It was building, becoming a fevered pitch. The same phrase was repeated, over and over and over.

Kevin had ceased answering his followers. His smile was like something straight out of Hell. As he stood before her, with the rhythm of the chants all around them, she could smell something new in the room. It wasn't the sweat of the townsfolk, and it wasn't the nakedness of Kevin. This was singular. The only way she might have described it would have been *white.* It smelt white. She had never smelt ozone before, but she imagined it might be something akin to this.

She thought about the other Kevin, the bigger one that had flashed into existence moments ago. She thought it was this Kevin she could smell.

There was a hint to smoked cheddar about it. In her panicked fever, it brought back more memories of her father.

Then the oddest sensation she had ever felt in her life hit her.

She was deflating.

Her eyes flicked from the urns on the floor to Kevin's hand. The needles on the end of the fingers were now sticking out of her chest.

It burnt. The needles were hot. She could sense her flesh searing where the needles penetrated her. That was the stink. Her flesh burning, cooking. There was a random thought about *long pig*, rattling through her head, but she dismissed it. She had to, she was too busy dying to think about cannibalism, and the smell of human flesh cooking.

All breath escaped her. She opened her mouth to scream, but the sound was stolen again. She blinked her eyes, but the world was nothing but a blur. She was convinced she was shrinking, but the four instances of sharp, burning agony were just a little too real for her to think about anything other than the pressing matter of her impending, and probable demise.

Kevin's face was close. Even through the blur of tears, she could see his every feature. She could see the dry skin on his forehead, she could see a few small black hairs sprouting from the end of his nose, she could see the madness and the fever in his eyes.

His teeth were gritted and were grinding as he twisted his hand.

Her world spun again as the untold torture of the needles gouged deep into her, piercing her, creating openings, became *everything*.

Four of them.

Without invitation, four members of the chanting crowd stepped forward, each of them holding something in their hands. All of them chanting. Another explosion of pain, easily doubled the first, wracked her as Kevin pulled the glove and therefore the needles from her body. Their exodus was a strange sensation. It was more deflation but this time it was agonising. She could feel her sad, pathetic, pain-wracked life oozing out of her.

The four townsfolk—she might have recognised them, had her faculties been working correctly, as her landlady, her employers, and the big man who she'd seen wearing the Stetson—approached her. Kevin stepped back, allowing them access to her. Her blood was dripping from the glove he had just killed her with. He stood back, admiring what he'd done.

More things were inserted into her. She flinched with each one. Her restricted movement causing it to hurt more with each piercing. Whatever they had done, were doing, hurt, a lot! However, it paled into insignificance next to the shame of dying in front of all these people. Yes, she was naked; yes, she was afraid; yet somehow, from somewhere, there was a feeling of strength. If she could have, she might have smiled. No one could hurt her anymore, no one could disappoint her, no one could bend her to their will like had happened all her life.

She embraced this death.

Welcomed it, even.

The four items inserted within her were tubes. Her flesh continued to burn, charring it. The stink that arose from her was—after she got over the agony—not unpleasant. It was the smoked cheddar again. All she could do was watch with a blurred fascination as her lifeblood flowed through them—filling the urns below.

She might have laughed if she weren't too weak.

The smell of cheese was overpowering.

Long pig, she thought again. The smell was cheddar, a ten-year-old treated cheese being smoked in a hickory smoker, not the smell of barbequed pork.

Lying bastards, she thought.

As she faded, as the darkened room around her grew ever darker, something embraced her. It was darker than the darkness, colder than the cold, and hotter than the searing heat of her flesh.

Whatever it was, it was here to take her.

Sweet death, come and claim what is yours, she thought.

Through the darkness, through the veil of life the other Kevin, the one she'd seen for just a fleeting moment, reappeared. His physical body was huge, double, if not treble the size of the original Kevin. This one was heavily tattooed. He kneeled next to her, raising his hands in the air. As he looked at her his almost inhuman eyes, dark in his pale face, watched as she slipped away.

Just once, before the honeyed oblivion embraced her, she smiled. She *should* have known better than to come here, to Needle Falls. But then, she'd never been one to make good decisions.

16.

THE VOICE WAS everywhere. It was her very existence. It was the air she wasn't breathing. It was the light she couldn't see and the scents she couldn't smell. It was inside her head, the one she no longer owned.

'BEHOLD, AMELIA CROSS,' it ordered. It wasn't a request.

She opened eyes she no longer had and observed a world she would never fit into. This wasn't the first time this had happened to her. She had never fit into her own world either. She had never fit into her mother's world; she wasn't allowed to fit into her father's. No matter where she went, she was always the outcast.

Always the victim.

The world shimmered, as if she were underwater, but there was no other feelings, no sensation of floating. There was no external stimulation at all.

She could see what was happening before her, but it was only as an observer, watching what was occurring as if it were playing out on a huge cinema screen, one that was wrapped tightly around her.

'OBSERVE,' the voice said.

Amelia could do nothing else *but* watch. She didn't want to. She *wanted* to die, on that strange table, with the tubes allowing her blood to drain out into the strange urns. She chuckled. It was a bitter laugh. Even in death, she wasn't allowed to do what she wanted, what she needed, what she so desperately longed for.

She adhered to the voice and looked.

Kevin was naked.

To her, it seemed he was always naked now, maybe he always had been.

This time, he was covered in blood. Almost every inch of his body, including his engorged cock, was covered in dark, viscous fluid.

He was holding an urn over his head. It was one he'd placed beneath her before he cut her, before he drained her. He was wearing the hat with the large antlers protruding from it. They, too, were coated in blood. He was chanting, mouthing words she couldn't understand. The urn was illuminated, just for a moment, the light brought about a change in Kevin. His face changed. His eyes shone with the same purple fire the urn did. His smile broke his features.

Before him was a table. On the table was a large contraption with small storage tanks attached to it. The contraption culminated in a hand-held device with a needle, or a small cluster of needles, at the end.

Slowly, with a reverence towards the contents of the urn, he poured the liquid into the storage tanks. It was no longer red, nor had it turned the sludgy, gloopy brown blood turns when exposed to oxygen. This was black.

He was still mouthing the words, and she watched from a distance that was both so close she could see every nuance of his actions but was also worlds away, as the tanks filled with … her.

Once full, he grasped the device, and the first of the naked townsfolk lined up in anticipation of what he was about to do.

The big man who she'd last seen wearing the clothing of a police officer, now nothing more than an overweight, middle-aged man, knelt before Kevin. Kevin touched him, embracing his shoulder. When he removed his hand, a bloody handprint impression was left.

Kevin picked up the device and pressed a button. The sound of electronic pins shocked Amelia. She marvelled that she *could* be shocked, even in this, that was either the afterlife or something else entirely. She recognised the sound. It was a tattooist's needles, the kind they used to pierce the skin, to colour the flesh. The storage wells the device was drawing from were filled with her blood.

The words, she thought. *They're sacrifices.*

From somewhere around her, and nowhere at the same time, something agreed with her.

Kevin went to work.

He drew the imprint of the bloody hand on the shoulder of the cop. The big man didn't flinch, even when his own blood began to run.

Kevin wiped away the drips and continued marking the man. He drew the handprint over some of the other tattoos, the words that were written all over his body. Once he was done, Kevin pushed the man away from him. Amelia marvelled at her blood staining the man's torso. It was a strange feeling. She knew she was already dead, yet she could feel herself beneath the skin of the man before her.

It was a violation, yet it was a rebirth too.

There was power within the sensation, power like she'd never felt, or held before.

Another member of the town stepped forward and dropped to her knees. It was Martha. Her head bowed as Kevin dipped his hand into the blood before putting it on her shoulder. He did the same with her as he'd done to the cop. He drew the hand, injecting Amelia into the woman's body.

Once again, the power coursed through her. She wondered how this could happen when her body lay lifeless, her blood congealing in the tubes that had been inserted into her, on the table, or the stage, or whatever it was, yet she could feel a tingle running through her.

'IT IS TRANSFERENCE,' the rich voice spoke. It was cold, and it fitted the stink of the room. It was white, like static when a radio wasn't tuned. It came from everywhere. She knew it was from the other Kevin she'd seen, the larger, more frightening version of him. Somehow, that Kevin, the god-like Kevin, was talking to her. 'FEEL ITS POWER AS IT PASSES FROM YOU INTO THEM.'

'Why?'

She marvelled at her question and the voice that asked it. It sounded like her, but she had no idea where it came from.

'YOUR STORY IS NOT OVER. THE POWER OF THE GLIMM IS STRONG. IT WORKS IN WAYS THAT SOME CANNOT FATHOM. OBSERVE, EMBRACE, AND FLOW ...'

Amelia didn't ask any more questions. She had no idea what The Glimm was, but she had a feeling she was going to find out.

Twelve of them were embraced with her blood and were blessed with the print etched into their flesh. She felt the raw power of the transference. It was an itchy, but formidable feeling.

17.

HE KNEW SHE'D been here. He wasn't wasting his time. He needed to call the lawyers and let them know he was on her trail. If she was using the name Kirsty, or Krystin, then she obviously hadn't wanted to be found. *Maybe Kevin knows something about what happened to her,* he thought as he walked along Main Street, looking in the shops, enjoying the ambiance of this quaint little town. If he was completely honest with himself, since the other night, after their kiss and all their text flirtations, he'd almost forgotten about Amelia. His whole reason for coming here had become second to him. All he could think about was Kevin.

Kevin and his strange ways, his pale skin, and his total lack of tattoos.

This set him aside from most of the residents he'd bumped into since being here. They, including the older folk, were covered in ink. He'd thought it strange when he first got here, but he was used to it now, and never really thought about anything but Kevin.

'Kevin,' he almost shouted down the phone as it clicked onto voicemail. 'Are you doing anything right now? I think I might have a lead on Amelia. Or a potential one, anyway. Well, give me a call back when you get this. I'm going to make my way to The Pickle for a bite to eat. You're more than welcome to join me.'

He cringed as he pressed the red button to end the call. It was the third voicemail he'd left for him today. He didn't want to come off as desperate, even if he was—just a little. He pouted at his phone wondering if there was a way he could log into Kevin's phone and remove the voicemail he'd just left, and the other two as well. Shaking his head, he slipped his phone into his inside pocket and made his way up Main Street, mentally leaving himself a voicemail, telling himself not to call Kevin again. He was heading to The Pickle, where he thought he might get himself a beer too. He did deserve one after all.

~~~~

Kevin didn't turn up, and he hadn't replied to any of the many voicemails he'd left. Carson had sat in the bar alone for a couple of hours, drinking and checking his messages. He'd forgotten all about talking to the owner of the café, to see if he'd been able to trace the guy who might know about Amelia. When he stood to go, he was a little unsteady on his feet, and in a foul mood. He checked his phone for the hundredth time. It was seven thirty, and already dark. He gritted his teeth as he left the bar, hoping to bump into one of those *good ole boys* who were about to give him a thrashing the other night. He felt the need to hit or be hit.

What did hit him was the night air. It smacked him like running into a brick wall. Suddenly, he no longer wanted to fight. He wasn't even sure if he could make it back to Martha's without being sick. *So much for my bravado,* he snarked to himself.

The night was clear, and there was a chill in the air, just enough for him to wish he had a jacket but not too much for him to be too uncomfortable. In the moment, this drunken moment, Needle Falls bored him. He longed for the excitement of the big city, the randomness of meetings and connections. Everything here seemed staged. Even meeting Kevin had felt like it had been pushed as an agenda. Martha's insistence that he go to The Pickle, the couple in the café always asking how he was finding things in their small town. 'Boring,' he slurred in his own inner monologue. 'That's how I'm finding things here. Fucking boring.'

'Well, that's nice, isn't it?'

The voice pulled him out of his grump. He turned, hoping beyond hope that the Gods hadn't granted his wish and put him in contact with his aggressors from the other night.

A smile spread across his face as he saw who it was.

Kevin shrugged, but his eyes were filled with mischief. 'You know, no one's keeping you here,' he said, his face relaxing into a smile.
~~~~

Carson, still more than a little drunk, threw caution to the wind and threw himself at the newcomer. Before he knew what he was doing, his arms were wrapped around Kevin, and they were kissing.

To his surprise, and delight, Kevin kissed him back.

All of a sudden, all thoughts of leaving this little town—of leaving Kevin—and going back to the big city were gone. Suddenly, he felt complete, like he could stay here for the rest of his life.

Every single last day of it.

18.

IT WAS PITCH dark. The velvety blackness tickled him. It had wrapped itself around him, setting him up in a cocoon. Carson awoke from a deep slumber. The sweet oblivion had been fuelled by beer, sex, and the heavy, comforting feel of a body lying next to him.

He was in a strange bed, he knew that much, and it took a moment of searching through his fuzzy memories to remember just where he'd ended up last night.

Kevin's apartment!

A grin broke in the darkness, one he didn't feel the need to share with anyone. There was a slight sickly feeling from too many beers at The Pickle, but he'd drank a lot of water before they'd retired to bed, and the physical exertions they'd put each other through must have burned off quite a bit of the alcohol. The only thing disturbing him was the strange cold in the room. It was as if every window in the house had been left wide open and winter had set in overnight.

He envisioned his dry, stinking breath steaming before him—it really was that cold.

There was also an unholy stink.

At first, a panic spread through him, as he thought it might have been coming from him. It had been a number of years since he'd had an accident in the bed due to too much drinking, and rough sex. A quick, flustered feel around him in the blankets put his fear to rest. It must have been coming from somewhere else, somewhere outside, as even thought he'd been drunk, he knew it hadn't been there before they'd gone to sleep. It was kind of sweet, but the sickly kind. He didn't want to remember it, but it reminded him of a time in his youth when he *had* shat the bed after a heavy night of drinking. It smelt like the kind of dump taken in the midst of a hellish hangover.

This thought turned his stomach, just a little, and he felt the contents churn.

He opened his eyes.

The darkness was almost as complete as it had been when he had them shut.

It took a moment for what little light there was to reveal the shadows of the strange room. He couldn't remember the layout … actually, now he came to think of it, he couldn't remember physically going to bed. He remembered the sex, but that had been instigated on the couch in the … *In the what*? *In the living room,* he answered, attempting to convince himself that he remembered actually being *in* a living room. He couldn't remember much of anything after seeing Kevin outside The Pickle.

You knew the smell wasn't there, he thought. *Do I though?* His mother had always told him that the first sign of madness was talking to yourself, the second was when you answered your own questions.

Suddenly, he was scared.

It was irrational, but he was.

Where was he?

Who was he lying next to?

What was the dark shadow looming over the bed, so close that, if it wanted to, it could reach out and stroke him?

'Thirteeeeeeeeeeeeeeeeeeeeeen!'

The hiss resonated around the room. As it did, Carson was already falling back to sleep, convincing himself this was all just a dream, and he only heard the word in his peripheral subconscious. He slipped into an uncomfortable doze that was filled with images of needles, dark wraiths, and crowds of naked people.

~~~~

The bedroom was freezing. It was so cold the bedsheets had stiffened, and the carpet, if it had been stepped upon, might have crunched underfoot.

Malic was fast asleep, the covers pulled up tightly over his head, keeping the cold from his ears and covering the tattoos that decorated
~~~~

his entire body. Moon, next to him, had buried herself deep into the covers too, subconsciously defending her heavily tattooed body from the strange, unexpected freeze of the night. Both bodies twisted and turned in the darkness as they fought the uncomfortable temperature drop. It wasn't only the cold they were fighting; it was the vile stink that had descended over the room too. If they'd been awake, they might have been gagging, holding back vomit from how dense the stench was. Rot, burning, defecation, death … everything bad had been cocktailed into the stink.

That was what it wanted.

The *it* was the thing looming over them. It was darker than the darkness encompassing the room. It was darker than any shadow that had ever been cast in the house. It was colder than the freezer in their kitchen, and it smelt worse than any garbage can had ever smelled. It brought with it a denseness, an oppressiveness that might have induced a headache in the sleeping couple that would bring an unease to the day ahead of them.

Long, emaciated fingers flexed over them, tightening the air. It orchestrated the cold, it directed the reek, it masked all sound.

Both bodies moaned as if deep into some disturbing fantasy. The tattoos on their shoulders, the last ones they had received, almost a year ago now, burned. The glow from the ink could be seen even through the blankets and the night clothes covering their bodies.

The handprint—Kevin's handprint—pierced the darkness, illuminating the entity standing watch over them.

The new light emphasised the darkness of the figure. It illuminated the depths of obscurity surrounding it. It sucked in the darkness as if feeding from some hellish mother's tit.

It might have illuminated the grin on its face as grey eyes glowed almost as bright as the handprints. It might have revealed this grin if there had been a face to show it, and not a singular black hole that rejected all light. The thing stood, it flexed its bone-like fingers in the night again, and the temperature dropped further. Malic and Moon moaned; they writhed as if in a sexual rapture, only one tinged in pain, agony, and torture.

Then it was gone. The glowing handprints were nothing more than tattoos again. The temperature in the room balanced, and the unholy stink of filth flittered away.

Both bodies relaxed, blissfully unaware of their supernatural visitor. However, they would be aware of something being wrong when they awoke to a world of headaches and aches and pains.

~~~~

The unholy visitor was busy that night. It appeared in many a bedroom in and around the town of Needle Falls. Twelve people in total were visited. All of them waking the next morning with aches and pains in their limbs, especially their shoulders. There would be headaches and stomach disorders galore in the town today.

None of them would have had a relaxing night. They would all wake filled with an anxiety they couldn't quite put their fingers on.
~~~~

19.

CARSON WOKE EARLY. The other side of the bed was empty. With a strange, guilty feeling, he got up and quickly collected his clothes. He'd been in this situation before, waking in a strange apartment, in an empty bed, where the person he'd shared it with had gotten up early and deserted him.

The morning was warm, which in itself felt odd, as he'd either dreamt it was freezing last night, or it *had* been freezing. Either way, he'd expected it to be chilly this morning, but he was wrong.

He crept out of the bedroom, peering his head around the doorway, not knowing what to expect. He could barely remember going to bed last night, and he didn't know if Kevin had housemates, or family, or anything. Nothing like that had cropped up in their conversation.

'Hello?' he whispered out of the door when he was mostly dressed. He felt a little silly, like he was falling into a trap or something. The dread blossoming within him was real. It was a flower opening in his stomach, one that should never have been there. It made him shiver, not from the cold but from something akin to fear.

'Hello,' he called again, just in case whoever might be in the house hadn't heard him. Again, there was no answer. The shaking in his bones receded as he listened to the silence. The only noises filtering through were from outside, on the street. They were normal sounds he associated with everyday life.

With his eyes closed and holding his breath, he took a step out of the room. He rested his hand on the banister that ran the length of the landing he found himself on. He looked over it. Downstairs was silent and still.

He took in a deep breath and leaned on the wall as he slipped his shoes on. There were four doors on the landing. One was the room he had just come from; another was a bathroom. The other two were closed, or almost closed. The room at the very end of the narrow strip was slightly ajar.

Thirteeeeeeeeeeeeeeen!

The hiss took him by surprise. His heart thumped in his chest as he looked around to find the source. Other than the sound, the house was silent and still. He shook his head slightly, and grinned. *Nerves,* he thought, attempting to sooth himself. He wondered what it was he had to be nervous about. All he'd done was get drunk, hook up with a guy he'd been flirting with, and ended up doing what came naturally afterwards. Something felt wrong though. Something was … *What, Carson?* he asked himself. *Something is what?*

He knew the answer was *off,* but he didn't want to voice it, either in his head or elsewhere.

The open door was calling to him.

He knew that sounded ridiculous. It was something out of a shitty horror film, a trope he always cursed the protagonist for doing. It was a tired and lazy plotline, but it was *exactly* what was happening to him right now.

He had a feeling that the hissed word, the single, but familiar hushed sound had emanated from behind that door, the one that was tantalisingly ajar. He didn't know if the cold he was feeling was real or if it was imagined, but the temperature had definitely plummeted. He was dressed in the t-shirt and jeans he'd gone out in last night. He had a coat, but he guessed it was somewhere downstairs, languishing on the back of a chair or hanging on a rack. He had absolutely no idea where it might have been. It could still in The Pickle for all he knew.

He wished he had it with him now. Goosebumps ran up and down his arms, and he rubbed at them, hugging himself in vain attempts to stave off the sudden cold.

Thirteeeeeeeeeeeeeeen!

Everything in his being told him to turn around, to get out of there ASAP. To forget this stupid door, to forget the cold, to forget the ache in his head and stomach from his overindulgence last night and just get the Hell out of there.

But something wouldn't let him.

He cursed under his breath as he took another step closer to the open door. Something crunched under his foot. Not really wanting to—in case he saw something he didn't want to see— but unable to help himself, he looked down.

The crunching was the carpet itself.

He had to take a double look, as his eyes fought to understand what he was seeing. The carpet around where he was standing was frozen. The grey had turned white. Frost covered the fibres, creating a trail that led to the slight crack in the door.

This alone should have been enough to make him run. His legs were screaming at him to do just that, but his brain, or something else, some external force, had other ideas. He took another step towards the mysterious darkness that seemed to be leaking from his destination, where the mysterious frost was leading him to. Where the mysterious voice was rasping from.

Sweet fucking Jesus, he shouted in his head. *Will you stop, Carson?*

He took another step.

The darkness leaking out onto the landing was fluid. It was oil attempting to mix with water. It dripped through as if there was a gulf of inky blackness, of liquefied nothingness waiting for him to free it, to allow it to wash over him, to engulf him, to swallow him whole in its eternal bleakness.

Where the fuck are these thoughts coming from?

He took another step, wincing at the crunch underfoot.

This was followed by another, and then another.

Before he knew what was happening, he'd reached the door, and his fingers wrapped around the doorknob. He'd expected it to burn with its dangerous cold, but it didn't. The metal was room-temperature. It was as if the cold, as if the steam decorating his breath was not real. He looked at the exposed flesh of his arms. It was almost blue, as if his blood was retreating back into his body to protect his internal organs from the intense cold he was experiencing.

He looked around again.

Everything else was normal. The other doors didn't look cold. Downstairs, over the landing, looked normal. There didn't seem to be frost anywhere else other than where he was standing.

Other than coming from out of this *fucking* door.

As his fingers tightened around the doorknob, something hit him.

It wasn't a physical attack, although the rawness of it made him reel back slightly. It was a godawful stink. He hadn't noticed it before, he'd been too nervous making his way through the house, but it had made itself known to him now, and it was disgusting. It was rotting meat, like when he had been a student and one of his roommates had left a burger in the back of the refrigerator for what must have been months. It had stunk the house out, and they'd thrown the majority of the food away for fear of it being contaminated.

He covered his nose, combatting the stench as he attempted to build up the courage to open the door. He imagined he could hear and feel flies buzzing around him, although none had shown themselves. He swallowed while still holding his nose, as he didn't want to taste the smell, and gripped the doorknob again.

The liquid darkness was still flowing from the door, but he dismissed it. Blinking rapidly, he pulled the door.

It came to him like an unwanted lover.

More darkness seeped from the jamb, but it was thinning. He thought it was either a manifestation of the warmth coming from behind the door—like heat flies they used to see on the pavement when they were kids goofing around—contrasting with the cold of the landing, or maybe it was the other way around.

Either way, he paid it no heed.

Thirteeeeeeeeeeeeeeen!

The hiss was barely audible now, like a radio blaring in an apartment two floors away, but it was enough to tighten his flesh, to cause his nipples to stiffen. He realised then, at that precise moment, that he really hadn't wanted to open this door. He no longer wanted to see what was behind it. All he wanted was to gather his belongings, leave this house, and get back to Martha's. There, he could crawl underneath his covers, close his eyes, and fall into a deep sleep. When he woke, hours and hours later, he'd remember all of this as some kind of fevered, alcohol-induced dream.

However, there were too many memories of last night with Kevin. They had done too much together to just dismiss this as a dream. Plus, the door was now open, and the second thing he realised was … his eyes were closed.

As the foul, frigid air washed over him, easing through his pinched nose, he gagged. He didn't want to know what was causing this stink, this cold, or the hissing voice. However, his body had other, rebellious ideas.

He opened his eyes and looked through the liquid darkness into the room.

A moan escaped him.

~~~~

As Martha struggled around the kitchen, her face was creased. Her red eyes spoke of a restless night, and her furrowed brow had deeper lines than usual as she gasped and winced at almost every movement she made. Her night had been filled with dreams, with visitations, with an anxiety she'd never experienced before and hoped she would never feel again. She rationalised it with what they had planned for tonight, for the night when everything changed.

For the night of The Glimm.

She muttered as she held her shoulder. She closed her eyes, squeezing them closed as if it would help ward off the pain, the agony, the burning.

Her latest tattoo was throbbing.

~~~~

A groan escaped Malic as he bent to pick up a tub filled with potatoes destined for the peeler. His back twinged, and the back of his thighs screamed. He'd woken like this when his alarm went off and snapped him out of a horrible dream where he'd been stroked, caressed by the rotting hands of a corpse.

He'd recognised her as he pretended to open his eyes.

Her hair had been lank and sparse. Her peeling skin was mottled; wet in places and crumbling in others. Her mouth had been full of teeth that looked strong and dangerous as the corpse grinned seductively at him. She'd been smiling as her freezing fingers touched his skin. He'd wanted to jump up, to get away from the wraith, to escape that hideous caress.

Now, even in his waking state, every time he felt an ache careen through him, he saw her. Dark against the darkness of whatever room he happened to be in, but every part of her visible. The rotted hole where her nose should have been, the holes in her naked torso where he and the others had inserted tubes to drain her of her lifeblood, everything they had done to her, was visible to him.

The worst part of it hadn't been his arousal at her nakedness and the memory of what they had all done on the floor around Kevin's table as she died. It wasn't the guilt of fucking Martha; it wasn't the excitement of ejaculating over Al Brescomb's face. Al, the police chief, had been a willing recipient of his seed as he fucked Luna in the hole she'd never allowed him to penetrate before Kevin and his promises of The Glimm.

No, the worst part of it had been her eyes. They glowed. They were filled with knowledge he didn't think he would ever be able to hold. It was an unholy understanding, one that at the moment, in the deepest, darkest part of his despair, he didn't want any part of.

He remembered the way his shoulder burned at her touch. It had taken everything he had not to shout out, to scream as the flesh beneath his latest tattoo bubbled and melted. The agony was the worst he'd ever felt in his life.

It had only lasted a singular moment, then the dead girl was gone. She disappeared into the day, into the unfamiliar darkness of the twinge in his back or the pull in his leg. He'd breathed a sigh of relief at her vanishing and continued on with his morning chores.

The memory of Luna thrashing and moaning on her side of the bed came to him. He'd wanted to turn to her, to hold her, to sooth her. He wanted to tell her everything would be all right, but he couldn't bring himself to do it.

He knew everything *would* be all right after tonight. Tonight was the night everything changed for them. The world would fall into order, and things would never be the same again.

'Will you get out of my way, you old fool?' Luna snapped as they passed behind the counter.

He wanted to snap back at her. He wanted to slap her across the face. He really wanted to grab her by the hair and smack her face down onto the sizzling grill in the kitchen, to hear her scream as he took her up the same hole she'd allowed the other men in the town to take her, right there and then.

He didn't do any of this, as he saw the same pained look on her face. He guessed his expression was either the same or pretty similar. 'Get out of *my* way, bitch,' he hissed.

She snapped her head around so quickly at the curse, he thought she might be smarting in an hour or two.

'What did you call me?' she spat.

Malic closed his eyes and exhaled. 'Listen, I'm sorry,' he whispered. 'I didn't get much sleep last night.'

'Me neither,' Luna replied. 'I had this crazy dream about someone called—'

'Kirsty?'

Luna nodded.

'Only, her name wasn't Kirsty,' Malic said, his voice barely a whisper.

'It was Amelia. Wasn't it? My shoulder's been burning all morning.'

'Mine too,' Malic said, rubbing himself absently. 'It feels like its burning.'

He turned away to look into the café as the bell to the door rang. Someone had entered, and with them came a disgusting stink, one he thought he remembered, possibly from his dream. He walked into the main café area to see who it was and what could be causing the hideous stench when he was hit with a wall of freezing cold air. In Needle Falls, the winters were harsh, and there were usually fatalities due to the severe temperature plumets, so Malic was used to the cold.

This was a different kind of cold altogether.

This was like jumping into a lake of ice.

It took his breath away. Gasping for air, he looked around to see who had entered but was no one at any of the tables. They would have had to pass him and Luna in order to make it to the restrooms. Shivering, he rubbed at his arms, absently going all the way up to his shoulder, which was suddenly stinging again. 'Hello,' he shouted.

There was no answer.

'Who are you shouting at?' Luna asked as she stepped out of the back room. 'Holy fucking Jesus,' she exclaimed, gagging.

Malic looked at his wife and noticed there was little colour in her face as she looked past him, into the main room.

'What is that?'

He looked back into the room as a sound caught his attention. The day outside had turned. It had been bright and sunny not two minutes ago. Now, it was as dark and as miserable as the first day of February. That was at least five months away. 'Who's there?'

'Thirrrrrrrteeeeeeeeeeeen.' The whispered reply swirled through the winter air like a cartoon swoosh of snow.

Goosebumps rose on his arms and his chest, and the agony in his shoulder he'd dreamed of, and lived through this morning, garnered his attention. Turning to Luna, he could see she was the same. She was grasping at her shoulder, shuffling backwards, away from the café, away from the cold and the smell, away from the voice. Her eyes were wide as they continued to stare past him, over his shoulder. Malic found himself not wanting to know what she could see.

Suddenly, her eyes were on him.

He watched her face fall. The eyes that were already filled with fear widened even more, if that was possible, and her cheeks pulled inwards as her mouth fell to match the rest of her features. What little colour she had, trickled from her, and suddenly she resembled an image of Jacob Marley he remembered seeing once when he was a child—the bandage around his head had worked loose, and his broken jaw hung slack by his chest as his eyes burst, filled with Christmas fury at old Ebenezer Scrooge.

The image had petrified him then and continued that now.

Thirrrrrrrteeeeeeeeeeeen!

He spun on his heel to face who, or what, was making the sound. Once again, he didn't want to, but he thought whatever it was had to be better than looking at Moon right then.

His shoulder throbbed with molten lava. He was sure his flesh, his bones were melting. *Maybe that's what the smell is,* he thought as everything in his world began to change.

A shadow had taken dominion in the corner of the dulled room.

It was only small, but there was a ferociousness about it that screamed of damnation and mercilessness.

The agony in his shoulder was spreading. Spiderweb fingers of magma spread from the tattoo towards his neck and through his chest. *Heart attack,* was his first thought, but he knew it wasn't. It wasn't shooting down his arm. It was travelling the other way.

The shadow shifted, and he watched it through someone else's eyes. It was a strange thing to admit, even to himself, but that was what happened. He watched whatever this spectral visitor was doing as if he were another person altogether.

Turning again to look to his wife, he could see she was watching the visitor too, with her hands up to her shoulder as if to stem the flow of pain that was trundling through her.

Only there was something different about her.

Luna looked different.

He wanted to scream.

He wanted to run but could do neither. All he could do was swing his head from side to side and watch the encroaching spectre and the woman who used to be his wife.

The clawing fingernails of madness tore through his sanity. He felt every single tattoo on his body—and there were a lot of them—itch. They screamed for his attention, but there was little he could do to satiate them.

The shadow was in his face now. With it came a deeper cold, one he couldn't fathom. He likened it to the cold of space, of nothingness, of the eternal misery of emptiness.

But it wasn't empty. With the cold came the stink.

It was the stench of a million people dead. The reek of corrupt corpses, of every vile, inhumane deed perpetrated by man, onto man.

It was the heavy, cloying whiff of every war man had perpetrated on his brothers.

With it came the promised madness that had been clawing at him, but there was something else too.

The shadow looked at him. The darkness beneath its hood was almost perfect. It might have been if it wasn't for the two silvery-grey, intelligent eyes staring out at him.

He screamed. Someone else behind him screamed too, as something reflected back at him in the dark mirror beneath the hood.

~~~~

Martha, Luna, Malic, Al the police chief, the three boys from the bar who had beat on Carson, the bartender, the girl from the grocery store, the three women from the beauty salon over the road from Malic's café, all of them had visitations that morning.

All of them fell to their knees, clutching their shoulders, the ones where the palm of Kevin's hand had been forever etched into their flesh using the blood and the life essence of Amelia, known to them as Kirsty. Each had been visited by a dark shadow, a faceless monstrosity that was neither there, nor not there. Their minds, not being able to comprehend this state of unbeing, had torn their own sanity away.

It had changed them.

It fulfilled its promise to them.

They had asked for change. To change their lives, to give them something more. In response, it had asked them to give something back. It had demanded sacrifice and worship, and oh, how that had been given.

The blood of twelve innocents infected their flesh, the essence of twelve victims adorned their skin, only they didn't quite understand what The Great Lord Glimm had promised.

They had never understood.

It promised them much. It promised to elevate their lives, to change them for the better. It promised them a world where they could be someone else other than themselves. Kevin had chosen them, just as it had chosen Kevin. He was to be its disciple, its right hand on Earth, much like it had chosen before.

These people hadn't known what they were doing, but ignorance was no defence when sweet, innocent lives were given up for its worship.

If it could have, it would have laughed, just like it had laughed before. The fools of this world were plentiful, and it knew it would laugh again …

Many times!
~~~~

20.

THE ROOM WAS really an anteroom. The door opened up to a smaller room that housed a staircase. If Carson hadn't been so scared and so sickened by the odour that was still lingering all around him, and not to mention freaked out by the liquid darkness he'd witnessed seeping from the jamb, he might have noticed the paraphernalia adorning the walls sooner.

The images were all black and white. At first, they looked artsy. Naked women in a variety of poses, some were innocent, but as he looked closer, towards the set of stairs, they began to turn fetish.

All the women were adorned in tattoos.

It wasn't until he'd built up the courage to step into the room that he realised the pictures were of celebrities. He recognised women on the walls from some of his favourite films over the last few years. The focus of the images were of instantly recognisable people. Pop stars, news anchors, politicians, even influencers from social media platforms, although he never really thought of those people as famous.

They were not all young either. There were more than a few photographs of older stars, of celebrities of yesteryear. The images fascinated him. They took his attention away from the awful stink and the frigid cold. As he stepped further into the room, towards the staircase at the far end, he noticed there were not only pictures of women on the walls. Again, the men ranged from very young to very old, but each of them were naked, each of them bathed in black and white, and each of them were covered in ink.

The pictures hung on either side of the staircase.

He didn't relish the idea of traversing the stairwell, but something inside him, some internal guidance system, told him he needed to. The dark and the cold called to him. As he rested his hand on the banister, the cold of the white painted wood scalded him. He registered the pain but put it to the back of his mind. He descended the steps one by one, enraptured by the artwork around him. A silent siren was calling to him from somewhere in the inky blackness below, and he was as helpless as a doomed sailor on hearing the alluring call from the depths below him. He flowed with the song, the call, the lull—he didn't know what it was; he just knew it was for him.

The cold continued to gnaw through his clothing, and the smell clung to the inside of his nostrils, yet he walked blindly, willingly into the all-encompassing, cloying obsidian.

His eyes were adjusting to the lack of light as he reached the bottom. He found himself in a large room, a very large room. For the amount of steps he had just traversed he assumed it must have been the basement of the house. He marvelled at the space even though he couldn't quite see it all.

The shadows down there were deep, and in some places, even with his adjusted eyes, he found it difficult to decipher what was waiting for him in the murky depths. He envisioned an evil mermaid, all claws and fangs ready to suffocate him, to pull him into her deep domain and keep him there, forever.

This was folly and he knew it. He could sense humanity but it was not quite in the way he might have expected it.

The hooded figure lifted its head and looked at him.

His scream was unreserved, and it was loud.

21.

AL BRESCOMB WAS on his knees. This was nothing new to him, not since he'd become embroiled with the crowd Kevin introduced him to. He never really had to be introduced, as he knew them all already. He was the chief of police in Needle Falls and prided himself on knowing everyone and everything that happened in the small town.

So, when Kevin Prince arrived with all of his Hollywood flair, it caused something of a stir. Al made it his business to get to know the youth and everything he brought with him.

The boy was charm personified.

He was only a small man, skinny, and pale, but he was an enigma, and there was nothing Big Al loved more than a riddle. The new boy was certainly that.

He had made it his mission to get to know the boy, to find out what made him tick. The only problem was, he got a little too close.

He made the mistake of listening to what the boy had to say.

He made the mistake of taking the time to *understand* what he had to say. He heard the talk of a better life, of something more than he had now. He bought into the grass being greener on the other side. He also bought into the power of The Twelve and the mythos of The Glimm. Kevin had told him The Great Lord Glimm had plans for him; all he required was offerings.

Kevin had been a celebrity tattooist. He had inked the top rappers, the metal stars, and all the A-list actors of the day, but had given it all up once he'd heard the calling of The Glimm. He'd managed to convince eleven others to join his cause, including Al's old friends Malic and Moon, old Martha from the bed and breakfast, and some youths from The Pickle and the beauty shop in town. There were twelve of them, and there were twelve for a reason.

Although what that reason was had been lost on him.

Kevin had told them about the rituals, the chanting, and the inking he would need to do to bring forth the God.

Al didn't know if he believed all the mumbo-jumbo at first. All he knew was that he was about to have a whole load of sex with some of the hot chicks from the beauty parlour, and with Luna, who he'd had a thing for since high school.

Once the first needle had pierced his skin and the surge of the sacred ink entered his flesh, everything started to become real. The power was within him. He no longer needed the little blue tablets to perform during the rituals; his cock was full, thick, and strong enough to go at any time it was required.

His wife had noticed his prowess too. She didn't know about the rituals and the promises of The Glimm; that was going to be a surprise for her. So, what had started as a bit of fun turned serious. Not just for him but for everyone involved. The inking became the ritual. The words etched into his skin began to mean something to him, to them, to The Twelve.

Suddenly, things began working out for him.

There was the raise in his wages. There was luck in his betting. There was a small, but serious lottery win. He was getting lucky with more of the ladies in town, the younger ones he'd had his eyes on. The ones he'd fantasised about fucking their mothers, he was now fucking them.

Then the sacrifices began.

Kevin told them they were required for the sacred ink.

He explained to them they were the ink, and that each inking brought them closer to The Great Lord Glimm's promises.

Strangers were brought into the fold. People passing through the town, vagrants, anyone who might not be missed.

Then *she* turned up.

She was welcomed into the town, made to feel special … She had to come of her own volition. She was to be the *twelfth.*

The rest of the town knew about their activities by now, including his wife, and they welcomed what was happening. It was for the greater good, and the original twelve were hailed as heroes. Kevin was the unofficial leader of the town and seen as the saviour of Needle Falls' ailing fortunes. The town was profitable again.

It was a community once more.

The Great Lord Glimm had done all of this for them, and now all they had to do was complete the last sacrifice, to use the essence of number thirteen and reap the rewards of their long, hard labour, albeit a labour of love.

So, this is how he found himself on his knees with an erect penis in his mouth, and his tattooed body being used by a man half his age while his wife watched, naked, pleasuring herself with three fingers. Three years ago, this would have never been a scenario he would have even considered. He would have smacked the person full in the mouth if they had even proposed something like this. He was no fag; at least he wasn't before Kevin, before the tattoos, and before The Glimm.

Despite the frantic activities he was performing, and the others in the in the room were doing the same, he was freezing cold. He couldn't understand how Franny, his wife, currently lounging back on the bed, her legs spread wide and her fingers doing their work on herself, was bearing up in the frigid temperatures. He looked up at the man he was fellating. His muscular body was tattooed in the exact same manner as his, as was the man who was currently behind him, entering him in a way he would have kicked some serious ass at even the suggestion of just a few short years ago.

Both men were sporting the same special tattoo on their shoulders. Kevin had called it *The Hand Of Glimm* when he'd inked them. He told them it was a special mark that not everyone could have, only his Twelve. Right now, Al's was burning. He didn't know if it was burning hot or if it was burning cold, especially because of the temperature in the room, but it was a distraction from what was happening, from their own little party celebrating The Glimm.

As the cold deepened, so did the nasty stink in the room.

At first, he'd thought it was coming from what he had been doing with the penis that had been buried deep inside him, but the stink had persisted. Not only that, but it had gotten stronger. The deeper the cold hit, so did the smell.

'Can't you smell that, honey?' he asked, removing the tattooed appendage from his mouth.

His wife of many years seemed unaware of either the cold or the stink as she continued writhing on the bed, lost in her own rapture.

'I can,' the big man standing before him said as he looked down at him. 'It fucking stinks.'

'I'm glad I'm not the only one,' the man behind Al replied. 'Can't you turn up the heating?'

'It's fucking September,' Al hissed as the boy slipped out of him—the hiss of air coming from his abused sphincter sounded funny. In the years since Kevin, this had become a regular thing, either with these boys or the girls from the beauty parlour, so they had gotten used to the noises that escaped them from time to time, but this was different.

Thirrrrrrteeeeeeeeeen ...

Al screamed as his shoulder suddenly gave way. It was an agony like nothing he'd ever experienced before in his long life, including taking a bullet back in the late eighties during an attempted bank robbery.

'Holy fucking Jesus …' he croaked as he fell, face first, from his position on all fours.

Both boys who had been abusing him fell too, both grabbing the tattoos on their shoulders. Their faces were creased in pain. He'd seen their faces look something akin to this before, but that had been in ecstasy. This was *not* the same face.

Something moved in the room.

Something dark.

Within it came a cloak of blackness that the two other boys saw too. Three pairs of eyes watched as it drew the light from the room, taking any heat with it. It swished across the room like a cold dark curtain. The boys both staggered away as Al watched from his position on the floor.

His wife had stopped what she was doing, and with a flushed face, was looking at the two boys as if they'd suddenly burst into flames. She was saying something, but Al couldn't hear her. The pain in his shoulder was an agony, but it was a silent agony. It took his breath from him. The boys were both on the floor now, their erections gone, replaced with the nubs of freezing cold, petrified penises.

Al was trying to scream, to shout, to get some help, as he thought his heart was about to give way. He didn't want to be found here, on the floor of his own bedroom, being Tower of London'ed by two young bucks. His skin was crawling. It tingled, much like pins and needles, but where that sensation can be a funny feeling, this was anything but. Every sensation was akin to being pierced with thousands of tiny needles. It reminded him of getting inked, but where that pain was pleasurable, this was intense, crippling.

Something was happening to him. He could feel it in every inch of his body, in every fibre of his being. It was torture, the likes of which he had never known.

The two boys were experiencing the same sensations, their faces were twisted into contortions he didn't think possible without external excruciating stimulation, the like that they were all experiencing.

His wide eyes fell on his wife. She was on the side of the bed, naked and shocked at what was happening before her. She was oblivious of the burning cold, of the acrid stink that was turning his stomach, of the dark figure caressing her breasts. Where its hands touched her, they left dark smudges like ink, the same ink they'd all been indelibly decorated with.

Blood, he thought. *It's not ink ... it's blood.*

~~~

Martha couldn't move. Her limbs just wouldn't respond to her brain's commands. This was either from the burning cold of the room or from the agony that was wickedly tickling her whole body. It started in her shoulder. She had fallen to her knees when it bit at her like a rabid dog, and she hadn't been able to move since.

The dark figure looming over her had a horrible stink to it. She had vomited from how bad it was and how deep the aroma permeated her being. Luckily, the vomit had been projectile and hadn't caught in her throat as she lay prone and helpless on the floor. The tears filling her eyes were thick, and in her scattered mind, visions were flashing through her memory.

She had no doubt the vile thing hovering over her was producing the memories, and the worst thing was she had no way of
~~~

turning them off. She was forced to live through every single perverse thing she had done, willingly, in the name of The Great Lord Glimm.

She had allowed herself to be violated. Both men and women, people she'd known her entire life, had entered her, spat on her, slapped her, ejaculated over her. She had allowed them to hit her, to fuck her, to violate her in every single way a person *can* violate another person. Two, three, even four people at the same time.

And she had enjoyed it.

She had welcomed the release of pure, unadulterated pleasure.

She had welcomed the sacrifices. She had been an active participant in the deaths of the innocents. She had willingly cavorted, naked and unashamed in their blood, revelled in their suffering. She had allowed her flesh to be infused, scarred in the sacred words, in ink derived from blood, from any of their bodily fluids.

She hadn't cared.

It was all done in *his* name.

She didn't know if he was a *he* or if he was an *it*. It didn't matter to her. Her life had changed for the better. The crippling arthritis that had crawled, uninvited into her body was gone. The debts she'd accumulated by the running of the bed and breakfast, and her love of gambling, had dwindled. Her fortunes were turning. Her once healthy libido had returned, and there was seemingly no end of people who wanted to fuck her, who wanted to use her tightening, newly firm, tattooed body.

Only now, as the dark, stinking figure stood over her, as she looked up at it from her position of weakness on the floor, she thought she might be dying. She was suddenly sorry for the things she'd done. She hadn't realised she was doing bad.

How stupid I've been.

Thirrrrrrteeeeeeeeeen ...

The hiss came from the figure, and with it came a new intensity to the agony in her body. The sensations were excruciating. The agonies in her shoulder, where The Hand of Glimm was currently burning, was spreading. It now had a grasp of her neck, of her chest, and the tendrils of pain were now stroking her face.

Each tattoo was nothing but a searing, slow death. The pain twisted and turned, it clawed and chewed, it fucked her with a barbed penis. She felt as if she were dying.

She would welcome it when it came.

~~~~

Billy and the barmaid from The Pickle were getting into it. They had found a young girl hitchhiking along the interstate that passed not too far from Needle Falls. Billy, with his handsome face and broad shoulders, had enticed the girl into the car. The presence of Natalie in the passenger seat had reassured her it was safe to get in.

Things turned nasty when Billy pulled over in a layby in the forest of pines that surrounded the small town. He'd removed his shirt, Natalie had done the same, before locking all the doors.

Their firm bodies, covered in tattooed words, each with a red handprint on their shoulders, had petrified the poor girl. As Natalie unlocked the door and dragged the girl out of the car, screaming into the trees, Billy followed, already unbuckling his trousers. He was ready to stick it to this pig. Since they'd been associating with Kevin, and his strange ideas of The Glimm, and the odd rituals they'd been performing, their pastime of raping and killing innocent boys and girls on the freeway had been kicked into gear.

Kevin had told them The Glimm would give them what they wanted, when they wanted it. There could be no worldly consequences for their actions, so the death and rape toll had doubled, tripled, even quadrupled.

The trees had a strange feeling about them today. As Natalie, topless and covered in the same writing he was, struggled to drag the girl into the scrub, Billy was looking around, sniffing at the air.

'Holy fuck,' he spat. 'Has something died out here?'

'Not yet,' Natalie panted as she dropped the struggling youth onto the pine needle-coated forest floor.

Billy laughed as he watched Nat kick her in the ribs, silencing her. It was then the wave of freezing air hit him. He noticed it affect Nat too. He'd always enjoyed watching her with their victims. She was gorgeous, physically fit, and nasty to the bone. She'd been nasty even before Kevin convinced her to join The Twelve he'd selected to summon what he called The Great Lord Glimm.
~~~~

They had been initially reluctant to join when they saw all the old *fogies* who were in there, but when he found out they would be fucking, and killing, and doing all sorts of other fucked-up, messy rituals, they both signed up, heart and soul. When he found out he had to fuck Martha from the bed and breakfast, he found it tough at first to get hard, but he'd been pleasantly surprised by how into it she had been.

Natalie found the same with Big Al, the police chief.

It had been fun.

The killings had been fun too, and their *extra* activities had been plentiful and consequence free too.

Life couldn't have been any better for a pair of psychopathic serial killers, and they had Kevin to thank for it.

Today, however, something was different. The area, their favourite area, was suddenly freezing. Natalie shivered as she tied the arms and legs of the young girl together, stuffing a rag into her mouth.

Billy squinted as he watched these proceedings. He looked at his watch. It read ten forty-seven. *In the morning,* he thought as he looked at the familiar killing ground. A dense fog was descending, and he could barely see the trees that were not ten feet away from him.

Once the girl was secured, Natalie looked around her too. He watched her face, as it bathed in the same confusion his had at what was happening. She wrapped her arms around her naked top half, hugging herself, staving off the sudden cold.

'What's happening?' Billy stuttered. The question was almost as much to himself as to his companion. 'It's fucking … freezing.'

Natalie was looking up at the minimal sky they could see through the canopy of the trees. It was just as cloudless as it had been prior to them entering the clearing. 'Why is it dark? And what's that fucking stink? Did you do the clean up after last time?'

'We both did,' Billy stuttered again, wishing for the t-shirt he had discarded. They liked to do this naked, so they didn't ruin their clothing. Today would just have to be different.

A shadow passed through the trees. They both saw it, but neither admitted it. Billy spared a glance at the petrified girl on the forest floor. She didn't look like she was suffering from the cold, the darkness, or even the awful stink, but then she was tied up on the floor of the forest being held captive by two semi-naked lunatics.

With a scream, Billy fell to the floor.

In his peripheral vision, he watched Natalie fall too, clutching the same area he was.

Her shoulder.

He felt as if the very flesh of his arm was melting. Like acid had been dripped on him and was currently corroding, eating through his skin, muscle, and bone. The sinew and the nerve endings in his shoulders were electric. He writhed on the forest floor, unaware of the pine needles penetrating his skin.

Natalie was screaming too. She was yelling and crying so loud he could no longer hear the whimpers of their captive over Natalie's screams.

His own too.

Something was happening to him. The pain was spreading. Fingers of torture were tearing from his shoulder, from his Hand of Glimm tattoo. Molten lava was entering his veins. It was dispersing through his body. Pure ice, or liquified metal, he couldn't tell what, consumed him.

The rest of his body was freezing, it was sick from the rotting stink, and he felt consumed by the dark shadow all around him. It passed through the trees, through the thick fog, coming towards him. This time, it didn't dissipate or undulate back into the darkness from whence it came. It lingered. It loomed over him.

It was looking at him.

Beneath a dark hood, there were two freezing lights. The kind of lights his fevered brain associated with nothingness, with desolation, with death.

The thing raised its head.

Another wave of nauseating stink oozed from within its folds. Billy saw what was causing the lights.

They were eyes.

Or something pertaining to eyes.

They were nothing but pools, puddles of silvery mortality.

Within those pools, he saw something, something that made him scream, and scream, and scream!

~~~
~~~

The girls of the beauty salon couldn't warm the shop floor today. They all took turns trying to turn the heating on, but even when they did, and they could hear the warm air streaming through the vents, they couldn't feel any of it. The three of them had shivered all through the morning. The customers who came and went were mostly oblivious to the biting cold.

'Maybe I'm coming down with something because of this fucking shop,' Tyler hissed as she hugged herself tighter.

'It's not the shop. It's whatever's making that stink. Can't you smell that?' June responded, her face creased as she held her nose while hugging herself tight, the tattoos of the sacred words of Glimm showing beneath her sheer white blouse.

'Go and catch Nicky. He'll be in the bar by now,' Alysia ordered as another shudder wracked her body.

'You go and see him.' Tyler shivered.

Alysia rolled her eyes. 'I will.' She shrugged. 'Anything to get away from this fucking stink and the cold.'

June stuck out her tongue as her colleague left the shop.

The instant the door slammed, the day went dark, and the stink trebled. In the middle of a gag, an involuntary act brought on by the stink, an agonising jolt hit her shoulder. Suddenly, her knees went weak, and it was moments later when they buckled beneath her. She fell to the floor unceremoniously, in the dullness of the day, just as a strange voice filtered into her head.

Thirrrrrrteeeeeeeeeen ...

~~~~

Alysia got no comfort from the cold in the street. The sky was almost as dark as night, and it seemed the smell had either followed her out of the shop or it was coming from out here in the town. She sniffed her hands, then underneath her arms, hoping it wasn't coming from her.

She was sighing with relief when something hit her.

She staggered, falling against a shop window as she did. Whatever had hit her shoulder had hit it with such force that she could
~~~~

still feel it. She corrected herself, looking around, hoping to see whoever, or whatever had struck her.

There was nothing, or no one, there.

She removed her hand from her smarting shoulder and looked at it. It took her a moment or two before she realised why it was wet. It was covered in blood. A strange, irrational panic exploded within her. She put her hand back to her shoulder and felt for something, anything that might have caused the bleeding, but all she found was pain. It was the tattoo that Kevin had done, The Hand of Glimm, that was bleeding.

It can't be, she thought. *That was a year ago. Why would it be bleeding now?*

But it was.

Thirrrrrrteeeeeeeeeen ...

The voice came from everywhere, all at once. Initially, she thought it was the wind whistling through the dark mid-morning, but something told her it wasn't, it *had* been a word.

Thirrrrrrteeeeeeeeeen ...

The stink was turning her stomach. It was physical, like sniffing ripe cheese, and the cold continued to bite at her through the thin white blood-stained blouse. One moment she was standing against a shop window, and the next she was on the sidewalk. She had fallen and fallen hard on the concrete. As her head collided with the paving flags, small stars with little dots of light all around them began to dance behind her eyes. There was something else too. It was dark, and it was dangerous; she could sense that. Her thoughts raced back to the rituals they'd performed. She thought about the sex, the bodily fluids ... She thought about the deaths, the sacrifices.

Was the dark figure coming for her?

She thought it might be.

Whatever it was, it lifted its head and looked at her. She could see her own reflection in the metallic surface of what might have been described as eyes.

It *had* come for her.

Waves of agony tore through her, and as she convulsed, through her double vision, she could make out someone running towards her.

She recognised who it was, but within that recognition was a mixture of both madness and fear.

~~~~

The Pickle wasn't the healthiest smelling place at the best of times. Nicky could never understand why people would want to spend their hard-earned dollars in such a shit-hole dump. He was bored. He'd been bored for years. He'd blown into this town ten years earlier, twenty-two and filled with dreams. He'd been on his way to an audition in New York City and had wanted to take the scenic route, to see a little of America, the country he loved.

His car broke down, he had no money and no means to get any, so he took a few shifts in the local bar.

'Ten fucking years ago,' he'd tell anyone who had a mind to listen. The ladies like to listen, as he'd been a good-looking guy back then, and he was still a good-looking guy now. A few extra pounds here and there, but not much had changed.

One thing led to another, and then another, and suddenly he found himself head bartender, earning a decent living, getting his fair share of pussy, all the alcohol he could possibly want, and a sweet little place in the apartment block directly behind the bar.

Life had been cruising at a decent pace, and then Kevin came along. Kevin with his dreams and his talk of how directors were now looking for older lead actors. 'The demographics have changed,' he'd say. Then he would start his talk of a better life, of dreams coming true.

Basically, he seduced him.

He tattooed him. He introduced him to a group of like-minded individuals who he already knew. He gave him a life filled with debauched sex, crazy drugs, and, eventually, when he was in too far, sacrifice.

Murder, he called it. Sacrifice, Kevin and the others called it.

He didn't mind. It had been done in the name of a God or something. He went with it, totally taken in the moment. And now, apparently, they were here, at the height of their quest. Just one more sacrifice and everything they'd ever wanted would be theirs, in their grasp for the taking. A better life for everyone.
~~~~

Hooray for that, he thought with a hint of sarcasm. *I refuse to be stuck here for another ten years. The place stinks like shit, its fucking freezing, and it's dark.*

He looked around, not remembering it being dark moments ago, right before he got lost in his own thoughts. *And that stink, it's worse than I ever remember it.*

It was so bad it made him heave.

He made his way to the door. He wanted to open it to let in some of the light of the morning, and maybe some of the fresh air of the day.

As the door opened, something brushed past him.

He didn't think too much of it at first, as there were always spiders and little *bastard* flies, no matter what time of the year. As he opened the door, he was hit by a wall of cold. A wall of the same shitty stink too. 'Holy fuck,' he gasped, gripping his nose.

His mouth was filling with saliva. He never did have a good gag reflex. He'd found that out in Kevin's basement, the hard way.

The cold tore at his shirt and the bartender's apron he always used. He'd lost too many nice clothes to awful stains over the years, so he'd taken to wearing the apron. It did its job against the beer and liquor, but it was useless against a sudden freezing wind. As he shuddered, he looked across the street and saw Alysia from the beauty salon. He grinned as he thought about the things he had done to her, and her to him. He squinted his eyes as he watched her stagger up the street. She looked drunk. He looked at his watch. He knew her—it wasn't like her to be drinking at this time of the day.

As he looked closer, he realised she wasn't drunk but in some obvious distress. Forgetting the cold and the stink in the street, he ran to her, but as he started his short journey, something gripped him.

It was an odd sensation. The instant he felt it, all joy, every happy thought he'd ever had fell out of him. He pulled his arm away but struggled to free himself. The grip was tight, and it burned his flesh. Reflexively, he turned to see who it was impeding him helping his friend.

There was no one there.

There was *nothing* there.

Where he expected to see the door to the bar and the empty room beyond, there was nothing but shadow, a shifting, grainy darkness that offered … nothing.

His arm was burning, and the vice-like grip had strengthened. It was forcing him to his knees. He screamed again but wasn't sure if any sound was made, as a thick syrup of the god-awful stench mixed with the cold and the darkness flooded his mouth.

He wanted to retch. He needed to vomit.

Thirrrrrrteeeeeeeeeen …

The voice hurt his ears even though it was barely a whisper. It made the sensitive membrane of his eardrum vibrate. The pain was lost within the agony of his enflamed arm, especially his shoulder. It was the tattoo, The Hand of Glimm, that was searing. He could hear his skin bubbling as if the ink itself was some hungry, self-aware acid. His flailing mind sent him a flashback of a film he saw when he was a kid. It was about an alien loose on a spaceship. Every time the monster was shot, its blood was acid, and it burnt through the ship. This felt like that same acid was eating away at his flesh, liquidising him, sizzling through him to get to his bones, his muscles.

His soul.

'Fuck …' was all he could spit through the vile ball of nothing in his mouth. Red-hot wires of torture were lashing out from his tattoo. They were reaching, grasping, scratching through his body. His neck, his face, his skin was tightening, stretching, retracting.

Ripping!

Whatever had hold of him suddenly released its grip.

Thirrrrrrteeeeeeeeeen, it whispered, or maybe it shouted—Nicky couldn't tell.

He staggered, he didn't know where he was going, he just knew he was heading away from the darkness of the bar, and out into the road. He found himself crossing the street. He needed to outrun the cold and the stink of decay, of death, of eternal damnation. He needed to get to his friend, who was lying on the street. She looked to be in as much distress as he was. There was blood on her white blouse.

When he reached her, he looked at her. A shaking hand moved her hair from covering her face, revealing her features. As he did, she opened her eyes.

Nicky screamed.

Alysia screamed.

The eyes that gazed up at him were different. They were wide with horror, pink, bloodshot. The burst capillaries within them was turning the pinks blood red.

But they were not *her* eyes.

They were the eyes of someone else.

Someone he recognised.

22.

'WHAT ARE YOU doing?' Carson asked the dark figure looking up at him. The cold of the house was biting his flesh, and no matter how hard he rubbed his arms, he couldn't stem the sensation.

'I've been waiting for you,' Kevin replied. His face hidden beneath the hood of the cloak he was wearing. Carson knew it was him.

Who else would it be?

'Why would you wait for me down here?'

'Your inquisitive nature drew you here. You were meant here, Carson.'

Carson attempted to smile, to laugh off the silly situation he found himself in. 'Kevin,' he chuffed. 'What are you talking about? I was just looking for you to see if you wanted to go and get some—'

'There'll be no breakfast,' Kevin said, his voice a void of inflection. 'You were brought to us to fit a purpose. You are Thirteen.'

Carson squinted; he gripped the wooden banister tight. He imagined it indenting beneath his grip like it did on superhero movies. 'Thir—'

'Thirteen,' Kevin finished. 'You were promised to us. You are the thirteenth sacrifice, the one who came to us of his own free will.'

Carson's head was shaking. 'I don't know what you're talking about. I never …'

Kevin's hooded head was nodding. 'You did. Last night, you gave yourself to me and my bidding. When we coupled, you sealed your deal with The Great Lord Glimm. It is you who will usher in the new era. You were foretold to me.'

Kevin tilted his head up towards him. His hood slipped, ever so slightly, but enough to reveal his pale face. There was no humour there. His eyes were the eyes of a shark, lifeless, black, yet filled with malice. 'The Twelve will take you this day,' he whispered.

'Thirrrrrrteeeeeeeeeen!' The whisper came from everywhere.

With goosebumps rising all over his flesh, Carson looked up the stairs towards the door at the top. The light was his salvation. He thought he could make it. Kevin was standing stock still. He didn't look in any hurry to stop him from doing exactly what he wanted to do.

'There'll be no escape,' Kevin whispered. 'Just like your cousin before you, and the others before her. You were all foretold.'

'Amelia?' Carson hissed as he turned back towards the man he had spent the night with, given himself to … *of my own free will,* he added in his head. 'You know her?'

Kevin nodded. 'As intimately as I know you,' he answered.

'She *was* here! Where is she now?'

'The town knew her as Kirsty, but The Great Lord Glimm knew her real name and her real purpose.'

'Where is she?' Carson demanded, a worm of anger, of panic, of adrenaline turned in his stomach.

'She has been shared among The Twelve.'

'What do you mean, shared? Did … did you rape her?'

Kevin's mouth smiled, but the rest of his face remained stoic. 'We didn't rape her. We shared her. She is in all of them. Her essence, what she required to live, The Great Lord Glimm needed for him to be able to grant us our gifts.'

'Who is The Great Lord Glimm? What the fuck is going on?'

'That, my friend, my lover, you will find out soon enough.'

Carson heard the door above him, just beyond the staircase, slam closed. An icy blast was carried, piggybacking on a sickening stench of horror. It spoke of blood, death, and, worst of all, damnation.

Kevin was on him in a flash, and Carson felt something sting his neck. Kevin's arms wrapped around him, and he wanted nothing more than to sink into this embrace, to fall asleep in the arms of his new lover. For the darkness to enfold him; to embrace the nothingness.

He wanted Amelia too.

He got everything he wanted.

23.

THEY WERE ALL in a café. He recognised it as the one in town, the one ran by the lovely couple Malic and Moon, whose real name was Luna, but Malic and Moon had a nicer click to it. It sounded like a TV show. It could have been Malic and Moon, detective agency, or it could have been a children's programme. One where Malic's best friend was the moon, and they would have all manner of nocturnal adventures together.

He was at a table facing the window. There was a steaming cup of hot chocolate before him, laden with small marshmallows—he thought there might have been too many as they were falling down the side of the mug, leaving snail trails of chocolate in their wake. *Is there even such a thing as too many marshmallows?* It was a funny thought, he liked it. He was waiting on Moon, bringing him a bowl of her famous spaghetti.

Outside the window, the town was beautiful. Snow lined the ground, and the trees in the distance covering the hills just outside of town were covered in white. The Christmas decorations were up all around the streets, and as the townsfolk were bustling here and there, doing their chores or maybe some last-minute Christmas shopping, Carson felt a sense of calm. It was warm in the café; it was safe. He was with friends. Amelia was here, as was Kevin, and some of the regulars from The Pickle, including Nicky the bartender and the girls from the beauty salon.

They were laughing. Carson was too, but he didn't know why.

'We're just waiting on the last two to arrive, then we're all here, and we can begin,' Kevin said. A genuine smile dominated his features, and the twinkle in his eye made Carson grin. He took a deep sip of his hot chocolate, or it might have been a bite of the melted sugary treat on the top of it, just as Moon arrived with his food. Malic came with her.

The bell on the door rang, heralding the arrival of two more people. It was Billy from the Pickle. Carson cheered and raised his cup. Billy had once tried to beat him, but Kevin had stopped it, and they had become fast friends. He was with his girlfriend. She was from The Pickle too, and even though Carson wasn't interested in girls, he had to admit that she was small-town beautiful.

The gang were all there, just as the day began to darken. They laughed and talked late into the night.

~~~~

The cold pushed him. He thought he could feel icy hands, icicle fingers hitting him in the chest, barging through him.

The stink did the same.

He thought he might have soiled his pants or was maybe waking in a septic tank. The smell was so deep up his nose he could taste it, he could feel it crawling into the pores of his flesh. *I'll be smelling that for weeks,* he thought.

With that thought, he suddenly realised he was naked. It was an ugly feeling to wake up finding one was naked in a strange, stinking location, especially twice in the same day. He shifted his position, trying to get comfortable and warm but found he couldn't move.

He wriggled, just a little, trying to move his hands.

But there was no give in his binds.

Binds?

On instinct, he opened his eyes.

There was nothing but darkness. An ugly realisation slowly trickled over him. He was wearing a blindfold. His stomach growled as it turned. Despite the frigid cold, a sheen of sweat coated him, and he wriggled even more. His arms were over his head. His wrists and shoulders were aching. He could feel them bound.

Panic.

It flowered slowly in the gestation chamber of his churning stomach and built quickly. It bloomed shortly after, and before he could even produce a single rational thought, it was fully grown and
~~~~

commandeering his every thought and action. He thrashed, he shouted, he screamed and kicked. Only he couldn't do any of these things; his binds were so tight.

Something was in his mouth. It was stopping him from shouting.

His feet were bound as tight as his arms and hands.

Eventually, the panic found somewhere to dwell within him. It steadfastly refused to leave, as waking up in this situation was not something he had ever envisioned, but thankfully a modicum of rationality descended over him. *Think,* he told himself. *Think. How could I have ended up here? What was I doing before?*

Kevin!

This thought brought its own complications. He remembered his night of passion with him, then remembered waking alone in the house. He remembered the cold, the stink, and the room.

Then he woke up here.

'Ah, you're awake!'

The voice was Kevin's. He would recognise it anywhere. He could sense someone standing before him, and when the hands were on his face, removing the blindfold, he felt ready for what he would see before him.

That was until he actually saw it.

He was in a dark, spacious room. He was trussed up on—it was either a table or a stage. When his eyes were working properly again, he saw it was circular and there were lights at individual points around it. He was in the centre. Kevin was stood before him wearing a long dark robe and some ridiculous headwear that looked like the skull of a stag, complete with antlers.

Without warning, Kevin reached into his mouth and removed the material that had been stealing his voice. Carson spat a dry spit and took in a gulp of air when his passageways were clear. 'What?' was all he managed to gasp.

'Shhh,' Kevin hissed, his forefinger over his lips. 'You're the thirteenth. You hold a revered place in our quest. You came to us of your own volition, and you give yourself to our cause.'

'I didn't give myself to anything, you fucking psycho,' Carson spat as he thrashed against the ropes holding him to the table. There was no movement in them. Whoever had tied him had obviously done it before and gotten good at it.

'Calm yourself,' Kevin soothed. 'Your fate was sealed the day you came into this town looking for your cousin. Don't you see the perfection of it? She opened the door to us, and you walked right through it. You wanted to be here. By your own admission, you said you thought you belonged here. How true that was.'

'I never came here for this,' Carson spat again. There was fire in his belly now; it was room sharing with the panic. It was causing some well-placed anger at his treatment. He knew if he could get out these binds, he could take Kevin and get out of here, out of this town. *Out of the fucking state,* he added in his head.

Kevin smiled as if he could read his mind. It freaked Carson out as the man who he'd shared intimacy with, an intimacy he never gave lightly, laughed. His eyes changed with the gleeful sound. They darkened, as if his pupils had expanded to take over all of his eyeballs.

There was nothing in those eyes.

An almost complete nothing.

Carson knew he would not survive this.

'I wanted to thank you, Carson. Being number Thirteen is an honour, one that, right now, you will not understand, but shortly, when the ritual, the pain, the suffering, and the sacrifice is complete, you will get an understanding of how important you are to us.'

'There have been others?'

Kevin smiled again, his strange eyes widening to almost inhuman proportions. He nodded. 'Twelve others. As I stated, you are Thirteen. The mystical number. The unholy number. You will be long remembered, Carson. This is written.'

'You killed Amelia,' Carson coughed, his throat too dry to speak correctly.

Kevin's smile was not built on good humour. 'We *used* her. It was written! Don't you see that? She was sent to us …'

Carson's head was shaking. 'She wasn't. She was running from an abusive situation. She was vulnerable, and you took advantage of that. You fucking killed her.' He could hardly believe the words were leaving his mouth. 'You fucking monster, you killed her. You and your fucking psycho town. You think you're on some kind of mystical trip, but you're just a fucking murderer. A sad, deluded murderer.'

Kevin's smile grew. He chuffed a little.

Carson's face fell when the next words from Kevin's mouth reached his ears. He realised all was lost to him. The reason he'd come to this small town in the first instance was lost to him. The words Kevin whispered spoke to him of the madness of the situation, of the desolation around him. Fear left him at that moment, as there was nothing left to fear.

'You can't make an omelette without breaking the eggs!'

The total lack of empathy in that one statement destroyed Carson. All he could do was close his eyes. His body went slack, and he resigned himself to the horrible situation.

He wanted to cry.

His tears might have been for himself, for falling for the wrong person again. They would have also been for Amelia. For the running she'd done, only to fall into the same dark grip, this time, of a cult of deluded freaks. The tears would have also been for the sadness and the cruelty of this world. For the beatings he, and people like him had taken, would take for the years to come.

They would be for all the awful cards he'd been dealt.

A noise from somewhere in the room, in the thick of the darkness surrounding them caught his attention. It distracted Kevin, and his smile widened again. He looked beyond Carson, into the depths of the blacked out room.

After a moment, he brought his attention back to Carson.

A heavy, shaking sigh escaped him.

Kevin climbed off the table and disappeared into the murky darkness. He returned moments later with four medium-sized urns and a glove with wicked-looking needles as fingers.

Carson's eyes narrowed in on the vicious instrument.

His heart was racing, his breathing had become both shallow and rapid. 'What is that?' he gasped. 'What are you doing with that?'

Kevin slipped the glove on his hand and flexed his fingers.

Through welling tears, Carson watched the tips of the needles glistening in what little light they managed to catch.

Another noise behind Kevin caught Carson's attention again, and reluctantly, he dragged his eyes from the weapons and back into the darkness. There were shadows shifting in the depths. He couldn't tell if it was his imagination or if there were people back there.

Either way, he figured it didn't matter.

Nothing much mattered anymore.

Amelia was already dead.

There had been no other reason for him to come to this town, and now that had proved to be his undoing.

More and more noises were coming from within the undulating darkness, but he no longer cared. Kevin had his back to him; he was looking into the same darkness he was. His arms were in the air, and his head was thrust back as if he were in the throes of ecstasy.

'Welcome …' His voice was loud, as if addressing a crowd.

Carson looked past his former lover, beyond the cloak, and saw there was indeed a crowd standing before him.

'Tonight is a momentous night,' Kevin announced.

The sounds from the darkness diminished, and the moving shadows within the shadows stopped.

'Tonight is the true night of the Thirteen. We can all praise The Glimm.'

'Praise The Glimm,' a choir of voices replied from inside the darkness. To Carson, the voices were genderless, there was no differentiation of age either, it was just a jumble of voices, a choir replying in unison.

'He is the thirteenth sacrifice, the final offering. Tonight, we ascend from our old lives and give ourselves up to The Glimm. Praise The Glimm!' Kevin continued.

'Praise The Glimm,' the shadows repeated.

Carson knew his time was up. He was in the presence of a cult, with Kevin as their leader. He looked at the glove on Kevin's raised hand and swallowed. He wanted to shout, to reason with the shadows, to scream at them, tell them how ridiculous this whole thing was. But he knew it would have been a lost cause. He *was* the thirteenth. That meant they'd murdered twelve before him. One of them was Amelia. He guessed they would be too far gone to repent their ways now. All he could hope for was a fast ending, as painless as it could be.

'Step forth and claim your fates, your destinies. There is one last mark of Glimm, and everything you have ever wished for, everything you have ever longed for will be yours. Come forth, come forth all!'

Kevin gestured towards the urns that were on the table before Carson. 'Come, collect the essence of The Thirteen, allow The Glimm to bless us all.'

The shadows within the gloom began to shuffle forwards. The dim lights blinked, then flickered out, casting Carson into a complete disorientating darkness. As the blackness swallowed him, he could feel the tears in his eyes running, he could trace their journey down his face.

Suddenly, strong beams of light split the darkness, emanating from twelve locations around the table—or stage, or whatever it was he was shackled to. They lit the room in a sick, greenish light. The beams were pillars in the darkness, and the strength of the light hurt his eyes. The only sound he could hear over his heartbeat was an odd hum. It took a moment for him to realise it was a mumbling of words. He couldn't make out what they were saying—it didn't sound English—but he could tell it was a chant.

It was a single phrase repeated over and over.

Then he heard the shuffling of feet. The shadows he could make out through the beams were moving again.

They were the shade within the dark.

Kevin hadn't moved.

He was motionless with his hand raised in the air like a cartoon impression of the King of Pop himself, with his one gloved hand raised high in the air. The proud antlers protruding from his head were motionless. He was uttering the nonsensical sentence too. Repeating it over and over again. Even through the pulsing of his blood pumping through his ears, the physical interpretation of his fear, Carson could hear the chorus of the nonsensical words ushering from what he presumed would be the townsfolk.

The beams turned off again, casting everything as black as death.

Movement within the blackness once again caught his attention.

The shadows were shifting. They were dancing, cavorting. Carson wished the lights would come back on so he could see what was happening. If this was to be his fate, then, from a courage he never knew he had, he wanted to see his murderers' faces as they killed him, as they sacrificed him for their stupid games.

As the shadows frolicked within the darkness, the beams of light began to pulse. The strobe effect made his head swirl, and he could feel himself moving in time with the rhythm and the chanting, which had picked up in volume and speed.

His head was swirling as the room spun faster. It was the only part of his body that could move freely. This fact no longer concerned him. His mind was racing. The strobing lights was now in perfect balanced rhythm, in exact time with the chanting, and it absorbed all his rational thoughts. The shadows were no longer shadows. They were wild animals running through a forest of light and dark. The sounds of the night were the song of The Twelve.

Faster and faster, the room span.

The light strobed wilder, the chant continued, the world spun.

Faster, and faster, and faster.

Carson could feel vomit, he had an erection, he could feel his heart pounding in ever vein in his body. It was an apple; it was rotting rapidly as if he was watching a time-lapse recording. It was being eaten by worms.

The world ceased to exist. It was nothing but a blur of strobing, chanting, throbbing … throbbing … throbbing.

Then, with one ear-piercing, wet scream … it all stopped.

24.

THE SHADOWS AROUND him twisted and turned. They writhed with a passion he hadn't witnessed before. They shifted through the darkness like angry wraiths. The chant was in complete unison, and he could feel his world spinning, turning, flipping.

This had never happened before.

It's the power of The Thirteen!

It was the only rational thought in Kevin's head as he struggled to stay upright, to hold his hand—the one sheathed in the special glove—in the air. The weight of his arm was causing it to waver, again in rhythm with the lights—the ones used to symbolise the twelve sacrifices. They lit up and turned off, they strobed. The mind effects were kicking his disciples into overdrive. They were thrashing wilder, and their chanting louder, until it was almost a shout.

He joined in the chant. He had no option, it had become everything. The room, the house, the town, the whole world consisted of strobing lights and ugly rhythmic chants.

Nothing else mattered.

'Hickula, tragantie a billinctus, shakker, toogorey!'

'Twelve, destiny calls, fulfil, encapsulate, embrace!'

'Hickula, tragantie a billinctus, shakker, toogorey!'

'Twelve, destiny calls, fulfil, encapsulate, embrace!'

Over and over, the chant continued. Faster and faster, the lights strobed. Everything became white in spite of the darkness surging all around him.

~~~~
~~~~

Kevin was no longer in a basement beneath his house. He was no longer in the darkness, and he was no longer surrounded by The Twelve.

He was nowhere.

An intense white light that his brain couldn't fathom held him. It encapsulated him, wrapping him in its starkness. None of his senses made any logic. His eyes, his ears, his smell, even his touch—everything was in a state of total flux.

Then suddenly, without warning, everything calmed. His head halted its journey around the room, and his eyes were finally able to focus. He was still in a world of intense light, but now he could differentiate between up and down, left and right. There was solidity beneath him. The chanting still swirled in his head, but it was now distant, as if it were in another room, on another level. It was far away, yet he could hear every single word.

Slowly, as his senses filtered back to him, he sensed the others with him. He couldn't see them, the light was too bright for his eyes to capture who they were, but he knew they were there. They were the ones chanting, they were the lights, it was them that held him in their embrace.

Eventually the light began to dim. As its intensity reduced, it revealed them.

They *were* here, they *were* all around him.

They were dressed in sheer white robes, covering them from head to toe, the hoods hiding their faces.

As he saw them, he counted them.

There were twelve.

He felt the need to vomit, or maybe crawl away, to find a dark place to hide until these people got bored and left, but he couldn't do any of those things. He was rooted to his spot. He couldn't move. He looked at his arms, then his legs—he *wasn't* shackled, but it felt as if he were, as he was not allowed to move. He looked at the ghostly figures before him. Anger swelled with the other sensations in his stomach, the ones he now recognised as varying levels of fear.

Who were they to restrict *him*?

Did they not know who he was, and what his role in this whole procedure meant?

He wanted to shout at them, to them. He needed to let them know that *he* was the instigator, *he* was the connection with The Great Lord Glimm, but his voice wouldn't work. It was as paralysed as the rest of his body.

As if sensing his thoughts, the twelve figures began to move closer. The nearer they got, the more definition he could see. They were a mixture of men and women, this he understood, but if they were *his* twelve, then how could they be doing this to him? He was their leader.

One by one, they lifted their robed arms and removed their hoods. As Kevin gazed upon their faces, the face of eleven innocents, eleven victims, the eleven sacrifices they had made over the last few years, flashed through his head.

He could see their pale faces, he could hear their screams as their blood was drained from them. He could see the lights in their eyes dimming as their lives filtered out through the tubes in the bodies, the same tubes *he* had inserted into them.

He opened his mouth to scream. He needed to scream

Nothing would come from him.

Only one figure remained hooded.

One anonymous member in a sea of faces he never thought he would see again. They were still hooded, coving their identity. He had an idea who it might have been, as there was only one face he couldn't see in the group.

Amelia, he thought.

Once more, as if reading his thoughts, she raised her hands, her cloak falling down her arms, revealing her pale, inked flesh. There were so many tattoos on her limbs, covering many deep scars in her flesh. Slowly, her hood was removed. Her blonde hair flopped out of it, covering her face. He already knew she would be smiling.

'Kevin,' she whispered.

He swallowed, still unable to move, unable to shout or scream.

'Do you remember us?' she continued.

He tried to nod; he tried to turn away from her. The last time he'd seen her, she had been drained of blood and her skin had been as blue as the images etched into her skin.

With wide eyes, he watched her draw closer. The others came with her, gathering close behind. 'You know who we are?'

I don't remember your names, he thought.

'We never *had* names, not to you, anyway,' she whispered again. 'You knew us as …'

'*Thirrrrrrteeeeeeeeeen!*' the others hissed.

'Thirteen,' Amelia laughed as she removed her robe, revealing her blue nakedness. Her nipples were purple, as was the tinge to all the extremities of her body.

She leaned in close.

Kevin found his voice then.

It was his turn to scream.

~~~

'ARE YOU PREPARED?' the voice asked from the blackness.

'I am,' Amelia whispered, her throat parched, her body aching and cold.

'TAKE MY HAND, AND I WILL WALK WITH YOU. TOGETHER, WE WILL GIVE THEM WHAT THEY HAVE REQUESTED FOR SO LONG.'

'What is that?'

'LIFE EVERLASTING,' came the answer from the wind.

Something touched her hand. Her revulsion at its caress caused her to snatch it away. Whatever it was, it was cold and wet. With it came a smell that didn't feel human to her—it felt as far from human as she could possibly imagine.

The smell was that of the sea. It smelt like a time she could remember when she was travelling. She'd ended up in a small town in Maine. It was a small fishing community and everywhere smelt like this. As if she had no other choice, she gripped the inhuman thing, and everything changed in an instant.

Suddenly, she was lighter than ever before. There was a dizzy, disjointed feeling of falling, of being nowhere, of being somewhere, of being everywhere. She was no longer Amelia, yet she was, more or less. It hurt her brain to even try to comprehend it. She was roasting hot, *and* she was freezing. She was as light as the very air itself and as heavy as a ball of lead.

A smile broke on her face.
~~~

The very same smile broke on the eleven other faces.

~~~~

Kevin screamed.

He was back in his basement. It was dark, but light was strobing. His disciples were still chanting, and the room was spinning.

The thirteenth sacrifice was still tied to the table.

The shadows in the darkness were still writhing. They looked to be dancing, swaying with the chant. His heart was thrashing. Every nerve ending in his body was tingling, pulsing. With each throb, another wave of agony, then panic, then euphoria, cycling back to pain, washed through him. His body wracked and shivered as he dropped to the floor. One of the needles of his glove snapped as it hit the black-painted surface beneath him. He looked upwards, towards the shifting darkness. They were closer than they had ever been. For the first time since he'd started this odyssey, Kevin was scared. Why should he be? He'd followed the rules of The Glimm to the very letter. The writings had been passed down to him, the same texts that had been followed for millennia.

On shaky legs, he eased himself back up.

His breathing was rapid, and it was making his head spin. The agony and the ecstasy coursing through his body was surging, pushing him on.

The eleven robed followers took another step closer. Their silhouettes becoming clearer.

He scrambled away from them.

'What are you doing?' he hissed, stumbling backwards until his backside bumped into the edge of the large table.

'Hickula, tragantie a billinctus, shakker, toogorey,' they hissed in unison. He knew this was what they were saying, but all he heard was '*Thirrrrrrteeeeeeeeeen!*

Thirrrrrrteeeeeeeeeen!

Thirrrrrrteeeeeeeeeen!

He clambered onto the table, attempting to get away from the town members, the ones he'd had so much control over. The very same people who'd followed him for all the years of this journey. He
~~~~

couldn't understand why they were turning on him now, not when they were all so close to fulfilling their every desire.

His limbs trembled, so much so he had to hold himself to lock them, to stop himself from falling off the table and into the swaying throng before him.

Somehow he knew if he fell into them, they would tear him limb from limb. They would destroy him, ruin him.

Suddenly, the twelve lights on the table snapped back on. The brightness took him back to the odd place he'd found himself in moments ago, with the sacrifices.

Luckily, this sensation was only brief.

As his eyes adjusted to the new brightness, he could see everyone standing before him. There were twelve of them, dressed in dark robes, their hoods covering their faces. He knew them all. It was Malic and Moon. Martha from the bed and breakfast. Nicky from The Pickle. It was Billy and Natalie. It was the girls from the beauty salon. It was Big Al and his officers. All of them were in his thrall, they would have done anything he asked. He had brought them this far; there was no way he couldn't back out now.

It's a trick, he thought. *A test to see if I have the endurance to go the distance. To see if I am worthy of The Glimm.* He began to laugh as he held his arms in the air. His broken glove once more held aloft, only this time it wasn't into the darkness but to a well illuminated room.

'The Glimm is with us,' he shouted. His voice sounded reedy, thin, and shaky, even to himself. 'Tonight is the night we take—'

'Thirrrrrrteeeeeeeeeen!'

The hissing interruption broke his stride.

'It's when … where we take what we've all—'

'Thirrrrrrteeeeeeeeeen!'

One of the disciples stepped forward. He couldn't tell who it was; or even if it was a male or female. Another stepped forward, then another.

Before he could continue, before the shortage of air in his chest allowed more words to escape him, they had all stepped forwards. His eyes crawled over them. He licked his lips. 'Tonight …' he continued.

As one, they began to undo their robes from the strings around their necks.

'Tonight …'

The robes opened simultaneously.

'We are gathered here to receive …'

They were all naked.

He recognised the tattooed bodies before him. All of them. The older ones and the younger. The men and the women. He knew them intimately.

They were the bodies he had personally inked. The ones he had physically, indelibly marked with his needles, filled from the sacred urns that contained the essence of twelve sacrifices. Each sacrifice had been the thirteenth member of their cult. They had been building and building to reach the heights of tonight.

The night of the true *Thirteen.*

At the sight of the bodies, he relaxed. They were his people, his followers, the twelve to his thirteen. Buoyed by this revelation, he continued his address. 'Tonight, we take our true thirteenth,' he started.

'*Thirrrrrrteeeeeeeeeeen!*' they all replied in chorus.

'Tonight, The Great Lord Glimm is within us. He will bless us with everything we have prayed for, everything we have worked towards, everything we have strived for. Tonight, we take it …'

The word *all* died in his mouth as every member of the twelve standing before, him removed their hoods. They all allowed their robes to slip from their naked bodies.

The first thing he noticed about them were the Hands of Glimm, the ones he had tattooed onto their shoulders from where The Great Lord Glimm had touched them. They were glowing. They were pulsating with a sickening purple luminosity. Blood, or something akin to it, dripped from each finger of the drawn hands. It dripped slowly down the breasts of the women and the chests of the men.

The second thing Kevin noticed made him scream like he had never screamed before.

Once his mouth opened and the ugly sound began to gush forth from him, it simply refused to stop.

25.

CARSON WATCHED EVERYTHING from his front row elevation. His hands were numb from the tight binding, and his back and legs were screaming at him. Even through the fear, the resignation to his fate, and the panic that had been an underlying sensation beneath his strangely calm exterior, he couldn't believe what he was seeing.

It was the wildest thing he had ever seen in his life.

It pushed the whole sensation of the man he'd been falling in love with tying him up and referring to the people he'd shared his everyday small-town life with lining up to kill him, to the back of his mind. He wondered if the drugs Kevin had given him were causing him to trip, or if his brain had taken stock of his situation and had developed something absurd to help him process what was really happening.

If it had, it had gone too far.

Or—and this was a stretch—maybe it *was* really happening.

As Kevin fell to his knees, as the bloody, wet screams began to flow from his wide-open mouth, a smile broke on Carson's face, one that fought against, and won, the tears staining his otherwise filthy face.

He simply could not believe what he was witnessing.

26.

IT SHOULD HAVE been his signature moment. It should have been the brightest peak of his existence. The Great Lord Glimm coming to *him,* to grant them everything that had been promised. Instead, he was on his knees before his subordinates, screaming so hard he'd lost control of all bodily functions. His bladder had emptied on the table. Dehydrated urine was running through the specially designed grooves, crafted to collect the essence of their victims, of their sacrifices.

He didn't care.

He was lost.

He was abandoned.

Everything was gone.

It was the end of their mission. The demise of their cult was upon them, and it was pushing him past his limits of endurance.

The heat from the glowing tattoos on each of their shoulders spiked the temperature of the room up from the freezing cold it had been. The stink filled his nostrils. It was the smell of rotten flesh, congealing fat and blood, and collapsing organs. It was The Twelve, the dead sacrifices coming back for him.

Only, that wasn't possible.

It wasn't The Twelve.

It was only number twelve.

Each and every face staring down at him as his screams of fear reached fever pitch was the face of the same, one person.

It was impossible. It just couldn't be.

Yet there it was, there *she was,* right before him, many times over. On each of the bodies—the old, the young, the male, the female—was the face of Amelia, or Kirsty, as they had known her.

The last one; their penultimate sacrifice.

Her youthful face was beautiful on all of their bodies. Her smile was filled with the secrets of youth, with the eagerness of a bright, elongated future. With each pulse of heat, of rot from the Hand of Glimm tattoos, Amelia's face grew happier. Her lips that should have been long gone, nothing but ash by now, were full. They were filled with a lustre that had been denied to her in life.

They parted as she laughed.

The mirth was real. There was nothing fake about the situation he found himself in.

'*Thirrrrrrteeeeeeeeeen!*' they hissed at the same time. Only there was a playfulness about the word now, like a cat playing with a mouse before getting bored and taking the final, fatal swoop.

In a wave of nakedness, the townsfolk, all of them wearing her face, swamped the stage.

Teeth were bared, hands were clawed, and all of them searching for purpose.

~~~~

Kevin felt every last scratch. He endured every bite, every tug at his limbs. Life, as he had known it, ebbed from his body in the mess of gore, of blood, of sinew that was all that was left of him. As his last breath prepared to leave his ravaged body, as his one remaining eye dimmed and his broken bones splintered, as his veins pumped the last of his much-needed blood from the many wounds he'd suffered at the hands of the eleven—or was it thirteen? he no longer knew, and more than that, he didn't care—he had the presence of mind to look at the real Thirteen.

His eyes met Carson's.

It was just for a fleeting moment before something behind the shackled man stole his attention. Dark bubble of blood grew and burst as he chuffed. It was darker than the darkness that was rushing towards him. It was dimmer than the glimmer of life he held on to. It was deadlier than death itself.

It was a shapeless, noncorporal mist. It was nothing, yet to Kevin, in the very last moments of his mortal life, it was everything.
~~~~

It was The Great Lord Glimm.

'You bastard,' he gasped before his earthly body was consumed by the nothingness.

~~~~

As Kevin's fight left him, as his body succumbed to the onslaught of his cult, they began to fall away from him, one by one.

Their bloody faces no longer portraits of Amelia. They were the faces of Al, of Malic and Moon. Martha's face was covered in blood, so much so that no one would have been able to recognise her, only that she was covered in tattoos, and was the oldest of the group.

Everyone fell from Kevin, to lie dead on the very table that would be their vessel to greatness. The same vessel that would grant them their every wish.

With each death, Carson's binds loosened.

He lay as motionless as the corpses surrounding him, unable to move his freed limbs.

His breathing was shallow yet rapid as he regarded the ugly scenes before him.

As his blood began to flow back into his extremities, the tingle was relentless. He flexed his fingers and toes, allowing the fluids to run back into them. Before long, when all feeling was back to a fashion, he wanted nothing more than to get out of this basement and out of this town. He would never look back.

He cursed Amelia.

He cursed Kevin.

But most of all, he cursed himself for allowing him to get into a situation like this.

'IT IS NOT YOUR FAULT.'

The voice boomed from everywhere, but mostly from inside his head.

'YOU WERE NOT TO KNOW, AND YOU WERE DOING THE RIGHT THING.'

He recognised it, although the last time he'd heard it, it was nothing more than a hiss.

'Who are you?' he asked, still flexing his arms, encouraging the blood to flow.
~~~~

'YOU KNOW WHO I AM, CARSON HESS. NOW, YOU MUST LEAVE THIS PLACE. THE GREAT LORD GLIMM'S WORK HERE IS DONE. LOOK TO SEE ME, OR HIM, NO MORE!'

With this creed, the presence he could feel in the room, the ominous threat, lifted. The cold dissipated, and the stink receded. He found himself alone with multiple dead bodies of the townsfolk of Needle Falls.

27.

CARSON FOUND THE keys to Kevin's car. Without thinking about it, he took them. He loaded his clothing and what was left of his possessions into the car, and without thinking of any consequences of his actions, he drove out of the town.

He didn't look back.

He was done with provincial towns. He'd found what he'd come for. His cousin, Amelia, was dead. There would be no trial of her mother now, and she would probably get out of prison, ready to reap her twisted revenge on a world she thought had treated her so badly.

This was no longer his problem. He could have cared less about Amelia's mother. His responsibility to that cause was in the past. There were other, more pressing concerns on his time now. Almost being killed by a lunatic, who happened to be his lover, even if it was just for one night, and the leader of a deranged death cult, had the effect of shifting one's outlook on life.

It gave a person other priorities.

When he'd been freed from his binds, when he'd danced around the dead bodies in that basement, doing his very best not to touch them, not to get anywhere near any of the gore that surrounded what was left of Kevin, he'd made his way upstairs to get his clothes, to get the car keys, and to get his rightful passage out of this shithole town.

As he'd entered the bedroom, he'd noticed one of the wardrobe doors was slightly ajar.

He didn't want to, but something called to him to investigate the space behind the darkness. His poor, exhausted heart was pounding again, and his wrists, where he had been bound, were throbbing. He licked his dry lips as he reached a shaking hand towards the partly opened door. A whisper filled his head. It was wordless, more of a sigh, but he recognised it as something akin to the voices he'd heard downstairs.

It sounded like it approved of his actions.

It sounded like he was supposed to find this door.

It sounded like whatever it was, it *wanted* him to investigate this space.

He'd opened the door fully and looked inside. There was one single item. It was on a plinth, in a position of reverence. His mouth dried as he looked at it. His ears began to burn and throb as blood, and indecipherable whispers rushed through them, drowning out any other sounds he might have been able to hear in the house.

His trembling hand reached in and took it.

He didn't know why, but he felt it had called to him. It knew his name. After everything he'd been through, after everything that had happened to him, and to Amelia, and to the others, the nameless ones he hadn't known, he thought he deserved this.

He took the item and stuffed it into his bag. He found a stash of money in one of the cupboards in the kitchen and took that too.

Now, as the sign telling him he was approaching the city limits of Needle Falls, he spared one glance towards the bag on the passenger side of Kevin's car.

It was lying on top of his belongings, the open zip framing it, a book stared up at him.

It had a plain, faded purple cover, but it looked ancient, like it had once been vivid and bright, but time had dulled it somehow.

In plain golden text on the front cover was one single word.

The word meant nothing to him, but it also meant *everything*.

The single word was …

GLIMM.

Beneath the word was a picture of an orb. It looked like it was made of glass, or maybe silver. It was glowing purple.

Using all his willpower, he pulled his gaze away from the book, just as the lights on the road that would take him from Needle Falls to wherever he wanted to go in the world changed to green. A smile broke across his face.

Suddenly, Carson Hess's future suddenly seemed a lot brighter.

Author's Notes

INK

David Charlesworth

LIVERPOOL HAS ALWAYS been a hotbed when it comes to nurturing creativity. Why that is? I have no idea. Be it something in the water, the sea air, or another weird, cosmic third thing, I don't know. Whatever the secret, we should be thanking it for Dave McCluskey and Peter Harper and their contributions to the arts. God only knows how Dave manages to conjure up the horrors he inflicts upon readers (and with such a rapid turnover too), and what Peter does with a paintbrush is nothing short of magical

I've had the good fortune of chatting with that pair online for a good few years now, but even though we barely live ten minutes away from one another, we've rarely caught up in real life. Which is a tragedy. Not only because we have a great laugh, but because that special "something" I mentioned before sparked. When we did meet, our conversation soon shifted from music and films to bouncing ideas for new books off each another, and then the idea to work on something together reared its ugly head.

I'll not get into too many details, lest any of those other projects come to light (especially the one about Bigfeets), but the strongest idea, by far, was also the simplest. *Let's see what we come up with if we both write a story about tattoos.*

I know Dave has created a tale that expands upon his already grand shared universe and world. So, I'm hoping my smaller, more intimate tale feels like a nice chaser/appetiser, depending on which story you read first.

Gemma's tale isn't based on true events, obviously, but its genesis was birthed from when my parents moved house when I was a teenager. Our quaint little home was far more crowded than it had any right to be. Because as well as myself, my parents, and sister, there was a woman living there who liked to stand just on the cusp of my bedroom from time to time. During the transitionary period, as we waited for the keys to our new home, I found myself living with an aunt … twelve floors up, in a block of flats. In a cupboard, no less! I'd be safe there, I thought to myself. From ghosts and aliens and any other cryptids that could pester people living in *normal* homes. And sure enough, things were fine. I was sharing that cramped little hole with almost a hundred books, so I was safe and entertained. But then I was ousted and forced the live in Milton Keynes for a while. Down there, ghouls are the least of anyone's worries.

I'm not sure what else I can add here regarding the story itself. But I'd like to thank my partner, Kathryn, for her inspiration and patience with my writing. I write for her, mostly, these days. Which is a blessing for me because she will always steer me right when it comes to humanising and grounding my character. But a curse for her because I mainly write bizarre cosmic horror that *chokkers* her head.

Luckily, that isn't this tale. So, I hope you enjoy the company of Gemma and Eva as much as me and Kath have. It's been a thrill to delve into this world of love, loss, and magic, and I hope you think of them the next time you have a pint of Tango and Gin.

Thank you for taking the time to read both the story and my ramblings here. I'm not the best at this kind of stuff, so I'll finish off by saying if you catch me in a pub, I'll get you a pint.

Cheers.

David Charlesworth
Liverpool
April 2025

INK

DE McCluskey

THIS MIGHT BE seen as a bit strange, me being involved in a book about tattoos, when the truth of the matter is, I don't have any. Not one bit of ink adorns my entire body. It's not because I don't like them (or because I'm scared of them) I just like the fact that when I go to conventions, comic cons, horror events, I am the unique one. Years ago, tattoos were for hippy types, rockers, or skinheads. Now, everyone Tom, Dick, and Harriet has them.

I am a fan of them. You only need to look at my internet history to see that … erm … I mean, I … erm, just like looking at them.

My other half—some say better half—has a few. A lot of my family have them. Our daughters have, or want, them.

I just don't.

Anyway. This story, for me, is less about tattoos and more about it being in the same universe as my debut novel, *The Twelve*. I love this Great Lord Glimm thing, and I definitely want to come back to it again. Also, eagle-eyed readers might have spotted a crossover into another universe, one of small metallic orbs called GLIMMERS, right at the end there. In this universe The Glimm are not the bad guys … I love the idea of it meaning different things in different worlds.

Anyway, if you haven't read *The Twelve*, go and do it, as this story (although it is quite standalone and you don't need to read it) might make a little bit more sense.

It came from a rather gruesome idea I had a while ago, one that I wrote as a short comic feature for a magazine that accepted it, but which folded not long after, so it was never produced. I'd called it Bob's Burgers. This was before the cartoon of the same name, but not the same idea, became popular. It was about a small burger van with a loyal customer base. Only he got his meat from grinding up lost customers. Anyway, one victim haunted the meat and therefore the stomachs of the people eating the burgers, and she possessed them to get her revenge on Bob. I loved that story, as the thought of haunted burgers still, to this day, intrigues me.

I don't want to ruin more food for my readers, so I've never adapted it into a story before (until now).

I want to thank David Charlesworth for coming up with this concept and for his patience in waiting for me to finish a million and one different projects before getting to this one. He is the author of a few books, but for me, his stand out ones are the DEATH HEAD VALLEY books, of which there are two, and possibly a third coming soon. Be sure to check them out.

The third member of the team is a long-term collaborator of mine, Ste (or Peter, depending how he feels on each day) Harper. You might know him as Folklore Art. He has worked on a number of my books, including The Glimmer Saga, *Mutant Superhero Zombie Killing Disco Cheerleaders from Outer Space (with Uzis)*, and many more. This whole concept was born in the pub, as these things sometimes are. His artwork is excellent, and you would do very well to check out his pop culture and his horror works. Excellent stuff.

I have to thank Lisa Lee Tone for her editing skills on these two shortish tales. She is a magnificent editor. I'm going to thank the long-suffering Kelly Rickard for her proofreading skills and managing to find something wrong on ALMOST every page. I also want to thank Lauren, my final proofreader before it goes out to Amazon. She also tends to find out some of the smaller mistakes too.

One day, I will shock them all and not make any—yeah, like that's going to happen!!!

Finally, a big shout out to YOU, the reader. If you are still out there reading my work, then I thank you, if you're not, then I can say whatever I want, as you'll never know.

Keep sweet, people, and read more books.

Dave McCluskey
Liverpool
April 2025

About The Cover Artist

John Zunski

I found John's work as I was idly flicking through the Deviant Art website. It's a site I used to go to find artists for my graphic novels. I found Andrew Maurice there who did fantastic work on my Interesting Tymes comics, I found Lukasz Marco who did Doppelgänger and Short Sharp Shocks, I also found the studio who did the art concepts for my DeathDay Presents graphic novel.

This piece jumped out at me, and it just shouted everything we and David wanted for this book. I messaged John and graciously he allowed us to use it.

From the bottom of my heart, thank you John. Please support his art, and he is also an author. Go and read some of his works.

John is a naturalist photographer based in western Montana, USA. He is also the author of Cemetery Street, Shangri-la Trailer Park, and Nightwatching. His work can be viewed at:

https://www.deviantart.com/johnzunski.

Printed in Dunstable, United Kingdom

65132420R00139